MIDNIGHT SHADOW

Laurel O'Donnell

Zebra Books
Kensington Publishing Corp.
http://www.zebrabooks.com

ZEBRA BOOKS are published by

Kensington Publishing Corp.
850 Third Avenue
New York, NY 10022

Zebra and the Z logo Reg. U.S. Pat. & TM Off.

First Printing: June, 2000
10 9 8 7 6 5 4 3 2 1

Printed in the United States of America

This book is lovingly dedicated to

All the people who read and enjoy my novels,
especially my dear sister Julie—
Your support and love are invaluable,
and my very good friend Care—
It has been my complete pleasure and honor to know and
befriend you.

And finally, as always, to my husband, Jack.
Through the good times and the hard times,
you've always been there as a partner and helper,
even when I don't see it.
Your love and friendship mean everything to me.

Prologue

England—1415

"... and he brandished his sword above his head, declaring, 'Tyranny will not be tolerated! All people will be treated fairly!' With that, the Midnight Shadow whirled away on his horse and disappeared over the horizon."

Bria Delaney sat on her grandfather's lap listening to the beloved tale of her favorite hero, but it couldn't erase her heartache. She glanced down at her lap and folded her hands. "I wish Father was here," Bria grumbled.

"Every man must fight against tyranny in his own way, child." Harry held Bria close to him. "Your father didn't want to leave you, but he had to fight beside the King. He is duty bound to the wishes of the crown." His old, wrinkled hand wiped a tear from her smooth cheek. He pressed a kiss to her forehead and brushed back her curly brown locks.

"I want to go with him," Bria said. "I want to fight against tyranny, too."

The rumble of her grandfather's laughter made Bria scowl fiercely. "They are armed men, Bria. What can a child do against an army? No. War is no place for you."

Bria crossed her arms and jutted out her lower lip. "I hate the French."

Harry chuckled, his entire body shaking. "Most of England does, my dear." He pulled her against him, hugging her. Then Harry set her on the ground, patting her bottom lightly. "Go. Mary and Garret are waiting for you."

"I don't feel like playing today," Bria said glumly.

"Ah, but who knows what grand adventure awaits you? If you brood all day in the castle, you might miss it," Harry reminded her.

Bria glanced up at her grandfather's warm, smiling face. Adventure. That word always seemed to stir her senses and rouse her imagination. The wet smear of tears on her cheeks was quickly forgotten.

Bria nodded and ran out of the room. She raced through the corridors of her father's castle, practically flying down a set of spiraling stone steps. As she burst from the stairway, a woman carrying an armful of laundry stepped into her path.

Bria twisted her body with the agility of an eight year old and barely missed knocking into her. "Sorry!" she called over her shoulder as she charged down a corridor to a large set of open double doors. She raced through the doors, leaping down the two steps of the castle to land in the dust of the inner ward.

The warm sun washed over her, forcing her to squint. She dashed through the inner ward, slowing long enough to leap over a puddle, then hurried through the outer ward, sprinting past the blacksmith's workshop, oblivious to the loud clang of metal against metal.

"Bria!"

A man standing near the outer gatehouse waved her over. It was Jason of Victors. She recognized him by his red beard and carrot-colored hair. His chainmail coif shone in the bright sunlight as if he had just polished it. His white tunic bore a flying falcon over a red cross, the crest of the Delaneys.

She hurried over to him.

"Good morn, child," Jason greeted warmly with a slight bow.

Bria smiled at him.

"I'm to deliver you a message," Jason added softly, almost conspiratorially. He glanced around the area, then motioned for Bria to come closer.

Bria anxiously stepped closer. "What message?" she wondered.

"Garret and Mary have pursued the French dogs onto Knowles's lands in the east woods. They are in desperate need of your assistance." Jason pulled back from her, nodding with a knowing look.

A grin burst upon Bria's face, bringing a happy sparkle into her eyes.

"Hurry now," Jason urged. "They may already be vastly outnumbered."

Bria wasted no time in darting beneath the outer gatehouse, remembering to turn and wave good-bye to Jason just as her slippered feet slapped against the wooden planks of the lowered drawbridge. She ran toward the meadows that surrounded Castle Delaney, her smile making her entire face radiant.

The sounds of horses' hooves, chickens clucking, and the distant sound of swords clanging grew farther and farther away as she left the castle and the village behind to enter the relative quiet of the grassy fields that surrounded Castle Delaney. As she bounded through the grass that rose almost to her neck, her mind replayed the story of the Midnight Shadow—the way he fought against tyranny and protected the weak. His generosity and his courage were unequaled. She wanted to be just like him.

She thrust at an imaginary foe, cutting down a stalk of grass with her hand. "Take that, you insufferable French cur," she growled. She spun and chopped at another stalk. "For England!" she cried.

Bria bounded through the stalks and into the forest that separated her family's lands from the Knowles's lands. She raced headlong into the brush, knowing the way well, having traveled it often to Mary's farm. Mary and Garret would be fighting the French somewhere in these woods, probably near the pond by Mary's house.

"Garret!" Bria called, halting to listen as she reached the edge of a small clearing. "Mary!" But there was no response, only the caw of a distant bird. Bria picked up her brown velvet skirt and raced deeper into the woods toward Mary's house.

After a minute she halted again, breathing hard. "Garret!" she called. "Mary! Where are you?"

She bit her lip lightly. Maybe she should go back. She looked over her shoulder in the direction of Castle Delaney.

The Midnight Shadow would never leave his friends alone in the woods at the mercy of the French. The thought pierced her mind and bolstered her courage.

As she moved slowly through the woods, the dried twigs and leaves crunched beneath her feet. She paused again to call out for her friends. "Mary! Garret!"

An eerie silence answered her. She looked around the quiet forest, her instincts telling her to flee. But how could she leave her friends?

Then she heard the crunch of approaching footsteps. "Mary?" she called hesitantly.

A figure emerged from behind one of the trees in front of her, but it wasn't Mary. As the shape neared, Bria recognized the boy and gasped silently. Randolph Kenric. He was bigger than she was and four years older. His brown hair hung loose around his shoulders. He looked like a wild animal.

The silence around her grew even more thick and ominous. Kenric was one of the meanest boys she'd ever met. He'd once skinned a kitten just to see how loud it could howl.

Bria stepped back. Her foot landed on a branch and snapped it in half. He turned his head and his brown hair fell into his eyes. He swiped the strands away to glare at her.

Bria took another step back.

Kenric smiled. "Ahhh," he said. "The heir to Castle Delaney. You're a little off your lands, aren't you?"

"I'm looking for my friends," she admitted.

"Which one? The peasant girl I shoved in the mud or the sniveling little boy?"

Anger pierced her, and her small fingers clenched into a fist. What gave him the right to treat her friends like that? Her eyes raked him with rage. "You're a mean cur, Randolph Kenric," she told him and turned to march toward Castle Delaney.

"Hey," Kenric called. "Didn't your father just leave to fight some war?"

Bria didn't answer him. She swatted aside a branch, continuing to move through the forest back toward her lands, her home.

Suddenly, she was yanked to a halt by biting fingers that dug into her arm. Kenric wrenched her around to face him. "Don't walk away from me when I'm talking to you," he commanded. "What kind of manners were you brought up with?"

"Let go of me," Bria ordered.

"Is that a command, your ladyship?"

She tried to pull her arm free, but he held her wrist tightly.

"I just asked you a question," he said innocently. "But you're too good for the likes of me, eh?" He chuckled low in his throat. "I'm not nobility like yourself, after all, just a poor cousin of the Knowles's. Shall I grovel before you, my lady?"

Bria twisted her arm. "Let me go," she said again, trying to sound commanding. But her voice caught in her throat as tears of fear stung her eyes.

"You need a lesson in humility." He began dragging her through the forest.

Bria dug in her heels, but her slippered feet were no help

on the leaf-carpeted forest floor, nor against Kenric's strength. She tried to pull his fingers from her wrist, but he held her tight. He pulled her deeper into the woods, into the darkness. "Stop it!" Bria called.

"You know, running through the forest alone isn't such a good idea," Kenric said. "You might fall into a bramble patch."

Bramble patch! Horror consumed Bria. She twisted and turned, trying to free herself, pushing at his hand with her free one. But his laughter rang out, as strong and vicious as his hold.

Kenric reached the edge of the bramble patch and stopped. Bria looked at the dangerous growth, the thorns like millions of miniature daggers. Some were long and straight like blades, others curved like hooks. All were sharp. She struggled against his hold, pulling at his grip, crying, "Why are you doing this?"

Kenric turned his dark smile from the spiked plants to her face. "Because I want to."

"Let her go!" a male voice commanded.

Bria looked up to see a man cloaked in black, a black mask on his face, a black cape on his shoulders.

The Midnight Shadow! He stood at the edge of the woods, his hands on his hips, his back tall and straight.

Kenric turned to look . . . and then broke out in a grin. "You must be joking!"

"I said let her go!" the Midnight Shadow repeated.

Kenric tightened his grip on Bria's hand. "Come and get her."

The Midnight Shadow moved forward, pulling a wooden sword from his belt.

Kenric tossed Bria aside. She landed hard on her hands and knees, the cluttered mass of branches and rocks of the forest floor scraping her flesh. Bria lifted her gaze in time to see Kenric pull a dagger from his belt as he approached the Midnight

Shadow—a *real* dagger, made of hardened steel. Kenric advanced upon the Midnight Shadow, waving the blade before him.

Bria climbed to her feet, dread constricting her chest as the Midnight Shadow took a brave step toward Kenric. They faced each other for a long moment. Then the Midnight Shadow swung at Kenric. Kenric ducked the blow, but the Midnight Shadow swung back, glancing a blow off Kenric's head, the wooden sword clunking against his skull.

Bria gaped as Kenric fell back to his bottom with a grunt. Joy exploded through her and she took a step toward her hero, but halted as Kenric shook his head, clearing it, and climbed to his feet. The Midnight Shadow arced his blade at Kenric's head, but Kenric caught the blow in his open palm. He yanked the wooden sword from the Midnight Shadow's grip and bashed him in the head with it.

Bria watched in horror as her noble hero fell to his knees before the evil Kenric.

Kenric reached down and ripped the mask from the Midnight Shadow's face, revealing a face Bria knew very well. She gasped. It was Garret!

Kenric laughed again, and again hit Garret's head with the wooden sword.

Garret toppled to his side and Bria lurched forward, seizing Kenric's arm as he raised the weapon to strike another blow. "Stop!" she cried. "Don't hurt him anymore!"

Kenric snorted and threw the sword down on top of Garret. He turned to Bria.

She took a step back, but Kenric locked his arm on her wrist. "Looks like your rescuer didn't save you after all."

"No!" she cried. But before the impulse to free herself overcame her fear, Kenric jerked her forward.

Bria felt herself falling, the thorns growing larger and larger as she plummeted toward the bramble patch. She reached out, attempting to brace herself from the fall. She turned her head from the thorns and squeezed her eyes shut. One of her hands landed on a small thorn and she cried out, pulling away from it. Other thorns stabbed at her arms, her legs, her back. The branches caught and snagged her clothing and her hair, pulling and ripping.

Panicked, Bria fought to be free. But the more she struggled, the more entangled her clothes and hair became, the deeper the thorns dug into her. Frightened, hurt, Bria stilled her fight. Her entire body was aflame with pain.

Through tear-filled eyes, she looked up and saw Kenric standing at the edge of the briar patch, staring down at her, laughing and laughing, his mouth big and wide, his thin lips stretched tight. Slowly, he turned away and moved off into the forest, his laughter still echoing in her ears.

Bria lay absolutely still, trying to calm her fear, trying to stop crying. She wanted her father so desperately. She wanted him to be home with her to protect her.

Then her thoughts turned to Garret. Where was he? Was he hurt? She had to get to him, had to reach him. Kenric had hit him hard. "Garret?" she called, but received no reply.

Her tears lessened as she concentrated on her friend, on helping him, on making sure he was all right.

Bria shifted slightly. Her hair pulled tight, caught and entwined in the thorny branches of the bushes. She grabbed the long lock around the top and pulled hard until she was free. The thorns in her arms burned hotly and she found herself crying again.

"Garret!" she called, worried for him. Worried that she would never be free. Still she heard no sound from her friend.

Tears continued to roll down her cheeks as she fought her way free, pulling and pulling at the nasty claws entangled in her velvet skirt. Tiny rivulets of blood trickled down her right arm.

"Bria?"

Instantly, she froze, looking toward the spot where Garret had fallen.

"Brie? Are you all right?"

She could barely make out his face through the blur of tears that filled her eyes. "Oh, Garret!" Bria cried, so relieved that she felt herself trembling. "I'm stuck. I can't get out."

"I'm coming," he said. "I'll help you."

Bria sobbed in release. Garret was all right! He'd help her get out of this. He'd help her free herself.

As Garret neared, Bria saw blood running from his blond hair, the crimson smear staining the side of his face. "Garret, you're hurt!"

Garret lifted his hand to his forehead. He brought his fingers away to look at the blood on the tips. Then he shook his head. "It's nothing." He grabbed a piece of her skirt and pulled it free of the thorns, then stood beside her and gently grabbed a lock of her hair, working it free of the bush.

As he leaned over her to ease her arm from the biting thorns, Bria noticed his black cape and mask were gone.

"I made a proper mess of things," he admitted quietly.

Bria looked away from him, tugging and pulling at her other forearm to free the brown velvet fabric of her sleeve from one of the brambles. Together, the children worked in silence until Bria was free of the bramble patch.

"Those thorns really got you." Garret gently wiped a spot of blood from her elbow. "Are you ok?"

"It stings a little, but I'm all right."

Garret looked at her for a moment, then hung his head, glancing away from her to the ground. "I never should have pretended to be something I'm not." He kicked at the cape and mask that now lay in the dirt.

"You were very gallant," Bria said, touching his shoulder warmly.

"Not gallant enough to protect you," Garret whispered. "Not as gallant as the Midnight Shadow would have been."

If it hadn't been so quiet in the forest, so still, Bria never would have heard his admission. She pretended she hadn't.

"Where's Mary?" Bria asked. "Is she hurt?"

"After Kenric pushed her in the mud, we ran away from him. She's all right. She's at her house waiting for us. I came back here looking for you." Again, Garret kicked at the fallen cape. "Little good that did."

Bria bent down and retrieved his fallen sword, holding it out to him. Garret stared at it for a long moment. Bria pushed it toward him again, an anxious feeling stirring the pit of her stomach. "Here."

Finally, Garret took it and placed it back in his belt.

She held out her hand to him and he clutched at her fingers. "I think I'd rather just go home now," Bria said softly.

He nodded, and they returned to Castle Delaney.

Bria never heard Garret speak of the Midnight Shadow again.

Bria squeezed her eyes shut. The shearing noise of her own hair being cut sounded loud in her ears as her grandfather ran the dagger through her long locks. Her shoulders shook with a suppressed sob.

"That's it, Bria," Harry told her.

Bria opened her eyes and glanced down at the floor. Her long brown locks lay curled around her bare feet.

Parts of her hair had been so tangled around the brambles, so full of thorns, that her grandfather had to cut off her hair to rid her of them. Now her once long locks reached only an inch above her shoulders.

Bria lifted a hand and ran it through her butchered hair. Sobbing quietly, she bent and scooped up the long strands in her trembling hands as if they were a valued treasure. She stared at the knotted mass of hair.

"It was unavoidable," her grandfather told her quietly, sincerely.

"Will Garret be all right?" Bria asked, wiping her sleeve across her nose.

Harry nodded. "He'll be fine," he said. "Just a bump on that hard head of his. You're sure you just stumbled into that bramble patch? And that Garret fell and hit his head?"

Bria looked away, unable to meet her grandfather's gaze. She'd argued with Garret to tell the truth so Kenric would get in trouble and be properly punished, but Garret insisted they keep it a secret. "Yes," she answered.

"Very well." Harry began to rise from his chair.

"Grandfather!" Bria said.

Harry looked down at her.

"Will you tell me the story of the Midnight Shadow?" she asked softly.

A grin stretched across Harry's face. "Of course." He motioned for her to move to the bed. They sat down together upon the soft mattress, and Harry picked Bria up and positioned her on his lap.

Bria settled into her grandfather's arms, looking down at the mound of brown hair she held in her hands. Someday Kenric would be punished. Someday he'd get what he deserved. Bria hoped she'd be around to see it.

Harry began, "He was known far and wide for fighting against tyranny and for upholding fairness. He was called the Midnight Shadow . . ."

Chapter One

Ten years later

Candles cast wiggling demons onto the stone walls of the dark room where a large bed held its sole occupant in lonely vastness. The shadows slithered across her pallid cheeks and moved over her neck like serpents looking for a tender spot of flesh upon which to inflict their deadly attack.

Lord Terran Knowles bent over her small hand, pressing his forehead to the slim fingers he held crushed in his. Her once warm skin felt clammy and cold. He didn't move for a very long time, and it appeared as if both he and the woman were dead.

But Terran wasn't about to let her die, not when he'd fought so hard to get her, winning her over another suitor. Not when he'd negotiated a dowry so grand it would provide enough funds to pay his knights and secure peace for his people and his castle for years to come. Not when he loved her. No, he couldn't permit Odella to die.

But how could he stop it?

Why, Odella? he asked silently. She'd been happy here at Castle Knowles—at least he'd believed her to be—and they were to be wed in a week. Why would she do this? Why would she poison herself?

He could think of no answer. Nothing! She'd always seemed cheerful, if shy. God knew he'd do anything to make her better, give her anything she desired.

A knock sounded at the door. Terran didn't respond. He wanted to be left alone with Odella. The door opened behind him.

"Terran?" a voice called, hesitantly.

Kenric.

His cousin moved closer. "I've brought a physician."

Terran's jaw clenched; his hands tightened to fists. "A physician will do her no good," Terran growled. "She poisoned herself. I want someone who knows about poisons."

"I can't find the herbalist," Kenric said. "And a physician—"

Terran whirled, his movements as lithe as a panther. He was off his knees in an instant, grabbing his cousin by the tunic and slamming him back against the wall. "Get me the herbalist," he snarled.

Kenric's black eyes were wide as he stared at his cousin for a long moment before nodding his head. "As you wish, m'lord," he whispered.

Terran released him, and Kenric walked swiftly from the room.

It took a long moment for Terran's anger to subside. *Physician. What good is a physician? I need someone who can help Odella. Someone who can cure her of the poison.*

Odella was like a glorious angel laid out in his bed, her hands folded on her stomach, her slender face somber and pale, her eyes closed. Her beautiful honeyed hair was tucked beneath her head.

She was a ghostly reminder of what she'd once been.

He remembered the first day he'd laid eyes on her, more than a year ago. He'd been riding into McColl Village to attend a tournament, arriving just as the merriment began. Odella had been dancing around a maypole with some of her ladies. He remembered her bright blond hair all but glowing in the sunshine, her laughter like music to his ears. He'd immediately fallen in love with her.

He won the tournament in her honor, defeating all who stood against him. After that, through months of negotiation, Terran convinced her father to betroth her to him.

In granting Terran Odella's hand in marriage, her father had given him the woman his heart desired and a bountiful dowry that would save his castle.

Now she lay dying in his bed. As he looked at her, lifeless and ashen, he wanted to cling to the memories until she regained her radiance. But somehow the images wavered and dissolved before his mind's eye into a mocking replica of what she used to be.

He rubbed his hands over his eyes, trying to hold fast to the memories.

I have to remain calm. She'll be as good as new soon. It won't be long before she's smiling again. It won't be long before I hear her laughter.

"Odella," he whispered. "Why?" He bent again at her side, gently taking her hand in his. "Why?"

Odella's head shifted slightly and Terran raised his eyes to her face.

In the flickering light of the candle, he could have sworn her lips moved. He stared at her for a moment, holding his breath, waiting for them to move again. It must have been his wishful imagination. Now they were still. Terran wiped his weary eyes, trying to clear them. But when he opened his eyes to look at her again, her lips were indeed moving!

He quickly boosted himself up on the bed. Her breath was

so shallow he could barely hear her. He lowered his ear closer
to her lips.

"Garret," she whispered.

Terran sat bolt upright, his jaw hard as granite. He must
have misheard her. But there was no mishearing her next cry.

Her lips moved again, her face contorting with pain "Garret," she managed to gasp.

Dysen! Terran reared back. *This cannot be! Why does she
call for another man?*

Then a thought struck him so hard he almost reeled. Could
she love Dysen? Could she have killed herself because she
couldn't be with Dysen?

Anguish and disbelief tore through Terran. He stood and
stepped away from the bed. How could this be?

He whirled away from her, clenching his fists. *God's blood.
Have I been so blind?*

Agony tore through him. *It cannot be!* he told himself. But
deep in his heart, he knew that he finally had his answer. Odella
had poisoned herself to escape marriage to him.

Chapter Two

The midday sunlight washed down upon the tilting field. A dozen knights were busy practicing their skills in the arena that had been set up in a field on the western side of Castle Delaney. Some of the men were on foot, clanging swords in mock battles. Others rode their muscular war horses, practicing battle maneuvers. Several men worked diligently on their jousting skills.

Bria pulled her knees up to her chest, staring down at the men in the field. She sat beneath a large tree, watching her grandfather give orders to one of the younger men as he handed him a jousting pole. Her grandfather indicated the quintain in the center of the field with a wave of his hand. The man nodded and spurred his horse forward, riding toward the far side of the field.

Someone plopped down on the grass beside Bria. She swiveled her head to see Mary adjusting her patched skirt around her legs. Her friend shoved a strand of unruly dark brown hair behind her ear and attempted to pat the rest of the flyaway strands flat. Her brown eyes twinkled with glee. "Has anyone arrived yet?'' Mary asked breathlessly. She liked this suitor business much more than Bria did.

Bria returned her dismayed gaze to the field. The young knight with the jousting pole had reached the far side of the field and was turning his steed to face the quintain. ''Two. No one interesting, though.''

Mary chuckled. ''I think if the Midnight Shadow himself walked through your door, you'd call him 'not interesting' to avoid marriage.''

''If the Midnight Shadow walked through my door, I'd jump at the opportunity to marry him!'' Bria exclaimed. ''But he isn't going to walk into Castle Delaney.''

The young knight in the jousting field spurred his horse and the horse charged forward, kicking up small puffs of dirt in his wake. The knight leaned forward in the saddle, leveling his pole at the quintain.

''That's your problem, Bria,'' Mary explained, watching him. ''No flesh-and-blood man will ever be as attractive as the imaginary one you've created in your head.''

The young knight hit the quintain, which spun rapidly. The soft bag hit him in his shoulder with enough force to throw him from his steed. He tumbled over the side of the animal, landing in a pool of dust.

Mary put her hands over her eyes and groaned.

Bria grimaced and murmured, ''Well, we know *he's* not the Midnight Shadow.''

Mary burst into laughter.

''Can you still meet me tonight?'' Bria asked, elbowing her friend.

''Of course,'' Mary replied.

Suddenly, the distant sound of trumpets filled the air.

Mary's eyes widened and she strained to see toward Castle Delaney, where the sound was coming from.

Bria rolled her eyes and crossed her arms, sitting back against the tree. ''Another suitor,'' she said with disdain.

Mary giggled and grabbed Bria's arm, trying to pull her to her feet. "Let's go see."

"Why?" Bria demanded, refusing to be lifted.

"With all that fanfare, he might be handsome!"

Bria huffed in disinterest. Mary yanked her to her feet and pulled her down the slight rise toward the road leading from the village to Castle Delaney.

Before them, Castle Delaney rose mightily skyward, its rounded towers standing as sentinels at each corner of the grand structure, connected by massive walls that protected the inner wards of the castle. The drawbridge was lowered, the portcullis raised to welcome the guests marching across the bridge.

Bria looked closely at the arriving guests, trying to discern their heraldry. The red flag one of the riders held fluttered in a gentle breeze, giving a teasing glimpse of the crest of a lion.

Bria's heart leaped slightly. She knew the crest. It was Lord Dysen and Garret!

Mary shook Bria's arm in excitement as she, too, recognized the heraldry.

Garret! She hadn't seen him in five years! Bria took a step forward, scanning the throngs. Dancing women waved translucent scarves as they moved to a minstrel's flute; men on stilts called out to the castle guards; a caged bear growled as a guard stuck the tip of his sword into its cage.

Bria scowled. Why had Garret brought such a show with him? He usually just arrived with his father. These performers must have cost enough to feed a village for a winter. *Oh no,* she thought. *Not Garret, too!* She groaned slightly and rolled her eyes skyward. *Please Lord, tell me Garret hasn't come for my hand in marriage!* But as she returned her gaze to the jugglers and minstrels disappearing into the castle beneath the gatehouse, she knew Garret had.

Mary grabbed her arm and pulled her toward the castle. Bria had been at her aunt's castle the last time Garret and his father had visited two years ago, but Mary had said he'd grown into a very handsome man. It was quite obvious Mary had been smitten by him, and still was. Her friend giggled whenever they spoke of him, and dramatically placed her hands over her heart whenever his name was mentioned.

But regardless of his newfound manhood and his handsome looks, he was still the Garret Bria had grown up with. He'd always be a brother to her. She couldn't imagine him being anything more.

Mary all but dragged her over the drawbridge and beneath the gatehouse. Inside the outer courtyard, the retinue had come to a stop. Jugglers with brightly painted faces entertained the peasants milling around. Children raced in and out between the legs of men on stilts, screaming in joy. Shouts of awe arose from the onlookers as one of the stilted men teetered and then caught his balance. Somewhere a dog barked. Several onlookers cried out in delight as a man slowly lowered a sword down his throat.

Even as Bria gaped at the numerous entertainers, Mary continued to pull her through the outer courtyard and into the inner courtyard, all but leaping up and down in excitement. The large space overflowed with the front of the procession, a garrison of armored knights, their plate armor glinting in the sun.

Had any knights been left behind to guard Castle Dysen?

Behind the soldiers, a group of actors recited poetry, and behind them a group of dancing gypsies performed wonders with their gyrating bodies.

Mary jerked her forward again, and they wove their way through the peasants milling about, past a rotund blacksmith grabbing his stomach in laughter at one of the actors.

Bria searched the crowd, but there was too much movement for her to focus on any one thing. It was a scene more befitting a holiday than the arrival of family friends. More jugglers rushed about tossing bags of beans, and musicians played merry tunes. Everywhere, people were laughing and cheering.

Bria moved past the jugglers and stopped dead in her tracks as a masked man clad in a black cape and wielding a shimmering blade stepped in front of her. Bria gasped, her heart pounding with the ferocity of a madly galloping horse. Could it be? The Midnight Shadow standing mere feet from her?

Suddenly, a woman tossed an apple into the air, and the masked man brandished his sword, instantly slicing the apple cleanly in two. Onlookers clapped at the man's show of skill.

Bria's body slumped slightly, her heart slowing. *He's just part of the show,* she thought. *Just part of the show.*

"There he is!" Mary exclaimed. She waved her hand high above her head and shouted his name. "Garret!"

Bria scanned the crowd, taking her gaze from the Midnight Shadow look-alike. "Where?" she demanded.

"Near the stairs of the keep," Mary answered, continuing to wave her hand.

Bria scanned the steps near the keep, but there were too many people. "I can't see him!"

Mary pulled Bria close. "There!" She pointed.

Bria followed her finger. She spotted Lord Dysen sitting atop a horse. He was speaking with someone on the stairs, but a man on stilts blocked her view of the person he was speaking with.

"Garret!" Mary screamed.

Bria pulled away from Mary and rubbed her ear, glancing at her in displeasure. When she turned back to search for Garret, she caught sight of a blond man dismounting a white horse, but she couldn't see his face as he disappeared into the crowd.

Mary squeezed Bria's wrist tightly. "He's coming!" she whispered loudly and jumped up and down in delight.

Bria grinned at Mary's thrill. She had to admit she was just as eager to see Garret as Mary was. She stood on her tiptoes, trying to see her friend amongst the crowd in the courtyard, but it was so full that every time she caught a glimpse of Garret, someone moved before her, obscuring her view.

"Bria! Mary!"

Bria saw a hand waving at them above the crowd. Before she could get a glimpse of him, the hand was gone, swallowed by the undulating crowd. Finally, the curtain of peasants before them parted and Garret emerged from the throng.

Bria's mouth dropped open. Golden blond hair swept down over strong shoulders. Garret was no longer the awkward, lanky child Bria remembered. His face had lost its thinness and had filled out; his jaw had squared. He was a knight now, a warrior. She felt an abyss of change open between them.

Then she looked into his eyes. There, in the twinkling blue depths, she found the Garret she knew and loved, the same boy she'd made a vow of friendship with all those years ago.

A smile of relief and of happiness stretched across her lips.

Garret stopped before her, his gaze sweeping her. For a moment, Bria thought he was going to take her hand and kiss it, marking a complete transformation into adulthood for both of them. Instead, Garret swept her into a tight embrace and whirled her around. Their laughter mingled.

When they parted, Garret swept Mary into a warm embrace. He kept his arm around Mary's shoulder as he looked at Bria in awe. "You've grown," he finally admitted.

Bria smiled. His sentiments mirrored her own. "I should hope so," Bria answered. "Last time I saw you, I was but a child."

"Yes." Garret sighed. "As was I."

Garret kissed Mary's head and Bria watched the red bloom over Mary's cheeks.

"And what of you, little woman?" he asked Mary. "What have you been up to?"

"Nothing," Mary whispered shyly, looking up at him through lowered lashes.

Bria realized with a jolt that Mary was flirting with Garret.

Garret's smile stretched wider, revealing perfect white teeth. And Garret knew it!

Their friendship would never be the same. The innocence of childhood had fled, and adult desires raged. He was a man now, and she and Mary were women.

"And what of you, Garret? I heard you went to war beside your father."

Garret's gaze swung to Bria, piercing her with the full intensity of his glorious blue-eyed stare, and he nodded, his eyes lighting up. "Have I got tales for you!" he began, but faltered. "Maybe we should speak of other things."

Bria glanced at Mary and frowned. "Why would we speak of other things?"

"Well, you're a lady now and—"

Bria smiled. "And maybe such talk offends me?"

"Well." Garret shifted from foot to foot uneasily. "Well, yes."

"When they didn't offend me before?" Bria asked, poking fun at him. Garret had often told her of the dreams he had of slashing down the French, of ridding the land of tyranny. "I'm still the same girl, Garret, as I'm sure you're the same boy."

Garret shrugged slightly.

Bria reached out to squeeze one of his biceps, firm with powerful muscles that distinguished him as a strong warrior. "These are real, aren't they?"

"I should say so!" Garret squeaked in objection.

A grin stretched Bria's lips and Mary covered her mouth against her giggles.

Garret glanced from Bria to Mary and back again. He shook his head, smiling. "Yes, you are the same girl." He grasped her hands tightly. "And it's good to see you. I missed you the last time I was here."

Bria smiled at him. "Me, too."

"Come on," Mary called. "Let's go watch the knights practice."

Garret nodded. "I'll meet you there. I must say hello to Lord Delaney."

Mary raced off through the crowd toward the practice field. Bria turned to join her, but Garret grabbed her arm.

"Do you still sword fight with your grandfather?"

Bria nodded, but quickly hushed him, looking from side to side to see if anyone had heard. Her father would never approve, so she and her grandfather kept it a well-guarded secret. Garret wouldn't know except that he'd followed her out of the castle one night long ago when the Dysens had been visiting. He'd discovered them fighting. She'd sworn him to secrecy.

"Have you beaten him yet?" Garret wondered.

Bria shook her head, a grimace of disappointment crossing her features.

"I've got a move guaranteed to disarm him. Are you interested?" Garret asked, a smile curving his lips.

"Am I!" Bria almost exploded with excitement.

"Meet me tomorrow morning in the field where you practice," he whispered.

Bria nodded.

Two swords crossed under a slitted moon, their metal blades clanging as they collided. The moon shimmered in the cold steel, its reflection clear and bright.

"Come on, girl, you can do much better than that." Harry watched Bria smile. She was beautiful. Who would have thought such a gangly girl would grow into such an elegant lady? Her long brown hair hung loosely in large curls about her shoulders, her lips were full and rose red, the blue of her eyes rivaled that of the sky—eyes that right now stared at him with the heated blue of a fire's core. She would indeed make a fine wife. It was just that defiant, determined streak she had to be wary of. Men wanted at least some semblance of subservience from their women.

The blades pushed hard against each other, then abruptly separated, the slender steel screeching as the weapons slid free of each other. Bria swung, but Harry backed away and her blade whistled through the empty air. She swung again, but this time Harry caught her swing and grabbed her wrist, bringing her in close so they were practically nose to nose.

"You're angry because your father finally made the decision to find you a husband." He pushed away from her and swung. "You're fighting with your emotions today, not with reason."

She ducked and spun away from him. "I am not," she insisted, then countered with an arc to his head. He blocked her blow, knowing she was lying because of the intensity with which she fought.

It took all his concentration to match her move and block it. "It's time, Bria. You should have been married long ago," he said.

She was quick, much quicker than he was. And she was smart, despite her emotions warring to take control. He could see her mind working as she lunged. But experience won out, and he was still able to thwart her strike. He caught her sword with his and twisted his wrist. He had disarmed her more than once with that move. It worked again tonight. Her sword went sailing through the air.

Disappointment surged within him. Even though she was getting better and better each night they sparred, he was still disappointed in her lack of self-control. But it was only a matter of time before she disarmed him. Then he'd have nothing further to teach her. That would be the biggest disappointment of all.

Bria cursed quietly and stomped after her sword. Before she could reach it, Harry put the tip of his sword to her neck. "Yield," he ordered.

Again, she mumbled a curse. "I yield," she added grudgingly, and moved to proceed past him.

But he kept the sword to her neck. "Why were you disarmed?"

He watched her jaw work as she clenched her teeth. "I was overanxious. I thought I had you that time. Just like all those other times." She shoved the sword from her neck and marched past him to her weapon, yanking it from the ground. She swung it through the air, hacking the breeze that assaulted her. "I'll never get it."

"You'll get it," he said, kindly. "You just have to learn patience. You want to win, but you're not willing to wait for an opening."

"You make your own openings," she countered.

"When you're good enough," he agreed, approaching her, "and when you realize you'll never be stronger than a man. You have to wait for an opening. You can't fight aggressively. You have to fight defensively. Always."

Bria rolled her large blue eyes. "I know, I know."

"But you don't know, or you wouldn't be disarmed."

She handed her sword to him. He took the handle of the weapon. "Don't stay out too long. Your father is suspicious enough."

"I know," she murmured. She walked toward the thick forest just beyond the clearing where two horses were tethered to a tree.

Harry shook his head in admiration. She was already better than most men he knew, but he dared not tell her that.

Suddenly, she paused and turned to look at him. Her long, dark brown hair cascaded over her shoulder as she stared at him. "Thank you, Grandfather."

Harry smiled and nodded. "It's my pleasure." She was his joy, his treasure. She was the only spark in his otherwise tedious life at the castle. He would grant her the moon—but teaching her to sword fight was a hell of a lot easier.

One of these times, he knew he'd have to stop her from riding out to her secret meetings with her friend Mary. The world was becoming much too dangerous a place for her to be out late at night on her own.

Chapter Three

Bria rode through the night, knowing the way to the pond in the east woods by heart. She knew where the land dipped, where it rose, where she had to duck to avoid the stinging slap of tree branches. So did her horse. They'd ridden this route together since she was ten—since her grandfather had begun teaching her to use a sword.

She tried not to let her frustration consume her thoughts. She should have had him! She had thought she did have him! Only one wrong move. *Damn.* That's all it would take in a real battle to cost her her life, all it would take for someone to kill her. One mistake.

Bria spurred the horse faster. The animal raced on, the night speeding by. The huge rock at the edge of the Hagen farm signaled that she'd crossed over into Knowles lands, but she didn't slow her pace. She turned right as she passed the massive stone toward the pond where Mary would be waiting.

As she topped a slight rise, the pond appeared, glistening in the moonlight. Bria slowed her horse and steered the animal toward the forked tree, actually two trees twined about each other so tightly as to become one.

Bria dismounted, throwing the reins around a tree branch. She turned and walked through the waist-high grass, staring at the dark pond. Long ago, soon after her grandfather had started teaching her swordplay, she and Mary had begun meeting at the pond. It was their secret place, a sanctuary where they could hide and tell each other their deepest desires. On some warm summer nights, when the moon was high and bright, Bria and Mary had gone swimming in those waters. She felt safe and comfortable here. They both did.

At the crunch of grass, Bria looked to her right. Mary bounded toward her, her dark hair alive with the moonlight's sheen.

As Mary drew closer, her eyes scanned Bria's disgruntled face for a long moment. "I'm sorry, Bria," Mary whispered. "You'll beat your grandfather yet."

"I know. It's just so unfair," Bria murmured. It was uncanny how sometimes each knew what the other was thinking or feeling.

"Unfair, is it? Your grandfather is so much older than you! It should take you years to surpass his expertise, if ever."

"Thanks a lot!"

Mary shrugged her shoulders. "You know what I mean. How would he feel if you beat him the first time you crossed swords?"

"But it's been hundreds of times!" Bria said with exasperation. "Hundreds of times, and I have yet to best him once!" Bria kicked at a fallen branch.

"It'll take time, but I know you can beat him," Mary assured her friend.

"Garret said he has a move guaranteed to disarm him," Bria said quietly.

"Really?"

Bria nodded her head. "He's going to show it to me."

"Isn't that cheating?"

Bria quirked an eyebrow. "Not if I win."

Mary's brown eyes widened in disbelief. Then she smiled and draped an arm across her friend's shoulders. Together they walked slowly through the grass. "Do you think your future husband will let you sword fight?"

Bria grunted. "Not likely," she murmured.

"What if it's Garret?"

"Mary!"

"You're so lucky!" Mary's enthusiasm bubbled over. "He's handsome and kind—"

"Mary, I can't marry Garret. It would be like marrying my brother!"

"But he'd let you sword fight."

"And we'd have to move very far from you."

Mary sighed, her excitement leaving her in a huff of exasperation. "No matter who you marry, you'll move away."

"So I won't marry!" Bria shrugged Mary's arm from her shoulders and raced off through the clearing.

Mary followed her through the tall stalks of grass. "You have to marry! You're a lady! That's your place—to produce heirs."

"What if my place isn't to produce heirs? What if my place is . . . to battle against tyranny?"

Mary giggled.

Bria stopped, striking a statuesque pose with her hands on her hips. "I am the Midnight Shadow!" she proclaimed in a deep voice.

"You sound like a woman."

"How's this?" Bria lowered her voice to a husky whisper. "I am the Midnight Shadow."

"That's pretty good," Mary admitted, amazed and surprised. "I think you've been practicing."

Bria smiled. Sometimes alone at night, she did. "Tyranny will not be tolerated!" she whispered. "All people will be treated fairly."

Mary grunted, the humor leaving her. "Then you'd have to battle Lord Knowles."

Bria broke her pose. "Now what has he done?"

"He increased our taxes again."

"Not so!" Bria gasped. That was the second time in a month. Trying to come up with the extra food to pay the collectors had been hard enough, but now it would be next to impossible for Mary's family to have a decent living.

"Mother and Father work so hard. They're up before dawn and work well into the night. I help as much as I can . . ." Mary shook her head, her dark locks swaying over her face. "But it's never enough. Lord Knowles always wants more, more, more."

Bria had no words to console her friend. She wished Mary lived on her lands, under her father's rule.

"Someone has to do something!"

Bria was shocked by the conviction in Mary's voice, the passion.

"It's not fair that we should have to work day and night! If Mother or Father gets sick, we'll starve!" Mary sighed. "If only the Midnight Shadow *were* real. He'd do something about this."

Bria remembered a time when she'd wished for the Midnight Shadow, too—when her father had gone off to war to fight the French and Randolph Kenric threw her into the bramble patch. She put an arm around Mary's shoulders. "I wish I could do something to help—"

Suddenly the sound of a man's laughter rang out through the forest. A second man's voice spoke quietly.

Silence settled around them again and the two girls glanced at each other.

"Let's go find out who it is," Bria whispered, feeling brave in the darkness.

"No," Mary gasped. "What if it's robbers?"

"They won't see us. Come on, Mary." Bria tugged her

friend toward the voices, pulling her into a group of thick bushes near a small dirt road.

An elderly woman's voice drifted over to them from the road. "I don't understand why you're bringing me here this late at night."

"It's necessary," a man replied.

Bria peered through the leaves. An old gray-haired woman stood near a man in the pale moonlight. She was dressed in a plain brown gown, a shawl wrapped around her shoulders. The man had his back to her, so Bria could not see his face. His leggings were black, his tunic pale. But what captured Bria's attention was the sword strapped to his waist. Bria swung her gaze down the road before them and saw another man not far away—a soldier, she guessed, by the chainmail he was wearing—but his tunic had no crest, no allegiance. He held the reins of two horses.

"Well, what is it you want?" the old woman demanded. "I'm sure it could have waited until morning."

"It's Widow Anderson," Mary whispered. "The herbalist."

Bria nodded.

"You want me to make you more potions?" Widow Anderson asked. "You still owe me for the first one. A lot of time and skill went into it, believe me. And if it's not used properly it could have deadly consequences. I took a great chance giving it to you."

"Yes, you did. And you've kept the secret well, as I instructed. It is with great regret that I must tell you there will be no payment," the man said.

Every one of Bria's senses flared to life. Something was wrong here, very wrong. Beside her, Mary shifted her position. Bria could feel the anger in her friend's stiff shoulders and clenched fists.

"No payment?" the woman huffed. "We agreed on ten gold coins." Her voice quickly changed from one of outrage to one of calm certainty. "I think you'll pay up."

"And I think you're mistaken." The man's hand dropped casually to the hilt of his sword.

One of the horses the soldier held whinnied and reared, and the man before the old woman turned suddenly, stepping into a beam of moonlight.

Bria froze as the ghostly light washed across his features. It couldn't be! She recoiled into the safety of the dark bush, praying he hadn't seen her. She'd hoped never to see him again.

"Listen, Kenric, you cheap worm, you'll pay what you owe." The old woman drew the man's gaze to her once again.

Kenric! Fear coiled around Bria's body, immobilizing her. Bria reached out for Mary . . .

But Mary wasn't there. She'd burst through the cover of the bushes and onto the road.

"No! Mary!" Bria whispered frantically.

But Mary moved forward, oblivious to Bria's warning, stalking toward Kenric and Widow Anderson.

Bria peered anxiously through the bushes, but remained hidden, unable to stop her pounding heart, unable to suppress the fear that encompassed her. It was Kenric, her mind repeated. Kenric.

As Mary stomped toward the duo, Kenric's eyes slowly turned and his lips curled into a contemptuous sneer. Fear gripped Bria's insides. Fear for Mary, fear for the old woman. Fear for herself. Her breathing came hard and fast as frightful images danced before her mind's eye. Haunting memories of Kenric's ugly black eyes glinting down at her. Falling into a thorny patch of brambles. Wicked laughter played over and over again in her ears.

Deep inside, she knew she should do something. She knew she should take a stand beside Mary, but she couldn't. She couldn't face Kenric. She could only watch in frozen terror as Mary approached Kenric, her tiny fists clenched at her sides.

Kenric surveyed the area around them, his gaze flashing past Bria's hiding spot and moving on. He turned back to Mary.

"That is quite enough!" Mary proclaimed. "You'll pay Widow Anderson, or everyone will know you cheated her." Her threat hung in the air.

"She'll get what's due her," Kenric finally said.

Bria didn't like the sound of his voice.

Mary seemed well pleased by his verdict. She nodded and smiled with satisfaction. Had Kenric changed after so many years? Was he going to do the right thing? Would he pay Widow Anderson?

Kenric drew his sword and plunged it into Widow Anderson's stomach.

Sheer terror held Bria immobile as Widow Anderson's mouth went round in a circle of shock.

Kenric's black, evil eyes shone in the moonlight. They were the most terrifying eyes Bria had ever seen. He smiled coldly as he pulled his sword from the herbalist's body. Widow Anderson crumpled to the ground like a scarecrow untied from its pole.

Bria struggled to regain control of her senses. "Run, Mary, run!" she shouted. A dark, shadowy presence swept over her as Kenric turned in the direction of her voice. She prayed she was hidden well enough in the bushes that he couldn't see her. He studied the area around her, his dark eyes narrowing as they tried to penetrate the darkness.

With a cry, Mary raced away into the forest on the opposite side of the road and quickly disappeared into the blackness of the thick trees, swallowed up by the woods. The soldier quickly gave chase.

Bria shrank back into the cover of the bushes. Kenric still held his bloodied sword, looking in her direction. He took a step toward her.

He's coming. He's going to find me.

Then another step.

Bria shot to her feet and whirled, dashing from the bushes, away from Kenric. She sprinted back through the tall grass, across the field, racing back the way she and Mary had come.

Her heart pounded in her chest and in her ears. Bria clutched the skirt of her dress, holding it high so she could run as fast as her legs would take her.

Behind her, Bria heard the crash of someone moving through the brush. Once again she was a child of eight, running from Kenric. She couldn't let him get to her. Sharp branches tore at her clothing, scratched at her flesh as she ran through the forest. She fought her way through the night, running for her life.

He'll kill me, she thought again and again. *He'll kill me this time if he catches me. Just like he killed Widow Anderson.*

Instinct brought her to her horse, which remained tethered to the branch of the tree. She pulled herself up onto the horse's back and immediately turned the animal toward the safety of her father's lands. All she needed to do was get to Delaney lands and she would be safe. Kenric was chasing her on foot. And now she was on horseback. She'd make it.

But the horse whinnied angrily as its head jerked forward.

The reins were still wrapped around the branch! Bria grabbed hold of the leather straps and pulled frantically trying to free them, but they became more entangled around the branch. With a howl of fear and frustration, she tore the straps free, yanking the small branch from the tree. She spurred the horse away as a threatening shadow crashed through the wall of bushes beside her.

The steed reared and Bria almost fell, but she clung tightly to the horse's mane, keeping herself in the saddle. The horse raced away over the land, knowing the way back to Castle Delaney by heart—a lucky thing, because Bria's hands were trembling so badly she couldn't have steered the animal if she wanted to. She urged her horse on, spurring it hard until she broke free of the forest. They raced over a small hill, galloping at a breakneck pace toward the castle.

Soon Castle Delaney loomed before her, but Bria didn't feel relieved. Fear held her in a tight embrace, erasing all other thoughts. She spurred her horse below the portcullis, ignoring the guard's call. As soon as they reached the inner ward she dismounted, practically throwing herself from the saddle. Her feet hit the ground first. Then she fell forward, landing on her hands and knees. For a long moment, she stayed that way, trembling fiercely, struggling to catch a breath, willing her pounding heart to slow down.

Kenric will kill me if he finds me.

He killed Widow Anderson. He murdered her in cold blood!

Mary! Bria quickly stood and took a step toward her horse, lifting her foot into the stirrups. But then she froze. Kenric would be waiting for her at the edge of the east woods. He'd know she would come back.

How can I not go back for Mary? He might hurt her. He might kill her!

Guilt and terror at what she had done, at what she was doing, weighed heavily on her shoulders.

She'd left Mary alone in the woods.

Suddenly, Bria bolted into the keep. She raced up a set of spiral stairs and down the hall. Garret would help her, she was sure of it. He'd return to the woods and search for Mary with her. She ran as fast as she could, finally skidding to a halt before his door.

Bria lifted her hand to knock, but suddenly froze, her hand raised in the air. He'd tried to protect her against Kenric a long time ago, but he hadn't been strong enough.

And now Kenric was even more evil.

What if Garret were hurt—or even killed—because of her?

Bria lowered her hand. She couldn't risk his life. She turned and raced down the stairs. She would get Jason of Victors, the captain of the guard, and bring a dozen men with her.

She could only pray Mary would remain safe until then.

Chapter Four

Garret emerged from the stables, adjusting his stockings. He glanced back over his shoulder at the wench sitting on a pile of hay, pulling her dress up over her ample bosom. He paused at the door to admire those luscious curves. She glanced up and caught him staring at her. She grinned and purposely dropped her top, leaning back so her breasts jutted out at him in invitation.

Garret chuckled low in his throat. "Wanton wench," he murmured. But he resisted the stirrings in his loins. He needed a few hours sleep if he was to meet Bria come dawn. He shook his head, laughing pleasantly. The women at Castle Delaney had always been very . . . accommodating.

He headed toward the keep, passing through the empty courtyard, whistling softly. As he approached the keep, the simple song died on his lips. A horse stood unattended in the middle of the inner ward. A scowl crossed his brow.

He approached the horse, patting its neck lightly. The horse whinnied and tossed its head. The reins jerked up with the movement before settling back to dangle over the animal's neck. Something on the end of the reins caught Garret's attention— something heavy enough to weigh down the leather straps.

Garret grabbed the bridle and patted the horse's neck again before picking up the reins. A branch was tangled in the leather straps. He worked the straps tree and inspected the branch for a moment before tossing it aside.

The courtyard was empty. *How strange,* he thought. Whose horse was this?

Garret had stepped up the first stair to the keep when the door flew open. Bria emerged from the double doors and their gazes locked immediately. A smile began to form on Garret's lips at seeing her, but ceased when he read the distress in her eyes. Her usually bright blue eyes were wide with fear. Her complexion was pale. Something was terribly wrong.

Garret bounded up the two steps to her side and took her hands in his. "Bria, what is it? What's happened?"

"Mary." Bria glanced over his shoulder toward the gate-house. "We were in the east woods and Kenric . . ." She turned those wide, blue eyes to him. "Kenric killed an old woman. And . . . I'm afraid for Mary."

"Where?" Garret demanded, straightening. "Where in the east woods? Where is Mary?"

Bria struggled to pull tree of his grip. "I need to find Jason. I need to call out the guards and go look for Mary."

"Tell me where she is," Garret demanded.

"I won't risk your life, too!" She shook her head frantically. "It's Kenric!" she exclaimed.

"And it's Mary!" Garret fumed. "Why won't you tell me—" Suddenly, understanding filled his eyes, followed instantly by indignation. His jaw clenched in anger. "You think I can't defeat Kenric."

"That's not it," Bria proclaimed.

But Garret knew the truth. He turned away. "If you won't tell me, I'll find her myself."

"No! Garret!" Bria raced after him and attempted to grab his arm, but Garret tore loose, whirling on her.

"I'm insulted you think so little of me," Garret said. Hurt twisted his heart. She was one of his best friends, yet had such little faith in his abilities.

"He killed an old woman."

"I've killed many men. Young men," Garret retorted hotly.

"She was weaponless! Kenric has no honor, Garret!" Bria argued vehemently. "This isn't a contest. He'd strike at you from behind, kill you by trickery, and I don't want a friend of mine killed."

"I can defend myself," Garret insisted. His pride had been wounded, and it was not so easily mended. "Are you going to tell me where she was or not?"

Bria hesitated for only a moment, carefully, thoughtfully, angrily perusing his face. Finally, she turned away.

Garret fumed. He couldn't believe she wasn't going to tell him, couldn't believe she'd leave Mary out in the woods in such great peril.

But then, much to his surprise, Bria swung herself up onto the lone horse in the middle of the courtyard and held out a hand to him.

"No," Garret insisted, something akin to panic building inside him. "I'll go alone. There's no need for you to risk your life. I'm a trained knight."

Bria glanced at him and Garret saw the resolution in her eyes. "She's my friend, too."

Garret cursed silently and grabbed her hand, pulling himself up behind her. He snatched the reins from her hands and demanded, "Where is she?"

They searched the woods for hours beneath the light of the moon, but there was no sign of Mary or Kenric or the old woman. It was as if Bria had imagined the entire thing. She knew that was exactly what Garret was beginning to believe. At dawn they went to Mary's home. Bria hoped beyond hope she *had* imagined the whole thing—that Kenric hadn't killed some old woman and that Mary was safe at home in her bed.

Bria glanced back at Garret, who was still sitting on the horse, before turning back to Mary's door. She lifted her hand to knock, but the door opened before her knuckles could hit the wood. Mary's mother, a thin woman with large blue eyes, stood in the doorway.

"Bria," she gasped. "Is Mary with you?"

Dread surged in Bria's breast. It hadn't been her imagination. "No," Bria said. "She didn't return home last night?"

"No," Mary's mother whimpered. She burst into tears. "Oh, Bria, I don't know what to do. You know Mary. You know she wouldn't stay out all night."

Bria looked in the direction of the pond. Dread filled her entire being. They had to go back and search again. They had to find Mary.

"George is out looking for her now," Mary's mother said.

"I'll look for her," Bria promised and returned to Garret. She couldn't lift her eyes to him, she couldn't look at him. This was her fault. She never should have left Mary.

Garret reached down and encircled her hand, pulling her up before him. "It's not your fault," he whispered.

Mary's mother stood in the doorway. "I'll stay here in case she comes home."

But Bria wasn't listening to either of them. She directed Garret to return to the pond. *I should have stayed with her. I shouldn't have left her alone.* She pictured her friend lying dead in the road, run through by Kenric.

They reached the pond and scanned the shore, but Mary wasn't there—as she hadn't been before.

"Mary!" Bria called desperately.

Pictures of Mary hidden in the bushes—raped, beaten, stabbed—played in Bria's mind. "Mary!" Bria repeated, her voice cracking with despair. Tears rose in her eyes. *I shouldn't have left her.*

Garret's arm tightened around her waist.

But Bria leaned away from him, resisting his attempt at comfort.

Garret nudged the horse forward slowly.

Bria searched the sides of the road as they rode by, hoping something would appear, something they'd missed before, some clue that Mary was still alive, a sign her friend was all right.

But there was nothing—no blood, no bodies, not even a sign of a scuffle. Of course, Kenric wouldn't have left any evidence of what he had done.

She'd never know what he did with Mary.

Deep down, Bria knew if Mary hadn't returned by now, she wasn't going to. Even acknowledging this to herself was admitting defeat. If she just kept looking, if she didn't give up, everything would be all right.

And then something caught her eye. "Wait!"

Garret pulled the horse to a halt and Bria dismounted, swinging her leg over the horse's back, never taking her eyes from what looked like a piece of red cloth stuck to the bark of a tree. She hurried over to it.

Bria stopped before the tree, looking at the cloth for a long moment. Finally, she touched it, then quickly pulled her hand back. Her fingertips were stained red. Sickened, Bria lifted her eyes to the piece of cloth again. It wasn't red. It was saturated with blood. The edges were still brown . . . the same brown as the dress Mary had been wearing. Bria crushed the material in her trembling hand. "Mary," she whispered, staring down at the red-stained fabric in her palm.

Garret moved up behind her. "It might not be hers," he said softly.

Bria turned to look at him, her vision blurred with tears. Garret reached out to her, pulling her close.

They both knew it was Mary's.

* * *

Terran stared out the window of his bedroom in Castle Knowles. *Garret,* he thought again. *Garret Dysen.* Even though Odella's father believed Terran to be a better match for his daughter, Odella's heart had already been taken.

The door squeaked open behind him. He didn't turn from the rising sun. What could he do for her? Would he release her to make her happy? Could he let her go to another man to give her life?

The footsteps of an invader entered the deathly quiet chambers.

"M'lord," Kenric whispered. His voice sounded like a scream in the soundless room.

Terran didn't answer him, didn't move.

Kenric lowered his voice even further. "The herbalist is missing."

Terran whirled. "What do you mean, missing?"

"She's gone, Terran. We searched everywhere."

"Then get another!" Terran demanded. "It's Odella's only hope. Bring me some concoction that will make her well!"

"I brought a physician instead," Kenric said softly.

"I told you I don't want a physician," Terran growled.

"Terran, be reasonable!" Kenric urged. "He's better than nothing."

Terran turned his gaze to Odella as soft footsteps echoed through the room. Her angelic face was so at peace, so soft and delicate.

A tall, thin old man stepped into his view. The old man bent immediately over Odella and a fierce protectiveness surged in Terran's chest. He forced the feeling aside and pressed his back against the cold stone wall. His eyes never left the physician.

"Terran, you should get some rest," Kenric advised.

Terran snorted his disagreement and crossed his arms over his chest. He was going nowhere. His cold black eyes remained locked on the physician. So help this man if he made one mistake, just one. He'd kill him with his bare hands.

The physician touched Odella's throat, her wrist, her forehead, then put his hand about an inch away from her lips. He held it there for a long moment, then slowly lowered it.

The physician lifted his gaze to Kenric, nervousness in his eyes.

Terran uncrossed his arms, ready for explosive action. "What is it?" Terran demanded. His gaze dropped to Odella. "What's wrong?"

"She's dead, m'lord," the physician announced.

Terran lifted his dark eyes to pin the physician to the spot. Rage and fear churned in his heart. The old man recoiled from his deathly glare.

"I'm sorry," the physician said meekly.

In one swift movement, Terran grabbed the physician by his tunic front and slammed him against the wall. "Liar," he snarled.

The old man quivered beneath Terran's twisted grimace. "I—I'm sorry, m'lord," he stuttered. Terran tossed the old man aside, and the physician quickly fled the room.

Terran's gaze slid to the woman in the bed. Her soft features were still, her eyes closed as if in sleep, her lips pale, but still pink.

Terran sat beside her on the bed, taking her hand in his trembling fingers, grief closing his throat. "Open your eyes, darling," he whispered. "Show that old goat how wrong he is."

But her eyes didn't flutter. They didn't open.

"Come, Odella. Don't be stubborn. Open your eyes." His voice cracked slightly.

Terran shifted his gaze from her cold fingers to her still face. She did not move. "Open your eyes, damn it!" he ordered through clenched teeth.

Her eyes remained closed.

Suddenly, grief consumed him and he swept her into a tight embrace, burying his face in her long golden locks. "Oh, no, no," he whispered into her hair. Anguish shattered his last shards of self-control. His utter misery rolled from his eyes, from his very soul, in a torrent of torment. "Odella, Odella," he repeated, over and over again.

Chapter Five

Exhausted both mentally and physically, Bria and Garret rode home slowly. They'd searched together and with Mary's father all day, but Bria knew it was useless. She knew that Mary's fate had been the same as the Widow Anderson's. But there was no proof. The bloodied cloth they'd found didn't prove much of anything. There were no bodies. How could she bring forth any accusations against Kenric when she had no solid proof?

It's my fault. If I'd stayed with Mary, she'd still be alive.

Or you would have been killed, a voice inside her reminded.

She looked over at the setting sun. Her stomach rumbled, but she didn't care. Grief and fatigue warred within her. The red sky wavered before her watery eyes.

"What should I do, Garret?" she whispered, staring at the castle as they approached it.

"Do?" Garret asked. "There's nothing *to* do. Mary could return to her house at any moment."

Bria closed her eyes. "You know she won't. Kenric killed her."

"You don't know that," Garret said. "She could be hiding in the forest or at someone's house. You didn't see Kenric kill her. Maybe she got away."

Bria opened her hand and stared down at the bloodied cloth. She knew Mary hadn't escaped. She would have gone home, or come to Castle Delaney. Grief welled within her. Her best friend. And it was her fault.

"Bria!"

Bria lifted her head to see her grandfather running across the drawbridge toward her. "I've been looking for you the entire day," he said in a worried voice. He came up short before her, reaching up for her, his old lungs fighting for a breath. Bria took his hand and dismounted.

"I'll stable your horse." Garret moved the animal off toward the castle.

Harry studied Bria's downcast face. "I'm so sorry." He engulfed her in a tight hold and rocked her slightly. "I heard about your friend."

"Oh, Grandfather." She pressed her face into his chest. All her grief and desperation and guilt came out in a torrent of sobs. Her grandfather's embrace tightened, and she knew she wasn't worthy of his comfort.

Her best friend was gone, and she'd abandoned her—had all but killed her. "It was Kenric," she wept. The entire story spilled out, ending with, "I know he killed her." Her grandfather stroked her back, comforting her as she spoke. "I thought of going to Knowles and telling him what Kenric did . . ."

"No!" her grandfather snapped.

Startled, Bria pulled back and lifted her reddened eyes to her grandfather. The terror in his gaze took her aback.

He shook his head as if clearing it. "I mean, it would do no good," he explained. "You're a woman. Knowles would never believe your word against his cousin's. Kenric is his trusted sheriff. Besides, then your father would find out you've been on Knowles's lands, and he strictly forbade that years ago.''

"I don't care if Father finds out. We're talking about Mary's murderer. Knowles should know."

"Knowles won't give a damn." Harry held Bria at arm's length and gazed into her eyes. There was a bitterness in his voice he couldn't disguise.

"But I'm a noble," Bria protested. "That has to count for something in Knowles's eyes."

"Even nobles lie, my dear."

"But what can I do? I left Mary there, Grandfather. I can't just . . . just leave her death unpunished."

Harry stroked her hair soothingly. "I don't think there's anything you can do. Mary wasn't one of your father's people. She's not your responsibility."

"She was my friend, Grandfather," Bria whimpered. "She was my best friend."

"I know, Bria. I know." Her grandfather wrapped his arm around her shoulder and began to escort her back into the safety of Castle Delaney. "But she lived on the wrong lands. She lived under the rule of a tyrant who has no sense of justice."

The fire in the hearth crackled and hissed angrily, the flames sparking and snapping. Bria thought they were yelling at her for leaving Mary. She pulled her knees to her chest. Even the fire didn't warm her cold, despondent spirit. She couldn't forgive herself for leaving Mary with Kenric. She couldn't forgive herself for thinking of her own life before the life of her friend.

"Little Lady?"

Bria would have smiled had she not felt so utterly miserable. It was her father's pet name for her. She turned to look at him over her shoulder. He was tall and handsome, with a commanding presence few others could claim. His dark brown hair was speckled with gray and his face was lined with wrinkles from the sun, from worry, and from laughter, but his blue eyes held wisdom beyond his years.

Bria adored her father. She hardly noticed his left arm, which hung limp and lifeless at his side. It was a dead weight, rendered useless in the war against France. When he had returned home three years ago, Bria had nursed him back to health, but he'd never recovered from the crippling wound.

"Is something wrong?" he asked.

"A friend of mine died today," she answered evasively. If he knew she'd spent the day on Knowles's lands, he'd have her head.

"Yes," he replied, taking the seat beside her. "I heard. And I'm sorry. But that's part of life."

"It doesn't ease the pain," Bria snapped.

"No, it doesn't," he answered.

"Especially when she was murdered."

Her father was silent for a long time as he stared into the fire. "I know you're sad, Bria, so I won't punish you for crossing over onto Knowles's lands."

Bria grimaced. She didn't care whether he punished her or not. She deserved to be punished for her cowardice. She deserved a whipping. She deserved a hundred lashes.

"But I will not have my order disobeyed again. Is that understood?"

Bria nodded.

"Stay off of Knowles's lands," he ordered. "Let this go, Bria. I don't want my only child hurt. Besides, you should be concentrating on choosing a suitor."

Bria looked away from him, her teeth clenched in anger. He was so concerned with betrothing her. But how could she concentrate on choosing a mate? How could she even care about her own future when her friend no longer had one?

She couldn't let Kenric get away with Mary's death. He'd been getting away with horrible things far too long. Someone had to do something.

Defeat, frustration, and grief swirled within her. What could she do? Who could she go to? Her father wouldn't accuse Kenric without proof of Mary's death, and he could ill afford to go to war with Knowles, even if he would risk his lands for a farmer's daughter who wasn't even one of his own people.

No, there'd be no help from him. Perhaps her grandfather would help, if she pleaded enough. But Grandfather was no longer lord of the castle. That was her father's role. After her father had come back from the war so wounded, her grandfather had magnanimously given the castle to his son. Now Father's word was law; Grandfather would obey his orders without question. There'd be no help from him, either.

But despite her grandfather's warning, despite her father's direct command, she had to do something. Something very drastic. Only one man could help her. Only one man could act upon the truth.

Lord Terran Knowles.

Chapter Six

Everyone had forbidden her from entering Knowles's lands—her grandfather, her father, everyone. So why had she rushed out first thing in the morning and gone straight to Castle Knowles's Great Hall, demanding to see Knowles? Because she couldn't live with herself without doing something to avenge Mary's death. And telling Knowles who had murdered the old woman—and probably Mary, too—was the only thing she could think of.

Surely Knowles wasn't as bad as all of the stories and gossip had portrayed him—a cruel tyrant who sat up in the towers of his castle, counting the coins he'd squeezed from his people. He couldn't be that bad. Surely he'd do something about Mary's death. He'd punish Kenric.

Bria sighed and looked around the hall. Near the back of the room, two servants scurried from table to table, cleaning up the remnants of the morning meal. One man was stretched out on the floor near the dying hearth, sleeping—or dead. Bria couldn't tell which.

Bria looked at the doors behind her again. She'd sent a serving girl to find Lord Knowles, since he hadn't greeted her when she arrived. It seemed like hours ago. Bria glanced back at the two women cleaning the tables. They hadn't offered her anything to eat or drink. What kind of lord was this Knowles to treat people so rudely? In Castle Delaney, servants would be rushing over one another to serve any guest, much less a guest of noble blood.

Bria shifted slightly and dusted off her blue satin skirt.

"He won't see you," a voice called from the doorway behind her.

Bria swung around, appalled at Knowles's lack of hospitality. But she froze in terror and shock as Kenric approached her.

Run! The thought exploded through her mind, but fright held her immobile as Kenric's gaze swept her body disrespectfully. She wanted to dash from the room and keep running, never looking back. She wanted to hide behind a bush, in a cave, in the forest, anywhere this man wasn't. But she stood absolutely still, clenching her hands before her. She couldn't help but glance at the sword strapped to his waist.

"Lady Bria." He greeted her with a slight bow. "What a pleasure to see you again." A smug grin slithered onto his lips.

She frowned at the mockery in his voice. "Kenric," she managed to say.

"I'm so sorry, but Lord Knowles is quite . . . indisposed." Kenric told her. "If you would have sent a messenger . . ." He shrugged.

"Yes," she murmured. *Run!* The thought again pierced her mind. *Run!* But she didn't move for a long moment as she fought to remain calm. "Then I'll be going." She moved to step past him, aware of the sudden tightness in her chest.

He reached out for her arm, his fingers barely brushing her sleeve. She tore her arm away as if his nails were tipped with poison. A smile quirked his lips. "Do you desire some refreshment?"

"No," she said quickly. "Father is waiting for me. I'd better leave." The tightness in her chest refused to abate. She found it harder to take a breath the longer she stood near the man.

"Tell me what you came for, and I'll relay the message to Lord Knowles." Kenric's grin stretched across his face.

Bria stepped quickly away from him, shaking her head. She turned toward the exit and all but sprinted from the castle and into the courtyard outside.

She took the reins of her horse from the boy standing in the courtyard waiting for her. Her fingers were trembling so fiercely that she didn't dare attempt to mount her horse. She turned to look at the door, half expecting to find Kenric lounging against the doorway watching her, but he was nowhere to be seen. Her eyes swept the keep, moving upward over the stone wall. Was he watching her, laughing at her?

Bria turned away from the keep and moved toward the outer ward. She clenched her fist around the reins to try to stop her trembling. Her palms were slick with nervous perspiration. *Damn him. Damn Kenric for being able to do this to me, to make me feel this way. I am a grown woman, not a child any longer. I am a lady.*

And he is a murderer, a small voice inside her reminded. He'd killed Mary, and all she could do was run from him.

Her slender fingers curled into tight balls of rage. *I should have wrapped my hands around his throat and choked a confession out of him,* she thought angrily.

She stopped at the gatehouse to glance back over the inner wall toward the keep. Peasants moved all around her. An ale-maker herded his oxen toward the inner ward, a farmer led his team of horses out of the castle pulling an empty wagon, a knight dressed in chainmail raced by her toward the inner ward.

So this wasn't the way. But what was she to do? How could she face Kenric and pronounce him a murderer? He could have killed her right there on the spot if she'd actually confronted him. She grimaced. He would have killed her without hesitation.

This wasn't the way to bring Mary's murderer to justice. But there was a way. There had to be a way. And she vowed she would find it.

Terran stared out of his bedroom window at the courtyard below, his gaze traveling over the inner ward to the outer ward. He felt alone. Trapped. He had never liked to stay at his castle, choosing instead the life of a warrior, traveling the countryside from tournament to tournament. For years he had enjoyed fame at all the popular tournaments and jousts across England, he had even traveled to France several times to participate in the festive battles. Each victory had brought him magnificent spoils—glorious suits of armor, strong horses. He'd even ransomed off two defeated French nobles for a hearty sum.

Freedom. Success. Now he was trapped in a place where his beloved had died with the name of another man on her lips.

Terran's bitter gaze moved over the people in the outer ward. All of them were scurrying about their work, doing their business of the day. A merchant drove toward the inner ward, yelling at a child who had run before his cart and spooked his horse. A boy herded a group of sheep toward the outer gatehouse. A man was speaking earnestly with another man holding a horse's bridle.

Terran's lips curled in disgust. These pathetic people with their dull lives, their mindless duties. He didn't know them. And they mattered not a whit to him. Life would continue for them just as it had yesterday and the day before that. It didn't matter to them that Odella had died.

Then his gaze came to rest on a woman standing near the outer gatehouse, holding the reins to her horse. She was staring up at the keep, almost as though she were looking at him. Her brown hair was nearly hidden beneath a sheer blue veil, and her satin dress glimmered in the sunlight. She was a noblewoman. That much was obvious from her dress and the way she carried herself. Who was she? Terran wondered. She looked so lost, so forlorn—as desolate as he felt.

A knock sounded at the door. "Come!" Terran called, annoyed at the interruption.

The door swung open and Terran glanced over his shoulder to see a servant woman standing just inside the door.

"It's good to see you up—" the woman began, nervously.

Terran cut her off. "Who is that woman?" Terran looked back out the window, toward the outer gatehouse, his gaze sweeping the area. The boy herding the sheep was still there. The merchant was still there, moving into the inner ward. The woman was gone.

"What woman, m'lord?" the servant asked.

"She's gone," Terran whispered, half to himself. He wondered if he'd imagined her.

The servant woman sighed in understanding. "Lady Odella was a good woman."

"I'm not talking about Odella. There was a woman standing near the gatehouse . . ." The servant's patronizing look annoyed Terran, and he waved his hand quickly. "Never mind. What do you want?"

The servant bowed. "They're waiting for you in the Great Hall, m'lord."

"With all due respect, m'lord," Kenric said to Terran, "you need a dowry to save you."

Terran sat stoically in his judgment chair at the far end of the Great Hall. Here he listened to the seemingly endless litany of peasant complaints, problems, and pleas for assistance. The room was usually brightly lit with torches, filled with servants scurrying about, loud with the conversation of peasants and farmers, but not today. He'd ordered all the torches to be extinguished, had sent the servants away.

Odella's smile haunted his memories. Her scent followed

him wherever he went. She'd been everything to him—his sunshine. Now he hated the sun for reminding him of her. His betrothed was gone, and he was in even more desperate financial straits than before.

How could he have known his own prowess as a knight, his own skill as a fighter on the battlefield, would cause his current financial woes? As his skill and reputation had grown, so had the fear and unease of his opponents. No one would face him on the field of battle. At first, this fear had been a great source of pride, but as the number of men willing to face him quickly dwindled, so had his treasury.

Eventually, he'd been forced to travel to remote provinces to find tournaments where he wasn't known. By then, his castle had fallen behind in its tithe to church and king.

But he didn't give a damn. Let the king take this castle. Let him take everything.

"M'lord," Kenric prompted, looking for some kind of response. "Terran, you're going to lose Castle Knowles in three months' time. You need to do something."

Terran grunted and turned away.

"You need to marry someone with a large dowry to save Castle Knowles. You need a betrothal—"

"I had one," Terran growled.

"Yes. Well, since that one is . . . no longer, may I suggest another?"

"No," Terran snapped. "You insult her memory by suggesting such a thing."

"M'lord," Kenric said, approaching him, "I know you loved her. But she is gone and you need to move on. The farms are not producing enough. The peasants are not happy."

"I don't give a damn," Terran growled.

"There's an easy solution."

"I know what you're going to say, and I don't want to hear it."

"You were betrothed once before," Kenric said. "From when you were born."

"I don't want to hear it," Terran repeated.

"The Delaney lands are very profitable. They could well support you and your lands. All you need do is marry Delaney's daughter."

"I don't want another wife."

"Delaney is trying to betroth her to another. Go and claim your rights. It will save your castle."

"Perhaps you didn't hear me. I don't want any other woman."

"You can grieve out on the cold ground, or you can grieve in your own nice warm castle. It doesn't matter to me, cousin. But this is an easy way out."

Terran's lip curled in disgust. "Delaney would never give her to me, not after what I did. Not with so many others vying for her hand."

Kenric smiled. "I'll take care of everything. You'll have the lady Bria's dowry to save your lands."

Terran couldn't care less. All he wanted was Odella, and he couldn't have her.

"Your time is running out," Kenric reminded him. "I know the thought of marriage is repulsive, but there's no other solution. I will handle Delaney's daughter for you."

Terran grunted and leaned back in his chair. "Do whatever you want."

Kenric bowed and moved out of the room.

Bria quickened her step and walked down the road toward Knowles Village. Her hand was wrapped tightly around the reins of her horse, her palms wet with nervous perspiration. *Damn him. Damn Kenric for being so evil.* No one else made her tremble this way.

No one else you know is a murderer, the voice inside her reminded.

"Excuse me, m'lady."

Bria glanced up to see a peasant hauling a cart filled with dried-out corn and rotten, worm-infested apples.

"Would you like to buy some of my fruit?" the man said.

Bria looked away from the horrendous fruit to stare at him. His brow was slick with sweat, his face reddened from exertion. He had a dark purple bruise on his forehead. "Where's your horse?" Bria wondered.

The man shifted nervously. "Well, I . . ." He squared his shoulders. "I owed taxes and one of the tax collectors took my horse as payment."

Bria scowled. Knowles's men. His evil was spreading everywhere. "If you have no horse, how will you work your fields?"

The man opened his mouth to reply, but promptly shut it. His shoulders sagged in defeat. "I . . . don't know. I will do what I can."

"Shouldn't you be working the fields now?" Bria wondered.

"Yes. But Lord Knowles just raised the taxes, and I need more income. My wife is working the fields, and I'm trying to sell this fruit. She would have done it, but she can't pull the cart."

Bria glanced back at the towering castle behind her, the fortress of Terran Knowles. Home of the ogre who refused to see visitors, but taxed his people to death. This was what Mary was talking about, she realized, what she must have experienced day after heartbreaking day. This was why she'd charged to the rescue of Widow Anderson.

Bria reached down to the belt at her waist and untied a small leather purse. Without a second thought, she handed it to the man.

He took the purse, shook it to hear the jangle of coins, then looked inside. "You want corn or apples?"

"I don't want any of it." Bria moved to step past him.

"But, m'lady," he objected, "surely you want something in return!"

"Keep it," Bria replied. "It's the least I can do for you and your family."

The man's eyes widened. "God bless you, m'lady. God bless you!"

Bria wished she had more to give to the poor man. She wished she had enough to take care of the entire village. They needed someone to watch over them, someone to protect them, someone to take a stand against that ogre Terran Knowles and Randolph Kenric and all of the other men under their command, she thought bitterly. What they really needed was a Midnight Shadow they could call their own. She sighed a tired sigh. If only her grand hero wasn't a figment of her imagination. If only the Midnight Shadow were real.

Chapter Seven

The fire from the hearth heated Bria's cheeks, as well as her anger. Her gaze was trained on the group of men gathered about her father, all come to Castle Delaney to win her hand in marriage. She'd been briefly introduced to all of them, but couldn't remember a single one of their names. Garret was the only man she knew.

They were all seated around her father, talking earnestly to him, no doubt boasting about their prowess in battle or the size of their coffers. She shook her head and turned her gaze back to the fire.

Maybe they should spend more time wooing me instead of my father, she thought with disgust. Not that she wanted them to pay attention to her. She'd done everything in her power to discourage their attentions during the last three weeks, which was undoubtedly why they'd turned their attentions to her father.

One of the castle dogs wandered by and nudged her fingers. Bria absently scratched the animal's head. She missed Mary so, and she couldn't stop thinking about that night. Maybe she shouldn't take all the blame. If Mary hadn't run out to help the Widow Anderson . . . Bria shook her head. For weeks, Mary had been angry about the taxes Lord Knowles was imposing on them. She would have run out to help Widow Anderson even if she'd been surrounded by twenty armed men.

Bria thought back to the poor farmer selling rotten apples and shriveled corn. He'd been so grateful for her assistance. The poor people of Knowles. What a tyrant! Bria began to shake her head, wishing she could help them.

Suddenly, she froze. Maybe she couldn't get everyone to realize Kenric was a murderer, but she could make Mary's death mean something. She could defend the people of Knowles Village. She could help them survive amidst the terror of Knowles's tyranny. Like the Midnight Shadow.

Well, not exactly like him. But she could help the people.

Laughter erupted from the group of suitors, drawing her attention. *The pompous buffoons. They could help Knowles's people—if they wanted.* But they were too self-absorbed to be any good to her, even Garret. She wished she could talk to him about what to do, what needed to be done to help the people. But he'd just brush her aside and tell her there was nothing *to* do. Bria knew nothing was further from the truth.

"You'll have to choose one of them."

Bria glanced aside to see her grandfather standing beside her chair. She grunted softly. "I'll choose the one who apprehends Mary's murderer."

Harry sighed. "Garret is a fine man," he encouraged, ignoring her comment.

"Garret is a good friend," Bria retorted, crossing her arms stubbornly and leaning back in her chair. "I just can't see him as my husband."

"You'd better see someone as your husband," Harry warned, "or your father will choose for you."

Bria's scowl deepened. "Maybe they can win *his* hand in

marriage.'' She jerked her head toward the group around her father. With that, she stood up and headed out of the Great Hall.

For the remainder of the day she avoided her suitors. She spent time embroidering, which she hated, but no one would think to look for her in the small room with the rest of her ladies. She spent time in the kitchens trying to help the cook, but getting in the way more than not.

Finally, she retired to her room, skipping the last dinner completely. It was only now, late at night, that Bria could finally relax. She sat on the window ledge, staring at the moon floating high in the dark sky. It was almost full, a sliver of it gone as if an artist had chiseled it away. Or maybe a lover had stolen a piece of it to give to his fair lady, Bria thought wistfully. She wondered if she'd ever feel that kind of love. She didn't think so.

Suddenly, the pounding of horses' hooves sounded in the courtyard. She glanced down from her seat on the window ledge as a group of five soldiers thundered in.

They came to a halt in the middle of the inner ward and dismounted. One man gave orders. Bria couldn't hear the words, only the resonance of his voice echoing off the castle walls. The men moved to obey his commands. The leader stood, his hands planted on his hips, gazing up at the keep. He reached up to slide his chainmailed hood from his head. Flowing black hair fell about his shoulders.

Bria squinted, trying to make out the man's face, but he was too far away and the night was too dark. She shrugged slightly. Rude of him to be coming this late at night, Bria thought. Her father was in bed and couldn't welcome him properly.

As if to confirm her thoughts, her father's personal servant rushed out in a long night dress to greet the leader, bowing humbly. One of the soldiers moved to the leader's side. Together they turned to gaze at her.

Bria straightened her shoulders. If she'd been closer, she would have been able to see his face, his eyes. As it was, she could see neither. But his gaze pinned her where she sat. Strangely, a tingle raced along her shoulder blades.

He gazed at her for a long moment and then turned toward the servant. After a moment, he followed the servant up the stairs and into the keep.

Bria watched until he'd disappeared inside the doors and they were closed behind him. She narrowed her eyes slightly, wondering who the arrogant lord was. She hoped he wasn't another suitor, but something in her told her he was.

The next morning, Bria stood in the outer ward, staring at the lowered drawbridge, wishing her father had asked her to go hunting with him. Instead, he'd taken her suitors. She was surprised when even Garret had gone.

"What troubles you?"

Bria shook herself from her thoughts and turned from the entrance to look at her grandfather.

Harry smiled warmly at her. "There are other places you'd like to be, eh?" He leaned close to her. "Me, too."

Bria smiled and returned her gaze to the soft blue velvet in her hand. She placed the fabric down on the merchant's cart and moved to the next fabric. Harry trailed behind her as she softly touched the material and then moved to the next fabric laid out on the wooden pushcart in the outer ward.

The merchant said to her grandfather, "Perhaps some beautiful satin will make her happy."

Her grandfather glanced at him, but didn't answer.

Bria didn't even look at the merchant. Her mind was occupied by the five men out hunting with her father. She didn't want to marry any of them. Bria shook her head, trying to shake the feeling of trepidation mounting inside her at her pending betrothal. She could only hope someone else would show up to rescue her from the sinking feeling growing deeper in the pit of her stomach.

"You went to Castle Knowles after Mary's death, didn't you?" Harry asked.

Bria was so unprepared for his statement that she turned to him, affirmation written all over her face.

Harry shook his head in disapproval.

"I had to do something!" Bria objected in a low voice. "I was hoping Knowles wasn't as bad as I was hearing."

"He's worse," the merchant whispered.

Bria's eyes shifted to the merchant as he presented her a piece of red satin.

"I'll never grace his lands again," the merchant continued. "His tax collectors stopped my wagon yesterday, demanding payment for my passage through their lands."

Bria perused the short man. His black hair was creeping away from his forehead; his eyes were lined with age. He had to look up to meet her gaze.

"Now, I consider myself a very fair man, as my prices are testament." He indicated the fabrics on the table with a generous wave of his hand.

Bria didn't move. "Go on."

"Oh, yes. Well, I was ready to give my fair amount. It's not unheard of for a lord to tax a poor merchant. After all, we're only trying to make a living. We work as hard as any man—"

"About the tax collectors," Bria reminded him.

"Of course. Sheriff Kenric and his men stopped me on the road and demanded payment. But what he asked was three times anything I have ever heard of! It was an outrageous amount. He might as well have stolen my entire wagon of fabrics. I usually have three or four tables filled with cloth. As you see, today I have but one."

Bria glanced at her grandfather. What Lord Knowles was

doing to the people of his lands, as well as those visiting, was preposterous. Anger surged through her so fiercely that she clenched her fist around the red satin fabric.

"M'lady, please," the merchant said gently. "The few goods I have left are quite delicate."

Bria immediately dropped the red satin and mumbled an apology. She moved on to the next piece of fabric and her breath caught in her throat. It was a rich, luxurious black velvet. Hesitantly, she reached out to touch the fabric, which caught the light of the sun and seemed to absorb it. It was beautiful— perfect! "Grandfather, don't you think this is what the—" She stopped suddenly, feeling foolish about speaking of her imaginary hero in front of the merchant. "Never mind." Though she didn't say it, this fabric was exactly what the Midnight Shadow would wear.

Bria stroked the material lovingly, sensing something powerful in its color.

A hand seized her wrist and she glanced up into her grandfather's intense blue eyes. "Bria," he whispered.

"What?" she asked, confused at his intensity.

"Don't do anything rash," he pleaded.

Bria shook her head in confusion. "I don't know what you mean." But even as she said the words, her gaze traveled to the black velvet. Exactly what the Midnight Shadow would wear.

"Have you decided upon some fabric?" the merchant wondered.

Bria lifted her gaze to the merchant, a reply on her lips, but over the merchant's shoulder through the inner gatehouse, she spotted a tall man with hair as black as the witching hour moving past the opening. Was it the man she'd seen in the courtyard the previous night? She dropped the black velvet back onto the cart. She wanted to have a few words with the man for arriving so late. "Excuse me," she muttered and moved quickly toward the gatehouse.

"Bria!" her grandfather called after her.

She raced after the dark-haired stranger, feeling the need to explain to him why it wasn't good manners to arrive so late—and, in doing so, discourage him from seeking her hand. She agilely dodged the other merchants in the outer ward.

She skidded to a halt just inside the inner ward, looking first left, then right. The courtyard was packed with peasants and knights come to see what the merchants were selling.

Bria exhaled sharply, thinking she'd lost him. But then the man revealed himself, rising from a bent position. He was tall, Bria realized, a good head above the tallest man in the crowd.

That did not dissuade her from her mission. Bria followed him as he continued into the inner ward toward the keep, skirting the crowd. She kept her gaze on him so as not to lose sight of him, though it would have been hard to do so. As he moved through the ward, Bria noticed his confident gait, as if he were used to getting what he wanted. Well, she thought, this was one woman who would sorely disappoint him.

She followed, studying his back. His shoulders were broad. He was probably a warrior.

Bria almost slammed into a woman carrying a basket of eggs, but she dodged to the left and moved around her.

The man paused to speak with another man, a peasant by the looks of his brown tunic and breeches frayed around the ankles. Bria tried to see the visitor's face when he glanced back toward the open gatehouse, but he turned away from her to the peasant, giving her only a teasing glimpse of his tanned skin. Then he continued into the keep.

Bria continued her pursuit, bounding up the steps. Inside there were fewer people, and she moved a little faster. He was directly in front of her, walking down the hallway. His black hair just touched his strong shoulders. At this range, she could see blue highlights in his hair as he moved past the torchlight. It looked thick and wavy, and she wondered if it would feel as soft as it looked.

She shrugged off the thought. He could have the most luxurious hair in the land, and it wouldn't make his late arrival any more correct.

"Excuse me!" she called.

He didn't stop.

"Excuse me!" she called louder. Her voice echoed in the hallway.

He halted in the middle of the corridor.

Bria slowed her rushed walk to stop directly behind him. She'd opened her mouth to reprimand him for his ungracious behavior when he turned. She stood, staring, unable to say a word. Her anger dissipated like water in a drought.

The visitor's face was rugged, a knight's face, but there was more to it. His jaw was strong and square, clean of stubble. His sensual lips were curved in a cynical twist. His nose was straight. But it was his eyes that captured Bria's attention. They were black, the darkest eyes she'd ever seen. Yet there was something gentle in them, something that called to her. His glorious hair framed his face with black waves.

Bria stared, unable to utter a word. For here she stood, face to face, with the most handsome man she had ever seen.

Chapter Eight

"You!" Terran gasped, recognizing the woman he'd seen standing at the gatehouse at Castle Knowles. What was she doing here? Who was she?

He could only stare into those blue eyes. Like rare gems, they shone and sparkled with an inner light of their own. His eyes perused her face slowly, savoring every gorgeous inch— her slightly uplifted nose, her high cheekbones, her full, kissable lips. He had a sudden desire to take her into some alcove and sample those lips to see if they were as soft and delicious as they appeared. Her hair was uncovered, and the wild, rebellious locks hung loose, curling around her cheeks and neck, as if to call attention to her most delicate attributes.

He'd never in his life felt this kind of desire. With Odella it had been different. He'd wanted to worship her beauty, not touch her. He realized with unexpected shock that Odella had been more like a prize to him than a flesh-and-blood woman. But this woman, God save him, this woman he wanted to kiss and ravish and worship in a very different way.

Is this some sort of witchcraft? he wondered. *How could I possibly feel such an attraction when I've only just come face to face with her?*

"Welcome to Castle Delaney," she greeted. Her voice was soft and husky. Terran found himself strangely mesmerized by the movement of her lips.

"Thank you," he said . . . and found it was all he could say.

"You arrived late last night," she said.

Terran stared at her. A scowl crossed his brow as her accusation penetrated his musings. He nodded. "How did you . . ." Then he remembered seeing the woman far above in the keep, watching. At first glance he'd believed her to be an angel floating far above him. But slowly he realized she'd been seated on a ledge and her ethereal glow was due to her white night dress and the light of the moon. "Ahh," he said. "It was you who greeted me with your silent gaze."

"I'm sure Lord Delaney would have greeted you himself if you hadn't arrived at such a late hour," she replied.

A grin curved his lips. This bewitching little nymph had spirit. It took courage for a woman to speak so boldly to a lord. He found himself liking that willful energy very much. "We rode long and hard, but could not have made it earlier."

She nodded, thoughtfully. "I see," she said softly. "And who does Castle Delaney have the pleasure of welcoming?"

Terran opened his mouth to reply, but closed it promptly. How much did she know about Lord Knowles? He wasn't oblivious to some of the foul rumors that had been spread about him. If she were anyone in the castle of importance, or even anyone who lived in the castle at all, she would already know of him. And most likely dislike him. "You may call me 'lord.' "

A frown crossed her brow and her lips gave a sensual little pout, but she assented with a nod.

"And you?" he wondered.

"You may address me as 'lady.' "

Terran chuckled. "This game could become most dangerous."

"Oh," she asked innocently, "how so?"

Was she truly so innocent, or was she enticing him? One side of his lips rose in a grin. "How so, indeed," he whispered. "Perhaps 'lady' would like to give me a tour of this grand castle."

Her gaze swept him and he felt his blood race. A mere look from those blue eyes was enough to call forth images of her naked body below his, her lovely lips parted in a moan of ecstasy.

"Very well," she agreed.

Terran stared at her, intrigued. She was either too trusting or a sly vixen. He would decide which.

He held out his arm to her, and she hooked her hand through it. Her touch sent tremors racing through his body. *God's blood! If a mere touch of her fingers gives me this much pleasure, I'll be in heaven tasting her lips.*

As they walked, he glanced at her out of the corner of his eye. Why was he so attracted to this woman? He was in mourning for Odella, and yet he felt as though . . . as though she was nothing compared to the vibrancy and life he felt from the woman beside him. He wanted nothing more than to kiss her and touch her. Maybe she could cure him of this horrible ache in his chest, this emptiness, at least for a few hours.

"You must have ridden a long way," she said.

The little vixen. She was trying to get information from him. "Long enough to need a hot bath," he admitted.

"I'm sure the servants saw to that last night," she said. "What would you like to see first?" she wondered after a moment.

"Nothing," a voice from behind them called. "If he wants to see the castle, he can find someone else to show him."

An old man stood just behind them in the hallway, and Terran's smile died as he saw the fury in the man's eyes. It was quite obvious the old man knew who he was and quite apparent that he didn't like him. This was the reaction Terran had prepared himself for. He sighed and calmly removed 'lady's' hand from his arm. "I'm afraid our excursion is over," he said.

"Grandfather!" she objected. "I'm more than capable of taking him—"

"Do as I say, girl," he commanded. "Come away from him."

Terran's jaw tightened at the way the old man spoke. There was no reason to be harsh with her. It wasn't her fault.

The woman stood her ground for a long moment, her chin raised slightly, her eyes flashing like lightning. Then she stalked away from Terran and joined the old man.

Terran bowed slightly to the old man before moving away from them.

"Grandfather! That was rude."

"He is not welcome here," her grandfather snarled, "and you will stay away from him."

"Who is he?" Bria asked, taken aback by his vehemence.

"It's best your father tell you." Harry took her hand and led her in the opposite direction from the way the man had gone.

Bria walked beside her grandfather, her curiosity more than piqued. Who was the man? Where had he come from? And why did her grandfather hate him so?

"We should start our practices again," Harry said. "Meet me tonight."

Lord Delaney and the suitors returned from the hunt that afternoon. Terran watched them dismount from a balcony in the keep. He'd been denied a room at the castle, further evidence

Lord Delaney wanted nothing to do with him. But that didn't dissuade Terran. He set up camp on the meadows just outside the castle.

Falconers rushed up to the men, removing the falcons from the hunters' wrists to bring the birds to the mews for a rest.

Lord Delaney was at the front of the group. The others followed him like lap dogs, vying for attention. Terran shook his head slightly. And then he looked closer at one of the suitors. Even from this distance, the blond hair and handsome face were unmistakable.

Garret Dysen. The man Odella had called for as death claimed her. Terran's jaw clenched; his shoulders became rigid. He had the sudden desire to run the man through.

Suddenly, a woman ran out to the group. She threw her arms around Lord Delaney's neck and spoke briefly with him. Terran recognized her instantly. It was 'lady' from the hallway. As he watched the vibrant little nymph, she exchanged words with all the men and then grabbed Garret's hand, pulling him through the inner ward toward the outer gatehouse.

A fierce rage seized Terran. What was this? he wondered, scowling fiercely. Where was she going with him? But then he knew instinctively: she was going for a tryst with her lover.

So, he thought, this Garret whom Odella had loved so much was a faithless dog. And his little vixen was just that—a temptress for all men to beware. Including him.

Chapter Nine

"Show me!" Bria whispered.

"All right," Garret exclaimed, "all right!" He laughed. "You certainly can be insistent."

She crossed her arms. "You haven't seen the half of it."

They were standing in a clearing just outside the castle, hidden from any castle occupant's view by a thick growth of trees. Bria had led Garret there because she didn't want anyone to see her using a sword.

Garret held out his sword to her. Her fingers wrapped around the handle. Bria swung the sword from side to side, testing it, feeling its weight.

Garret moved away from her to the outer edges of the clearing and searched the ground until he found a large branch.

When Bria turned to him, he was approaching her with the branch, swinging it in circles first around one shoulder, then the other. He hefted it once and then held it before him like a sword.

Bria took a step forward and crossed her sword with the branch.

"By now your grandfather knows all your moves," Garret said.

"He taught them to me," Bria answered with a slight shrug.

"Then you have to come up with new ones. And don't think about just using your sword. Use your body as well."

"My body?"

"Sure," Garret said. "For example . . ." He swung the branch at her several times, slowly. Bria easily blocked each move. Then he grabbed her wrist and moved toward her, stepping on her toes lightly with his.

"Garret!" Bria cried. "Isn't that cheating?"

"Not when you're not as strong as your opponent." Garret shrugged slightly, still holding her wrist. "And don't use your feet just to step on someone. Kick with them." He brought his leg around to kick her softly behind her knees, making her buckle. He quickly helped her right herself, pulling her closer. "Or you can use your shoulder to ram them," he added.

Bria nodded. "I see."

Garret drew closer to her, looking at her over the crossed weapons. "You're guaranteed to win," he whispered.

Bria smiled. She could just picture her grandfather's face when she beat him! His surprised look, his . . . suddenly she realized Garret was leaning closer, his eyes closed, his lips puckered. "Garret!" she protested, pushing away from him.

"What?" he demanded.

"Don't do that!" Bria said.

"I just thought that since we might marry—"

"Stop it!" Bria said. "Don't talk like that."

Garret frowned. "You know that's why I'm here."

Bria backed away from him. Everything felt too strange. It would be like kissing a brother. Not like kissing . . . well, not like kissing the man she'd met earlier that day. "I said stop."

"But, Bria—"

"I have a sword, you know." She waved it before her to keep him at bay.

"All right," Garret assented, holding up his hands and taking a step away. "But when we're wed—"

"I said stop it!" Bria cried, dropping the sword. She turned and raced back to the castle. She wasn't ready to talk to Garret about marriage. She didn't even want to think about it.

But there was something she wanted to think about. Another man taking her into his arms and kissing her—a man with midnight black hair.

As she moved back toward the castle, she saw the cloth merchant she'd been speaking to in the inner ward packing up his cart. She stopped as she spotted the black velvet draped across the side of the cart wall. He smiled tiredly as she approached. She reached into the cart and ran her hand across the softness.

"It certainly seems to be calling to you, don't you think?" the merchant said. "I've seen it happen often. Some women and some fabrics are just meant to be together."

Bria studied the velvet for a long moment. Strange as it was, it did seem as if the cloth was something she had to have. She couldn't take her gaze from its black sheen.

"Would you like me to have a horse's width brought up to your room? It would make a fine dress."

The ghost of a grin appeared on her lips. A dress wasn't exactly what she had in mind. "Make it three horses' widths."

The merchant bowed slightly.

Bria turned a brilliant smile on him and raced inside, moving toward the Great Hall. She didn't quite understand the surge of excitement that blossomed in her chest, but something inside her was telling her she'd just made one of the most momentous decisions in her life.

Dinner was being served as she entered the Great Hall. The smell of spiced duck filled the large room. She took only two steps before she faltered, coming to a dead stop. The cloud of elation she'd brought into the room with her immediately darkened, turning into a thick fog of disheartenment. One seat was empty on the raised platform at the far end of where she always sat to eat. It was between Lord Prescott and Lord Brent. Funny, she remembered their names when she least wanted to. She winced slightly and glanced over her shoulder at the double doors. There was still time to run.

Before she could make her escape, Garret entered and moved past her, whispering, "Coward." He moved around her and walked confidently up the long aisle to his seat at the head table.

Bria ground her teeth. There would be no escape from her suitors wherever she went. She could avoid them for only so long. It was time to face her future. She straightened her back in resolve and walked up to the head table, smiling as graciously at her suitors as she could while gritting her teeth. Lord Brent smiled up at her like a tiger spotting its kill as she sat next to him. Thankfully, a large portion of duck and bread was set before them and everyone set about immediately to eat.

She reached for the food and stopped, slowly glancing around her, noticing that the conversation in the room had lowered to a murmur. She lifted her gaze to the rear of the Great Hall. A tall man dressed in black moved up the middle aisle toward her, toward the head table.

Bria gasped. It was the man she'd met in the hallway, her "lord." She straightened, trying to see him better past all the servants who scurried about the table to accommodate the nobles.

His black hair hung to his shoulders, glimmering in the light from the torches on the wall, the dark strands framing his face. Somehow he was even more handsome than she remembered. His black tunic clung to his broad chest, open in a V shape to reveal the strong, smooth skin beneath. She followed the opening in his black tunic down to his waist, where he wore a black leather scabbard. His muscled thighs were clad in tight black leggings and his black leather boots barely made a sound as he moved toward her.

But again his dark, brooding eyes caught her attention, making her heart hammer in her chest. They were locked on her. A tremor raced up her spine.

He stopped before the head table, and his gaze shifted from her to pin her father to his chair. For the first time, Bria realized her father's hands were clenched in fists atop the table.

"Lord Delaney." The man's deep voice sent shivers through Bria's body.

"Good day," her father answered amiably enough, but Bria heard the barely restrained tension in his voice.

"Since you didn't greet me last night when I arrived—"

"It was very late," her father answered.

The lord continued as though her father hadn't spoken. "I will state my intentions now. I've come to marry your daughter."

Excitement flared through Bria. Her heart raced. He'd come to seek her hand! Bria had guessed as much. Still, the words gave her a thrill she'd never experienced. The thought of being encompassed by those strong arms sent shivers of excitement racing up her spine.

A murmuring of objections came from the lords seated around her at the head table. How could they hope to compete with her "lord"?

Her father slowly rose from his chair. He was shaking his head as if in amusement, but there was a serious scowl on his brow. "Lord Knowles, I'm afraid that's quite—"

Lord Knowles? Bria's mind repeated the name over and over, first in confusion and slowly in mounting anger. "Lord Knowles?" Bria gasped. Any thought of finding excitement in his arms quickly vanished. Anger and humiliation washed through her. How dare he deceive her? He was her enemy!

She was on her feet as she pounded the table with her fists. "Never!" she ground out between her clenched teeth.

That drew his gaze. The two beacons of darkness centered on her.

"I'll never marry you," she vowed, storming from the table.

Chapter Ten

Terran watched with keen interest as his future wife left the room in a huff. The little firebrand from the hallway was Bria Delaney! He studied the sway of her shapely curves as she stormed from the room and realized he could do worse, much worse. At least he knew how she felt from the beginning. There'd be no surprises like the one Odella had presented upon her deathbed. No, Bria was not like Odella at all.

He turned to glance at Garret Dysen, who sat but a few chairs from him. Hatred burned keenly in the man's eyes. Terran's jaw clenched as anger and resentment burned inside him. It had taken him by surprise that Odella had loved Dysen, but it was no secret how Bria felt about him.

Terran mentally shook himself. That damned Kenric said he'd taken care of everything.

"You're not welcome here," Lord Delaney snapped. "I suggest you leave."

Terran turned to glare at Lord Delaney. The room was so quiet that Terran swore he heard the anger sizzling through his host's blood. "I'll leave when I have my betrothed," Terran answered.

"You broke that contract when you chose to take a new wife," Delaney answered.

There was such blatant hostility in his voice that Terran decided he liked the man. He certainly had no problem expressing his dislikes. "We never married," Terran growled. As if it was any of his concern.

"Lady Bria deserves better than you," Lord Brent said.

Terran pinned Brent with a searing gaze. He was an older man here to obtain a rich dowry, no doubt. "Let any man who doubts the legitimacy of my claim challenge me in a joust."

"No," Delaney roared. "I forbid it. There will be no fighting at Castle Delaney. We will settle this like civilized men."

"There is nothing to settle. The dowry was set by my grandfather and your father. I will adhere to the terms, as will you," Terran ordered.

"That is impossible," Delaney said. "I have just sealed Bria's betrothal to Lord Garret."

Surprise rocked Terran and his glare shot to Garret. Odella had killed herself out of love for him. Now the man was betrothed to his future bride! *Will this man ever stop dogging my every step?*

Terran's gaze moved over the other suitors. By the displeased grumbling and the shocked looks on their faces, Terran knew Delaney had made a snap decision to thwart him. His stare slammed back to Delaney. He smashed his fist on the table. "She is mine. I will not permit such insolence!"

Amid the stares of disapproval, Terran quickly composed himself. He straightened and forced his voice to be calm, hiding the fierce rage that burned within. "If you persist in being unreasonable, I will take it up with the king. I'm sure he'll see it my way." He turned and quickly left the room, fighting to keep his feelings inside. But as he entered a spiral stairway, his rage finally surfaced, burning like molten lava in his veins.

He pounded the wall once, hard. A savage growl tore loose from his throat.

God's blood! Must Dysen haunt me all my life? No matter. Bria will be mine in the end. I will see to it.

"Knowles! Where are you?" a voice called from the hallway.

Terran stepped out of the stairway to confront the anger he heard in the man's voice. His own fury flared upon seeing Dysen standing in the middle of the hallway, searching for him.

Garret spotted him and stalked toward him. His fists were clenched at his side, his shoulders bunched, his eyes narrowed to twin orbs of flame. He stopped just feet from Terran. "Stay away from her, Knowles," Garret snarled.

"I can hardly do that when she is to be my wife." Terran fought to retain his calm, but deep inside he felt none of the even-temperedness that he put on.

"Did you not hear what Lord Delaney said? Lady Bria will be *my* wife."

Terran lowered his chin and glared. "That remains to be seen."

"Look, Knowles," Garret said, "I respected your right to Lady Odella when you won her. I expect you to do the same."

"Yes," Terran growled, feeling the fury rise within him, "except you neglected to tell me that you had already won her heart."

Garret's mouth dropped open, but he promptly closed it.

"Your name was the last thing she ever said."

Garret's brows drew together in agony, and for a moment he looked away from Terran. "Yes," he admitted, "we loved each other." When he lifted his gaze, there was bitterness and rage glittering in his eyes. "But when her father chose you, we agreed to abide by his decision. I left her with you."

Terran straightened slightly. *Perhaps Dysen is more honorable than I've given him credit for. Perhaps he did love Odella, and she loved him. Perhaps everything I thought was love was*

*nothing of the sort. Could it be I only loved Odella as I'd love
the spoils of war?*

"And you tormented her so much she took her own life,"
Garret added.

The words snapped Terran out of his ponderings. His fists
clenched. The accusation was insulting. "I think your giving
up on her love drove her to it, not me."

Fury flamed in Garret's eyes. "So you've come here to get
even?"

Terran began to turn away. "I've come for my wife."

Garret seized his arm, halting him. "You think you can go
from one woman to the next without a thought to their feelings?
Well, it isn't going to work this time. You won't have Bria."

"Is that a threat?" Terran asked, jerking his arm free of
Garret's hold.

"Consider it a challenge. Tomorrow on the tilting field."

"I'd have it no other way."

Two swords crossed in the moonlight, their metal blades
clanging as they collided.

"Come on, girl," Harry goaded Bria, who was standing
mere inches from him, trying to stare him down. "Concentrate.
You want me to defeat you?" He swung his sword around to
the side and in.

Bria just barely blocked it. She swung and the blades pushed
hard against each other, then abruptly separated, the slender
steel screeching as they slid free. Bria swung again, but Harry
backed away and her blade whistled through empty air. She
swung a third time, but this time Harry caught her swing and
grabbed her wrist, bringing her in close so they were nose to
nose.

"You have to control your anger," he warned, "especially
when you fight." He pushed off of her sword and swung.

She ducked and spun away from him, then countered with

an arc to his head. He blocked her blow. She lunged and then feinted left.

It took all his concentration to match her move and block it. She was quick, much quicker than he was. And she was smart. He could see her mind working even as she lunged. He caught her sword and twisted his wrist. He'd disarmed her more than once with that move.

But tonight it didn't work.

Bria held her wrist firm and angled his weapon into the ground.

Disappointment settled heavily about his shoulders. How many times had he told her she couldn't win against his strength? But just when he was about to overpower her and push her sword into the earth, she lurched forward, planting her leg behind his, and shoved him hard with her shoulder.

He went over like a felled tree, slamming into the ground on his back. Startled, he took a moment to recover and catch his breath. He began to rise, only to find the tip of a sword at his neck. Her blue eyes glinted, the full moon reflected in her bright gaze, a triumphant smile curling her lips.

With a sigh, he settled back against the grassy bed of the ground. "Well done," he said.

Bria's smile grew. "Yield," she commanded.

His head came up quickly. "Don't press your luck," he said.

Bria withdrew her sword and laughed in pure delight. She threw her head back and joyful glee churned merrily from within her throat. "It worked! I did it!" she proclaimed. "I actually did it!"

Harry pushed himself to a sitting position. Every muscle in his body ached. The fall hadn't done much to help his brittle bones either.

Bria danced happily around him, spinning wildly, as if she'd just won her first joust.

Harry planted his hands on the ground and began to ease himself to his feet.

Bria stopped her dance of victory and moved to his side, grabbing his arm and helping him to his feet. "I'm sorry," she said, "but I've never won before. Garret said I could beat you if I used my wits and body. He said there were other ways to win a battle!"

Harry nodded. "Your skill has increased."

"Increased?" Bria exclaimed. "I beat you!"

"I'm not the young man I once was, or I doubt you could have accomplished that." He knew that he was lying to save his wounded pride.

Bria took several instinctive steps toward the tethered horses.

"Stay on our lands!" Harry shouted after her.

Bria stopped cold. Harry watched her happiness fade as she stared at the forest, and he immediately regretted his words. With her friend dead, she had no reason to go racing off into the woods.

He placed an arm about her shoulders. "Mary knows," he whispered. "She knows you beat me."

He felt the agony written in her eyes, the grief etched in her brow. She threw her hands around his shoulders. Harry held her close, sharing her pain, soothing her with gentle touches and whispered words. But he knew nothing he said or did could replace her lost friend.

Later that night in her room, Bria stared out the window at the moon. The round circle shining in the cloudless night sky reminded her of a wide, shocked eye—shocked because of her instant reaction to Lord Knowles. She tried to push the attraction aside, but it lingered.

Terran Knowles! How dare he show up at her own castle, demanding her hand in marriage, looking like some valiant knight? Giving her hope there was someone out there she wouldn't mind marrying? And then revealing himself as her most foul enemy! The cur.

Bria turned away from the moon, trying to push his accursed image from her mind. She concentrated on her victory earlier that night, the joy and excitement she'd felt when she'd defeated her grandfather. Her first impulse had been to run off and tell Mary. Her friend would have been so proud of her.

She threw herself down upon the bed. If only she could make Kenric and that deceitful Knowles pay for their vile behavior.

Her hand brushed something soft, and she glanced down to see she was sitting on the black velvet she'd bought from the merchant. She picked up the material and held the fabric against her face, then draped it across her shoulders and leaped on the bed. "I am the Midnight Shadow," she said softly, striking a pose with her hands on her hips. A feeling of power and righteousness filled her—a feeling very similar to what she'd felt after giving the poor farmer the coin in the village of Knowles.

She'd felt so full of confidence that she could make a difference, a confidence renewed when Garret had shown her how to win the fight with her grandfather . . . and it worked! Because of her new assuredness, she was able to defeat him. She felt strong and unbeatable, confident enough to take on the world.

Then the questions came from deep inside her, questions which now repeated themselves over and over in her mind: *Confident enough to take on the world, yes. But confident enough to avenge Mary's death? Confident enough to stop Kenric's reign of terror over helpless farmers and merchants? Confident enough to wage a secret war against that monster Terran Knowles?*

She stared at the midnight moon and thought of a different kind of midnight, one in human form. The Midnight Shadow would know what to do.

Bria shook her head and lowered her hand so that the fabric fell from her face and shoulders. The feeling of confidence and strength that had surged through her quickly faded. He was only a legend, not someone real. Yet why couldn't someone become the Midnight Shadow to give the people hope?

She dropped to the bed. *I could be the Midnight Shadow,* she thought for a fleeting moment. Then a wistful smile crossed her lips. She could be, if she were more courageous. Then an idea came to her. Maybe she couldn't be the Midnight Shadow, but she could help the people that Knowles and his men harmed, starting with Mary's mother.

The sun was just rising over the horizon as Mary's mother, Sandra, walked back toward her house, carrying a bucket of water from the stream. She'd awakened early to begin work in the fields. The day of searching for Mary had cost them dearly. She and her husband, George, hadn't worked the fields that day. To make up for it, they'd worked through two nights.

Then disaster struck. Exhausted, George fell sick.

Now Sandra had to work the farm alone until George was well. She doubted they'd have enough crops to pay Sheriff Kenric and survive the winter.

She lifted her gaze from the ground to the house. A shadow shifted behind one of the trees in the forest just beyond the small thatched house. Panic seized her. Robbers, she thought. Or worse yet, tax collectors!

She dropped the bucket and raced toward the house, calling, "George!" Her heart pounded as she thought of him hurt inside. She couldn't live if something happened to George. She couldn't bear it!

Sandra shoved the door open and almost hit George in the face.

"What?" he asked, startled by her urgent tone. "What is it?" He leaned heavily on the table in the center of the room.

Relief swept through Sandra, but she stepped outside to look for the shadow. Had it been an animal of some sort? A witch?

"What's that?" George asked, pointing at the ground.

There by her feet, in the dirt just before the door, was a small bag. She bent and scooped it up. The faint clink of coins reached her ears and she cast a quick glance at George. His brown eyes were wide and he gripped the table for support.

Sandra pulled the string on the bag. Slowly, it opened in her hands. The sight that greeted her made her breath stop. She clutched at her chest.

George joined her, taking the bag from her hand. He dumped the contents out into his open palm. It was gold, more than he could have made from his harvest!

Sandra looked for the person who left the bag, for the shadow she'd seen in the forest, but no one was in sight. Her eyes shifted to the money in her husband's hands.

Slowly, a smile lit George's face and laughter began to churn from his throat.

Sandra sat heavily in a wooden chair, staring at the gold coins. Relief and exhilaration surged through her. They'd survive. They'd live through the winter. Sandra felt wetness on her cheeks and lifted a hand to swipe at the cool moisture. She was crying, but not tears of sadness. They were tears of relief and gratitude.

Chapter Eleven

Bria pulled her knees to her chest, watching the knights practice their skills in the field. She'd felt a strange satisfaction in watching from behind some trees as Mary's mother found the pouch she'd left. The warm feeling still lingered. She was sorry for taking it from her father and fixing the books so he wouldn't notice it missing. But Mary's family needed it more than her family, and she'd vowed to repay her father . . . somehow.

If she was going to continue helping the people, she needed to figure out some other way to get money and another way of helping Knowles's people besides giving them coin.

Bria winced as one of the young knights tumbled from his horse after being hit by his opponent's lance. Dark clouds brewed on the horizon, threatening rain since the early morning, but Bria had ignored them, choosing to come out and watch the men practice in the tilting yard.

"You seem particularly offended by my presence."

Bria glanced up and saw Lord Knowles standing above her. Despite her vow of anger, she felt a moment of breathlessness.

He looked at his hands as he pulled on a pair of black gloves. His black hair fell forward, obscuring her view of his face except when a breeze blew his hair aside. He wore a black tunic over his strong shoulders, and black leggings over his powerful legs. Behind him, his ebony horse whinnied softly, tossing his mane. Bria shook herself. "I wasn't the one who refused to see you when I came to your castle," she retorted.

He shifted his dark gaze to her, snapping on his second glove.

Bria raised her chin and stood squarely facing him, planting her hands on her hips. "I wanted to tell you one of your people was murdered. By your sheriff."

Terran shifted his dark gaze to her. "Then he deserved it."

Bria clenched her teeth. What a fool she was for thinking to confront him with the truth. "She was my friend, you dog," she snarled and whirled to walk away.

His hand shot out, capturing her wrist. "All your suitors have left," he said in a deceptively soft voice. "You *will* be my wife."

She bridled as anger seared through her. He shrugged off Mary's death as if the news had been a fly buzzing about his head that he swatted away with a simple flick of his wrist. He'd dismissed every word she'd said and then expected to marry her?

"Not all my suitors have gone," she replied defiantly, struggling to be free of his hold. But he was much stronger, and she couldn't break his grip. "Garret is still here."

Knowles grunted softly. "I will deal with him in a moment." He lifted those black, cold eyes to her. "He will be gone by this eve."

"My father will never consent to my betrothal to you," she retorted. "You overestimate your importance, Lord Knowles."

"You overestimate your own worth," Knowles responded.

"You were betrothed to me before you were even born, and your father will adhere to the letter of the law."

Doubt and disbelief crept into Bria's self-righteousness. "You lie," she finally declared.

"Ask your grandfather." He released her wrist as if it were nothing more than an old rag, then turned and led his horse down the slight hill toward the tilting yard.

Fear gnawed at her confidence. If he was telling the truth, why had she heard nothing about it for all these years? This past year, relations with Knowles had become strained, but none of Bria's questions to her father or grandfather about it had been answered. When she questioned the servants, she'd discovered Knowles had become betrothed, but she'd thought nothing of it at the time.

She watched him walk to the fence of the tilting yard. His gait was powerful, demanding attention. He immediately attracted Garret's gaze. Garret spurred his horse to the wooden fence that separated the practice field from the spectators, racing his horse boldly toward Knowles.

A sudden bout of fear seized Bria, and she began to walk quickly down the hill. As Garret's horse neared the fence, her anxiety increased, as did her pace, until she was almost running. Bria reached the fence to hear Garret's reply to something Terran had said.

"You got lucky with Odella," Garret snarled. "But your luck has run out."

"Prove it," Terran replied, without looking at Garret.

"No!" Bria gasped, boosting herself up onto the wooden fence. She held the top rung with a tight grip.

"I'm more than ready," Garret sneered.

"Garret! Don't! You can't win!" Bria cried.

Garret's eyes shifted to her and he spurred his horse to Bria. He gazed down at her for a long moment, his blue eyes full of hurt pride. "I know you don't have faith in my ability as a fighter. I will do this to prove myself.'' He turned the horse, presenting her with his back.

Bria opened her mouth to protest, but Garret was gone, moving his horse toward the other end of the field. She looked quickly left, then right, then all around the field, hoping to find someone who could put a stop to this madness. Several squires practiced their swordplay nearby. They'd have no power to stop the dueling knights, and the other knights wouldn't dare question Garret and Knowles's right to do battle.

Terran swung himself up onto his horse and entered the tilting field. He rode past her, sitting tall in the saddle, his black eyes locked on her.

Her eyes swept his confident form. His mastery of his animal far surpassed Garret's. Bria's heart beat hard with dread. She thought of racing back to the castle to get her father or grandfather to stop the fight, but by the time she returned, the battle would be over.

The two opponents went to opposite ends of the field and were handed jousting poles by their squires. They turned their horses and Terran spurred his steed first, heading toward Garret.

Garret responded in kind, leveling his lance at Terran, driving his horse forward with a firm kick.

Bria's mind reeled. It was all happening so fast! The fools weren't even wearing helmets!

There was a low thump as Terran's lance struck Garret in his chestplate. Bria held her breath as Garret dropped his lance and teetered in the saddle. Somehow, he managed to hang on to the reins and stay atop his horse.

Terran reached the opposite end of the field and glanced over his shoulder. When he saw his opponent was still seated, he grabbed another lance and turned again, relentless in his assault.

Garret caught his balance and seized a pole from his squire, spurring his horse to meet Terran. The horses' hooves pounded the earth, dust exploding into the air behind them.

"Come on, Dysen!" a man called from beside Bria.

Bria couldn't tear her eyes from the joust. The pounding of her heart matched the thunder of the horses' hooves.

Garret hit Terran hard in the shoulder, knocking Knowles's lance free.

Bria gasped. But Terran was not unhorsed. He turned a scathing gaze to Garret.

A grim smile crossed Garret's face. Men around the field cheered as he rounded on Terran again, a lance in his hand, readying for the final attack.

Terran seized the final lance and turned on his opponent. His horse exploded toward Garret. A burning intensity lit Knowles's gaze. Lowering his head, he gripped the lance tightly, then leaned away from Garret's thrust and jerked his lance just in time to hit Garret squarely in the stomach.

It was a brilliant move. If Bria hadn't been so horrified watching Garret fall backward off his horse and crash head first into the dusty earth, she would have marveled at Knowles's expertise.

Garret's head hit the ground hard and his body crumpled after it. Then everything was still. He lay unmoving.

Silence encased the yard.

Terran brought his horse around and threw his lance to the ground.

For a long moment, Bria couldn't move. She couldn't breathe. "Get up," she whispered to Garret. But the moment stretched on and Garret still didn't move. Bria ducked beneath the planks of the fence and raced onto the field.

Garret's squire reached his side first and bent to him. Still Garret had not moved.

Bria couldn't run fast enough. *If I just make it to his side, he'll be all right,* she told herself—promised herself.

As she reached his side, Garret's squire lifted his head to her and she read confusion and dread in his young blue eyes.

Bria turned her gaze to Garret. He lay on the ground, his

arms out to the sides, one knee lifted as if at any moment he'd get up. Her eyes shifted over his body to his face. She began to tremble and tears filled her eyes.

Garret's eyes were wide and glassy, staring blankly up into darkening clouds.

Behind her, thunder rumbled.

"No!" The wretched cry tore from her throat as she collapsed to her knees beside him. "Garret!" She lifted her hands to help him, but she didn't know what to do. She didn't know what to touch to make him better.

Bria lifted her shocked, hurt gaze. Panicked, she glanced around her at all the men looking at her. Sympathy, horror, and anger met her gaze. But she didn't give a damn. Her friend—her friend, for the love of God—was dead. There was nothing they could do.

Finally, she locked eyes with Terran, who stood across from her. She opened her mouth, but the only thing that came out was a sob.

She rose to her feet, stepping across Garret's body to confront Terran. "You wretched beast," she snarled. "You killed him." She hit his chest with her open palm. "You killed him." As the tears fell from her eyes, she stared at him, daring him to deny her claim, daring him to . . . comfort her.

But he simply stood there.

Finally, Terran turned his back to her and moved out of the practice field. Men parted to let him pass as if he were Death himself walking upon the earth in human form.

Bria's chest contracted painfully as a sob shook her body. The tears that had welled in her eyes overflowed, rolling down her cheeks.

Garret was dead. Mary was dead. How many more of her friends would die because of Terran Knowles? How many more?

The sky opened up and a heavy rain fell.

Chapter Twelve

Hurt and rage were still fresh in Bria's heart. Garret's death was so pointless, such a waste of a wonderfully promising life.

She sat quietly alone in her room. She held the black material in steady hands, pulling a stitch through the soft fabric, the battle replaying again and again in her mind. It could have been an accident.

But Terran's words echoed in her mind. *I will deal with him in a moment. He will be gone by this eve.* He'd known what he was doing. He had eliminated his competition with ruthless efficiency.

Thunder rumbled around her, shaking the entire castle.

Bria glanced up at the ceiling as if any moment it would tumble down around her.

The shock she had initially felt was slowly wearing off. In its place, a fierce anger shrouded her. What right did that man have to think he could just walk into her castle and demand her hand in marriage? Just who did he think he was?

And he killed my friend to achieve it.

The thought of his total lack of regard for life made her cold. But she had known that from the beginning from the way he overtaxed and all but starved his own people. What kind of lord was he?

She pulled through another stitch. It was time someone showed that heartless cur he couldn't treat people, be they peasant or noble, the way he did and get away with it. It was time to take action.

There would be no more senseless killings. There would be no more injustices to the people of Knowles. Mary would have wanted it that way.

Bria pulled the final stitch through the dark black material and stared at her labor. It was one of her finest works. The sewing was precise and sturdy, reinforced by double stitches.

She set her work on her lap, staring at the dark material. It was perfect—a hooded cloak made of the richest, blackest velvet. Simply perfect.

Exactly what the Midnight Shadow would wear.

Bria stared into Lord Dysen's watery brown eyes and clasped his old hands tightly, sharing his pain and agony, but her loss could never equal his. He'd lost a son. She'd lost a friend.

He lifted a hand and placed it on her cheek. "God be with you, child," he whispered, then turned, his great blue cloak flaring out behind him. He exited the double doors of the keep, moving toward the funeral procession that awaited him. Her father stood near Lord Dysen's horse, waiting to wish him luck. Hunched against the downpour of rain, they clasped arms. Bria watched them stare into each other's eyes. They needed no words. Their deep friendship sheltered them from much, but the death of Garret wounded them both.

There had been talk of bringing Knowles to justice, but as they'd questioned the squires and the spectators around the tilting field, they learned the challenge had been a fair one and the battle had been fought honorably. Garret's death had been a horrendous accident; he'd taken a bad fall that had broken his neck. Though all the facts pointed to this, Bria refused to believe it. How could she when Knowles had threatened Garret just moments before the joust?

Her father and Lord Dysen exchanged words, and then Lord Dysen glanced back at Bria, sheltered inside the keep, before mounting his horse and leading the solemn procession toward his homelands.

If no one has the courage to put an end to Knowles's tyranny, then I will, Bria vowed as she looked at Garret's coffin atop a wooden wagon pulled by two black horses. The conviction she'd felt as she sewed the cloak still burned in her heart, in her very soul. The preparations had been made. All the years of practice with her grandfather would finally be put to use.

Her father walked slowly up the two steps to the keep and to her side. Together they watched the horses and the wagon carrying Garret's coffin move off through the gatehouse.

Her friend. Tears rose in her eyes as she thought of her betrayal of Garret. She hadn't believed in him, not since he had faced Kenric those many years ago and lost. Not then. Not now. Because she couldn't keep her distrust of his skills a secret buried deep in her heart, he had faced Terran . . . and lost. She was a curse to anyone she called a friend.

Her father brushed a kiss against her temple and moved deeper into the keep.

Bria continued to watch until the procession had moved out of the castle toward the village and finally out of sight. As the Dysen entourage disappeared on the horizon, a fork of lightning erupted in the sky and wormed its way through the darkness, lighting the courtyard.

Across the courtyard, next to the blacksmith's shop, Bria spotted a dark form. As she watched, another spear of lightning flashed through the sky, washing over Terran Knowles before leaving him in shadow again. Bria's jaw clenched and she raced out into the blackness of the storm toward him, running beneath the awning that sheltered him from the rain.

She stared at him for a long moment, studying his black eyes, the scowl that lined his forehead. His thick hair fell wet and heavy over his cheeks. "What are you doing out here?" she demanded. "How dare you offend Garret's family by spying?"

Terran's jaw clenched.

"Isn't it enough that you murdered him? Must you defile his procession, too?"

Terran seized her shoulders and slammed her up against the blacksmith's shop. "Enough!" he roared. "Enough of your insults. I have endured them from your father and grandfather, even from Dysen. But I will not tolerate them from you."

Bria's mouth dropped open for only a moment before her shock vanished, replaced by fury. She opened her mouth to reply, but Terran slammed his open palms on the wall on either side of her.

"I said enough!"

For a long moment, Bria could do nothing but stare at him. And slowly, a realization came to her. She was alone with him. And he was close—very close. His hands were on either side of her, effectively trapping her. His lips were but inches from hers. Her eyes scanned his face, his rugged square jaw, his sensual lips, his dark eyes. Lightning lit the sky above, but Bria barely noticed except for the reflection in his eyes. Was that remorse in them? Or was she imagining it?

He leaned closer to her until his face was beside hers, almost cheek to cheek. Bria stiffened. What was he doing? But she didn't protest. His hair brushed and mingled with hers. "I didn't mean to kill him, Bria."

She felt a soft wave of hot breath on her neck, but his words were so soft Bria wasn't sure he'd spoken them at all. She turned her head to try to see him, and he shifted his gaze to look into hers with eyes that seemed a little lost.

In the next moment, he was brushing his lips against hers,

seeking, exploring. She was unsure of what to do and found herself frozen, half wanting him to kiss her, half wanting to flee. His touch was gentle, almost soothing. Not at all what she had expected.

He pulled slightly back to look into her eyes, studying them as if waiting for her to deny him.

But she couldn't. She didn't want to.

He cupped her neck and pulled her to him, claiming her lips with a more urgent need. A fierce, reckless desire seared through her. His arms pulled her tight against the length of his body.

Her world spun out of control. He coaxed her lips open to his exploration and when his tongue entered her mouth, warring with her own, Bria felt the ground rumble beneath her feet.

He kissed her fully, expertly exploring every part of her mouth. Then he pulled slowly away, ending the kiss, leaving her weak and confused.

He stepped back, taking his strength and support with him.

Bria's knees buckled and she almost fell, but he reached out to steady her. Humiliated and awed by her reaction to his kiss, she expected to look up and see him laughing at her. But when she gazed into his eyes, she found no laughter there. He appeared just as baffled as she.

Before Bria could comment, he turned away from her and walked across the courtyard. He did not hunch against the rain, and as if by his command, the downpour faded to a light mist. Bria stared after him. Her heart was still floating in her chest, her body strangely separated from her mind. She knew she should feel ashamed and manipulated, but she didn't. She'd enjoyed his kiss. And what scared her the most was that she wanted to feel his lips against hers again.

Suddenly, Bria saw a dark shadow moving across the deserted courtyard. She recognized the figure immediately as he began to slowly climb the stairs toward the castle walkway. *What is he doing?*

Bria glanced at the sky and the dark storm clouds once more

before hunching her shoulders against the weather and heading out toward the stairway. She sloshed through the puddles and mud of the courtyard, racing toward the stairs. *He shouldn't be out in the rain,* Bria thought.

Bria held a hand up to protect her eyes and saw the shadow pause at one of the crenels. She ran up the stairs, slipping once on a slick stone, but quickly righting herself and moving after him. As she approached him, she saw he was staring out at the fields just beyond the walls. Bria looked out over the battlements, following his gaze, trying to see what he was looking at.

Looming on the field, marring its perfect green grass, were the white tents of Lord Knowles and his followers. His red flag drooped beneath the rain.

Bria glanced back at the man. "Grandfather," she called over the loud whistle of a sudden gust of wind. "You shouldn't be out here," she added as she reached his side.

"Bria," he answered, and she heard the utter agony in his voice. "I'm so sorry."

"It's all right." She tried to soothe him, blinking back the rain as it splashed her face. "Let's go inside and we'll talk about it." She gently tugged his arm.

But he remained motionless. "You don't understand, child," he said softly. "This is all my fault."

"Don't be silly," she replied. "I can't—"

"But I'm going to stop it," he said. "You won't have to marry someone like him." He stared with icy eyes at the white tents below.

Bria shuddered at her grandfather's cold tone. She removed her hand from his arm, trying to see into his eyes. "What have you done, Grandfather?"

Thunder crashed around them, shaking the castle.

Harry turned his eyes toward the tents. Bria followed his gaze. He was waiting for something to happen. But what? She held her breath, anticipating the worst, expecting the sound of agony or the scream of murder. But for a long moment, nothing happened.

Bria began to doubt the intent in her grandfather's words. Maybe she'd misread the threat in his voice.

But then, suddenly, she saw a man running frantically from the rear of Lord Knowles's tent toward Castle Delaney. Confusion and trepidation flared to life inside Bria. She anxiously brushed the water from her eyes. What had her grandfather done?

Suddenly, bright flames erupted up the back of one of the white tents, dancing in defiance against the rain.

"No," Bria gasped. She looked at her grandfather and saw a satisfied grin on his lips. "No," she repeated.

Flames burst to life behind another tent, then another.

Bria turned and ran across the walkway and down the stairs. She raced through the courtyard toward the inner gatehouse and then the outer gatehouse. She slipped once, falling in the mud, and then climbed to her feet. She shouted orders to the outer gatehouse guards to bring buckets of water before running into the fields toward the burning tents.

As she approached, she saw the fire had grown to engulf most of the tents. Men, coughing and hacking from the heat and black smoke, were milling about. Bria headed for the first tent. The flames snapped and cracked, reaching toward her. She stumbled back beneath the heat, holding a hand before her face. She glanced at the other men—servants, by the looks of their clothing—and shouted, "Is anyone in there?"

Their befuddled looks caused her to take action. She dived into the tent, screaming over the roar of the fire, "Is anyone in here?"

Through the thickening black smoke, Bria saw a pile of blankets. She dropped to her knees and crawled over to it, feeling around beneath them, but the blankets were empty.

The thick smoke encircled her, trying to cut off her air. She coughed and lifted her arm to her nose, trying to breathe through the fabric of her dress. Her eyes watered and she brushed at them with the palms of her hands. She turned to leave, only then realizing that the black smoke was hiding the exit.

Panic welled within her, but she fought it down, desperately searching for escape. Above her, the roar of the fire crescendoed, and she looked up to see that the fire had already engulfed the top part of the tent. With a loud rumble, the entire tent began to shake.

A scream welled in Bria's throat. A burning piece of wood landed beside her, making her leap to her feet.

Suddenly, from out of the black smoke, a dark shape emerged. It was the devil himself, his eyes glowing red. She reared back, but he caught her arm and hauled her into the smoke and the burning walls.

Chapter Thirteen

Bria clenched her eyes tight against the smoke and a blast of hot air assaulted her face. Then, suddenly, a cool mist sprayed her forehead, her cheeks, her neck. She opened her eyes and found herself outside the burning tent, standing in the rain. She coughed harshly, gasping for breath.

It was a long moment before she was able to lift her watery eyes to the dark shape standing at her side, a moment longer before she realized that the man who stood before her, lit from behind by a dancing red light that could come only from the fire, was Terran Knowles.

Her fogged mind pieced together the quick turn of events that had led her here, and she finally whispered in shock, "You saved me."

His dark eyes narrowed. "And you burned my tents."

His accusation came as a blow and her mouth dropped open. Then her brows drew together as her anger reared, her narrowed eyes matching his. "What would I be doing in your tents if I set fire to them?"

"Caught in your own trap," he snapped.

Hurt and disbelief constricted her chest. How could he believe that after the kiss they'd shared? With a snarl of frustration, Bria attempted to turn away, but was stopped short by a shackle on her arm. His large hand was wrapped around her forearm. She turned her gaze to meet his furious eyes. "Let me go," she commanded, trying to break free, but his grip was tight, his large fingers digging into her flesh.

"So you can try to poison my drink or hire someone to kill me?"

"I did not try to kill you."

His eyes narrowed even further. "No. Killing me wouldn't achieve your goal."

"What are you talking about?" Bria demanded, stilling her vain attempts to free herself.

"The papers. That's why you set fire to the tents."

"What papers?" Bria asked.

"The betrothal papers," he snarled. "You hoped the papers would be gone, too, burned with the tents."

"What betrothal papers?" Bria demanded, confused.

"These papers." He reached inside his black tunic and produced two sheets of parchment that he held in a clenched fist. He pushed them at her, leaning close to her face to growl, "You didn't think I'd be stupid enough to let them out of my sight, did you?"

Bria stared at the papers. Betrothal papers. Could she really be betrothed to this man, to her enemy? Part of her wanted to cry out in excitement, but part of her refused to believe it. It couldn't be! She would have known! But what else could make the suitors leave without so much as a fight and make her grandfather attempt to burn the tents? Betrothal papers!

Terran stepped back from her, releasing her arm. He quickly put the betrothal papers back inside his tunic, sheltering them from the rain.

A shiver raced along her shoulders as she looked into his

black eyes. *Those are the eyes that showed no emotion when you tried to tell him of Mary's murder by his dog of a sheriff,* she reminded herself. Her gaze dropped to his lips. *But those are the lips that kissed you with such warmth and passion.*

"Bria!" a voice called out from behind her.

Bria forced herself to turn away from Terran to see her grandfather racing toward her across the fields as fast as his old legs would carry him. He lost his balance and fell to one knee a few feet from her. For a moment, Bria couldn't move. Shock held her immobile. How could she marry Terran? How could part of her want to?

Harry's gaze remained on her as he knelt in the mud, and for a moment he looked like a penitent man, begging for her forgiveness. Then he scrambled to his feet, reaching for her. He grasped her arms desperately. "Are you all right?"

Bria nodded, searching his eyes for answers.

"Since our tents have been so grievously ruined, I'm sure Lord Delaney will have no objection to our staying inside Castle Delaney," Terran said from behind Bria.

Harry looked up at him, his mouth open as if in objection, but no words came forth.

"Good." Terran marched away from them toward the castle. Two servants followed him, as well as the men he had arrived with. All glared at Bria as they passed.

When they were well away from them, Harry swept Bria into his arms. "Bria," he whispered as he held her tightly against him, "I never meant . . . you could have been killed."

Bria pushed away from him so she could look him in the eyes. "Grandfather, am I really betrothed to Knowles?"

Harry looked away from her, and Bria could see the agony etched in his furrowed brow. "I never meant for this to happen. When I was Lord of Delaney, old Lord Knowles, Terran's grandfather, was a powerful man. We wanted our lands united. I was just as greedy as he was. We pledged our first girl to his son, or the other way around. Knowles and Delaney lands would be united. But he had a son, and so did I. You were the first girl on either side."

He looked into her eyes. "Do you understand? I was young then. I wanted more power. I wanted more wealth. I didn't care about the future. I didn't care about . . . anything. Bria," he said desperately, "I would give anything to destroy those papers, to take back the betrothal."

Bria stared at him for a long moment. He seemed infinitely older, the weight of her destiny on his shoulders. Finally, sympathetically, she patted his hand. "It's all right. We'll find some way out of this." She took his arm and together they followed Terran into the castle.

Tonight it begins, Bria thought. Her grandfather leaned on her as they moved up a slope. *Betrothed to Terran or not, it begins tonight.*

Terran watched Bria enter the hall, holding on to her grandfather's arm. Her face was covered with soot and her hair was in a wild disarray of curls, but she still managed to hold her head high, her back straight. Damn, he thought. She still managed to look beautiful.

He shook his head, trying to see beyond her beauty. He'd underestimated her. He wouldn't have thought her capable of burning his tents. She was an opinionated woman, yes, but it took strength of character to act on such beliefs, a strength no woman he'd met thus far had. She'd be a difficult woman to keep firmly beneath his rule, a woman who would need to be watched every moment of every day.

He found his eyes lingering on the way her brown curls reflected the light of the fire from the hearth, found his gaze captivated by her lips as she spoke soothingly to her grandfather. And he remembered their kiss. It had fueled the spark she'd started with her defiance—passionate, uninhibited.

He had thought briefly that one kiss, one taste of her lips would be enough. Far from it. That one dangerous kiss only made him want to taste the rest of her. It was a feeling unlike any other woman had given him, and there'd been many willing to give themselves to the victor of the tournaments. One taste of their practiced lips and bodies had been more than enough.

But Terran could watch Bria every moment of every day and never be bored. He shook his head, trying to free himself from the spell she was casting on him.

But that wasn't why he wanted her as a wife. He needed her dowry. If she were the ugliest woman in the universe, he'd still marry her in order to pay the king's tithe, to save his lands. It didn't matter that she had eyes as infinite as a clear blue sky, eyes he could lose himself in, or that her kiss was earthshaking.

The only thing that mattered was her dowry.

Chapter Fourteen

"Stupid peasants," the tax collector muttered, weighing the sack of coin in his hand as he glanced up at the half moon high in the night sky. All of their pleading for leniency, all of their groveling for mercy, had made him very late. His wife was going to yell and curse him, accusing him of stopping at the inn for a round of ale with the boys. It was almost midnight already.

If Kenric wasn't paying him so well, he'd be damned if he'd do this dirty work. He spit on the ground in front of the farmer's house he'd just left. He turned to his horse and was about to mount when he heard a sound behind him, a soft sound like the fluttering of cloth. He whirled toward the noise, his hand going to the hilt of his sword. But the field before the farmer's house was empty. He shrugged slightly. Maybe it was the wind.

He turned back to his horse and put his foot in the stirrup. Again the muffled sound of fluttering clothing, now louder. Closer. He whirled and drew his sword. "Who's there?" he demanded of the darkness.

But no one stood before him. A gentle wind blew about him, moving through the trees with a whispery softness. The shadows thrown by the trees shifted and transformed as the moonlight filtered through the swaying branches. He relaxed slightly. He was hearing things.

Then he felt something sharp against his throat. He shifted his gaze to his side and his eyes went wide as he saw a man dressed all in black, a cloaked hood concealing his face. Where had he come from? He wasn't there mere seconds before. It was as if he'd formed out of the darkness itself. Fear gripped the tax collector's heart.

"Drop it," the masked man said in a firm whisper.

The tax collector held up his sword and released it. It thumped against the earth.

"The bag," the masked man ordered again in a whisper, holding a black-gloved hand palm up.

The tax collector began to tremble as he handed the bag to the robber. The robber palmed it, then grabbed the tax collector's hair and shoved the tip of the blade against his throat.

"Tell Lord Knowles his tyranny will no longer be tolerated," the masked man whispered against his ear. "Tell him the Midnight Shadow will see to it."

The Midnight Shadow shoved the tax collector into the dirt.

The tax collector lay still for a long moment, terror keeping him pinned to the ground. He slowly lifted his head and looked about him for any signs of his assailant. But the field was empty and still.

The Midnight Shadow was gone.

"I've been waiting for you. You awaken late."

Bria whirled to see Knowles moving toward her. The red light of the hallway torch flickered over his black hair, casting his face in shadows. *Does he know?* she immediately wondered. *Has he come to confront me?*

She lifted her chin slightly. "Do you always hide in the dark waiting to accost ladies as they emerge from their rooms?" she demanded. Her heart pounded in her chest. *He startled you,* she told herself, *that's all.*

He straightened at her barb, but feigned disinterest. "I was waiting to accompany you to break your fast."

A rush of relief spread through her. *He doesn't know!* The relief was followed quickly by a moment of excitement—to sit next to him, to speak with him of his castle and lands. *What am I thinking?* Bria wondered. *I have to keep in mind who he is.* "I don't think my father would care to have you in his hall," Bria answered tartly.

Terran drew up slightly, his demeanor becoming cooler. "I don't think he'd object to having his son-in-law dine in his hall."

Bria turned away from him, shaking her head. "Surely you see it is futile. My father will not betroth me to you."

Terran stepped up close behind her, and a shiver raced up her spine. She held her breath, waiting.

"If you speak to him, perhaps he will change his mind," Terran murmured.

Bria felt that rush again, that anticipatory anxiousness. "Why would I speak with him?" she asked.

"Because you want to be my wife," he whispered against the nape of her neck. His hot breath sent shivers shooting down to her toes. She closed her eyes, relishing the feeling. She opened her mouth to deny it, but no denial came forth.

He chuckled low in his throat and brushed a kiss against the soft skin of her neck. "You are mine. You have always been mine."

Bria half turned to him and something caught in her throat as she saw just how close he was. He was going to kiss her.

When he spoke again, his lips caressed her hair. "I will not give you up, my lady."

The sound of approaching footsteps caused Terran to step

back from her. Without the warmth of his body radiating over her, the spell was broken. Bria stumbled forward, quickly moving away from him. She trembled as she hurried down the hallway, feeling his gaze upon her. The pace of her steps increased until she rounded a corner to a spiral stairway. She stopped and leaned against the stone wall, almost as if she were hiding from his view.

What is happening to me? Every time Terran is near, I lose my senses. It must be because I am so tired. I barely slept at all last night. She had lain in bed, excitedly replaying her daring exploit with the tax collector over and over in her mind.

Yes, she thought. *I'm just tired.*

And in danger, another voice reminded her. *He may have just been your suitor before last night, but now the real war has begun. You've made him your enemy now.*

With that certainty, Bria moved toward the Great Hall to break her fast.

Kenric sat in Terran's judgment chair in Castle Knowles, staring down at the tax collector who had returned empty-handed. "The Midnight Shadow?"

"Yes," the man replied. "I swear he just disappeared with the bag, or I would have chased him down."

Kenric's eyes narrowed. "That's a good story," he commended. "Now give up the bag."

The tax collector's eyes widened. "I don't have it, I swear!"

Kenric nodded at one of his men standing near the door. The man approached the tax collector. "Make this easy on yourself Give it up."

"I don't have it! This man just appeared out of the night and stole the bag from me at sword point!"

"Yet you have no proof."

"What was I to do?"

"Die." Kenric nodded at the soldier behind the man.

The soldier pulled his sword from its scabbard and plunged it into the tax collector's back.

The man stared at Kenric with large eyes before slumping lifeless to the floor.

"The Midnight Shadow," Kenric muttered. "Such nonsense."

Chapter Fifteen

Terran sat in the back of the Great Hall watching the head table. Bria, her father, and grandfather all sat there, looking righteous and proud.

Terran ripped off a chunk of venison. He watched Bria as he slowly, thoughtfully, chewed his food. Her long brown hair was wound tightly in a braid that ran down her back along her spine. He only glimpsed it when she turned to exchange a word with her father or grandfather, who sat at her side like sentinels.

Terran tore his gaze from her. She was no Odella. She was bold, headstrong and determined. But those qualities only made her more appealing, more of a challenge.

Terran didn't mind that there was no chair at the head table for him. The Delaneys had chosen to ignore the betrothal, to ignore him, by denying him a place at their table. Their action intrigued him. It showed their anger and their hostility toward him, yet Delaney had not challenged him outright, nor even banished him from Castle Delaney. *As if this slight will make me leave,* Terran mused.

He wasn't leaving until he got what he came for, a wife and a dowry. Still, it had made him furious to see his betrothed sobbing at her lover's side, the way she clung to him, held onto his arm, touched his shoulder. He shook his head. At least he knew she loved another man. Yet she had responded to his kiss, had actually kissed him in return. Could he be wrong about her relationship with Dysen? Or did he simply not satisfy her?

Terran threw back a drink of his ale. When he set it down again, his gaze came to rest on Bria. *She can't be trusted,* he told himself for the hundredth time. *She thinks the worst of me. She'll betray me at the first opportunity that arises.*

His jaw clenched and his eyes narrowed slightly as he watched the little nymph at the head table delicately bite a piece of bread. *I will enjoy changing her mind about me,* he thought, *night after night.*

"He's watching you again."

Bria already knew it. She could feel his dark gaze upon her, and her body responded instantly, a delightful shiver of want coursing through her. He'd been following and watching her since the afternoon meal.

She glanced back over her chair to see Terran Knowles standing at the opposite wall, his arms crossed over his massive chest, his feet planted firmly shoulder width apart. He just stared at her, making no pretense that he wasn't watching her.

A tingle raced up her spine at being the object of his intense stare. Bria turned back to the fire, her anger at her immediate response to him mounting. He was, after all, her enemy. He wouldn't listen to her about Mary or Kenric, and yet he affected her in an instantaneous way. It was frustrating and confusing. "I don't understand why Father won't throw him out of Castle Delaney."

"He doesn't want to start a fight," Harry answered.

Bria shook her head. "Ever since he came back from the war, he'll have nothing to do with battle. He's already angry over the incident with poor Garret." Bria shifted in her seat.

Harry laid a hand on her shoulder. "It was an accident, Bria," Harry explained patiently. "It could have happened to anyone. Garret fell from his horse and twisted his neck."

"I know," Bria whispered. She knew the words Terran had spoken were the truth. He hadn't meant to kill Garret. "But that doesn't make it any easier."

"He'll become tired of the pursuit and return to his lands," Harry whispered.

Bria turned to cast a glance at Terran over her shoulder. He was still leaning against the wall, watching her with an unwavering gaze. Again her insides turned to liquid. She felt everything in her melt beneath his gaze. She just hoped she could keep her distance from him until he left.

"You must be careful meeting me at the clearing. Don't let him see you."

"I won't let him see me. But you'll have to bring my sword."

Harry nodded and Bria rose from her chair. She bent over to kiss his cheek and felt the tension in his corded muscles as she rested her hand on his shoulder. "Don't worry," she whispered. "It will all turn out fine."

"Bria, don't underestimate him," Harry warned. "He's no fool."

Bria smiled warmly at her grandfather and headed toward her room.

"Lady Bria," someone whispered as she neared the kitchens.

Bria looked up to see Deb, her personal servant, motioning for her to come closer. Deb's gaze darted left, then right, scanning the surroundings of the dark hallway. Bria moved to her and Deb quickly ushered her into the kitchen.

"What is it, Deb?" Bria asked. "What's wrong?"

Deb grabbed her hand, leading her past a young boy fanning the cauldron flames with a bellows. They moved deeper into the kitchen until they were alone near the stacks of bagged vegetables piled shoulder high. Deb turned to Bria, her eyes filled with concern. "Is it true, m'lady?"

"Is what true?"

"Are you really going to marry Lord Knowles?"

For a moment, Bria wondered how Deb could have known, but then quickly remembered she'd scolded Deb countless times for spreading gossip through the castle. "No, it's not true. I will not marry him," she told Deb.

Deb breathed a sigh of relief. "The Lord be praised. You will be saved."

"Saved? From what?"

Deb glanced around the kitchen, making certain no one else was within earshot. She turned back to Bria. "They say he killed his betrothed."

"What?" Bria gasped. Now it was her turn to glance around the kitchen. Knowles had been watching her all day, but it seemed for the moment she'd eluded him.

"The poor girl loved him so much," Deb said, more than bubbling at the prospect of repeating gossip. "But he didn't care about Lady Odella. Why, he didn't even attempt to keep his mistress a secret, either. He was only marrying her because of her dowry."

"That doesn't surprise me," Bria said. *Mistress,* she thought. *That doesn't surprise me, either.* "Go on. How did he kill her?"

"Well, the poor girl was brokenhearted. She wanted to end their betrothal, and he just poisoned her. Killed her in his own bed. They buried her but a month ago, and here he is tryin' to get your hand in marriage." Deb shook her head.

A scowl marred Bria's forehead. She couldn't picture Terran Knowles poisoning someone. He was a fighter, and poison had always been the coward's way to kill someone. Bria looked at the servant girl for a long moment. She was a wealth of knowledge, knowledge that she needed. "Are you still seeing that innkeeper?" she wondered.

"Yes," Deb replied, bowing her head somewhat shyly.

Bria nodded. "He must hear all the gossip about Knowles."

Deb nodded. "Oh, yes, Scott does. Being that he works near the village just beyond Castle Knowles, he hears plenty, m'lady. Why, little Ben Johnson was nearly killed the other day when—" Deb stopped herself short. She curtsied to Bria. "My apologies, m'lady. I know how you don't like me to gossip."

"It's all right, Deb. I need to know as much as I can about my suitors and how they rule their lands, don't I?"

Deb burst into a wide smile. "Of course, m'lady. Of course you do."

"Now tell me about little Ben Johnson."

Deb nodded. "Two of Knowles's tax collectors were riding through town when little Ben—he's the alemaker's son—ran out into the street after a toy. One of the horses spooked and reared, nearly throwing one of the tax collectors from his saddle. Little Ben went to apologize to the man and those ruffians beat the poor child! Just for scaring a horse!"

Bria's jaw tightened and her eyes narrowed slightly. "Is he all right?" she asked after a moment of controlling her anger.

"Yes," Deb answered. "Scared to death of the tax collectors now, if he wasn't already. He'll steer clear of them."

"Tell me what else you've heard," Bria urged.

Deb's face all but glowed. There was nothing she liked more. But before she began, a boy raced through the kitchens, brushing past her skirt. He carried a handful of carrots. Bria recognized the dark hair and wiry body instantly. Her eyes widened, following the boy's path through the kitchen. "Wasn't that Garret's squire?"

Deb nodded her head.

"Bradley!" Bria hollered.

The boy skidded to a halt and returned to Bria's side, an

apologetic look on his face. "I didn't step on your toes, did I, lady?"

Bria shook her head. "What are you doing here? Why didn't you return to Castle Dysen?"

"Lord Knowles took me on as his squire, lady," Bradley replied, looking shyly away, shifting from foot to foot.

"You're Knowles's squire now?" Bria asked, amazed.

"Aye, m'lady," Bradley answered. "Please don't be mad at me. When Sir Garret died, I just didn't know what ta do. My father is poor an' we have no coin ta—"

"Did you approach Knowles?"

"Oh no, lady!" Bradley exclaimed. "I was too afraid of 'im. Lord Knowles came ta me."

Bria was dumbfounded. It didn't make sense. When Bradley was lost and alone and unsure, Knowles had taken him under his wing—but Knowles wasn't that kind of man!

Bradley took a step back toward the doors. "If'n you'll excuse me." He held up the handful of carrots. "I'm tryin' ta make friends with Lord Knowles's horse."

Bria could only stare at the boy as he turned and raced out of the kitchens.

"Lord Knowles must have put some kind of spell over the boy," Deb said.

Bria scowled. It just didn't make sense.

Bria rubbed her eyes as she mounted the spiral stairway to her room. She feigned fatigue, but inside she felt a renewed vigor for the events to come. After Bradley had left, Deb had given her very valuable information she could use for weeks to come. She felt vibrant and anxious and even a little frightened at what the future held. She had a lot of work to do.

She paused immediately at hearing footsteps behind her. She turned to see Terran stalking after her. Her heart began to race as he approached. "Good eve, Lord Knowles," she called.

"Good eve, Lady Bria," he said with an ingratiating smile, a brilliant smile, a perfect smile.

She shook her head mentally. *What am I thinking?* She looked again and saw a different smile as he moved toward her beneath the flickering light of the torches. The smile was wolfish, predatory. But something in it caused her pulse to quicken. "Why have you been following me all day?" she wondered.

"I enjoy watching you," he said.

A thrill raced up her spine. "Thank you," she replied, embarrassed at her self-consciousness. It wasn't a compliment she had ever received.

His smile grew wider and more genuine.

It left her breathless. He was so handsome, more handsome than she'd ever known a man could be. Frightened by this newfound sensation, she backed to her bedroom door. "Well, good night, Lord Knowles."

"Good night, Lady Bria," he whispered.

His voice sent waves of warmth through her body. Bria quickly entered her room and shut the door, hoping to seal out her feelings as well, but that was not to be.

In the darkness of her room, giddiness and breathlessness swirled inside her. What was happening to her? What was this feeling? She had to remember that he was a cruel lord and treated his people badly. But why had he helped Bradley? And why was she feeling this warmth for Terran? She begged for it to stop, chastised herself for feeling anything for him.

The strange, unwanted feelings remained to torment her, and she knew of only one way to rid herself of them.

Terran had expected to be lectured about hounding her in her own castle. He hadn't expected her large blue eyes to stare at him with such . . . surprise.

Her silence had given him a chance to study her face—her

perfect little nose, her high cheekbones and full lips. Had she lingered a moment longer, he would have kissed her again, he was sure of it. As it was, his blood boiled in his veins at the mere memory of their kiss.

Terran shook his head. Lust. He'd felt it before. Not this strongly, and certainly not for someone who wanted nothing to do with him. Could that be part of her intrigue? Or was it simply her womanly body that called so strongly to him?

He realized suddenly he was staring at her wooden door and turned away. He would begin his pursuit again in the morning. Perhaps he'd find her alone in the garden, or in a hallway, to discover her further.

Terran entered his room and shut the door. He sat at his window in the dark for a long time thinking about his betrothal to Bria. What would have happened had he not initially rejected his betrothal to her for Odella? Would she still despise him?

The sound of horses' hooves echoed in the courtyard. He glanced down and saw a lone figure riding through the inner ward toward the outer ward of the castle. Familiar long brown hair waved behind her, uninhibited. Terran's eyes narrowed as he leaned a little further out the window to watch her path.

Where could she possibly be going this late at night?

The next morning, little Ben Johnson's mother stretched and yawned. Her first thought was for her son, Ben. The tax collectors had beaten him soundly for spooking their horses, leaving him with a bleeding nose, a fat lip, and bruises on his face. That had been two days ago, but she worried they'd return to exact more vengeance on her family.

She hurried to the main room to check on him.

Ben was already awake, sitting up in his straw bed, playing with something. His black hair bobbed and fell over his bright eyes.

Ben's mother relaxed and smiled, moving to her son. "Good morning, Ben," she greeted, sitting beside the bed.

Ben threw his arms around his mother's neck and gave her a big hug. "Mother, Mother! Look at what I got!"

Ben's mother looked down at the small wooden horse her son was proudly displaying. She scowled slightly. "Where did you get that?"

"The Midnight Shadow gave it to me," little Ben replied, his face aglow. "He came last night and gave it to me. He said to stay away from the tax collectors."

Horror spread over Ben's mother's face and through her heart as she glanced around the room. She drew Ben closer to her heart as if to protect him. "Someone was here? In the house?"

Ben nodded. "But he was nice, mother. At first I was afraid. But then he gave me this." He hugged the wooden horse. "Oh—" Ben rummaged beneath his pillow for a moment and produced a small bag. "And he said to give this to you."

Wary, Ben's mother took the small bag from her child. She pulled the drawstring and cautiously peered inside. Then she quickly turned the bag over and five gold coins spilled out into the palm of her hand.

Her eyes widened at the sight. "Oh, thank you, Lord!" she exclaimed, hugging her son.

"The Midnight Shadow is a good man, isn't he?" Ben asked, innocently.

"Yes, Ben," his mother replied. "A very good man."

Chapter Sixteen

"Who is this Midnight Shadow?" Terran demanded, slamming his fists on the wooden table, making the wood reverberate beneath his fury. He stood, rising to his full height to tower over Kenric. The two tax collectors standing behind Kenric shrank back. "How dare he steal my coin?"

Terran's voice echoed through the Great Hall, spearing from one side of the room to the other. A servant cleaning the wooden table paused to look up at him, but quickly bowed her head and continued her work.

Kenric had arrived at Castle Delaney late in the day with word of Knowles's new enemy. The Midnight Shadow had struck again in the night, robbing two tax collectors as they returned to Castle Knowles.

"No man will steal from me," Terran fumed. "This I vow. I will have this Midnight Shadow."

Kenric dismissed the two tax collectors with a wave of his hand. The two men practically raced for the double doors at the back of the room. "My lord," Kenric whispered, leaning in to do so, "this cannot continue. We need to pay the men to defend Castle Knowles, and need I remind you we have only two months before we must pay the king?"

"It will not continue," Terran vowed. "I want him taken."

Kenric nodded, bowing. "As you wish." As Terran sank back into his seat, Kenric joined him at the table, sitting opposite him. He was silent for a moment before asking, "How are things going with the marriage plans?"

Terran's eyes narrowed. "It would have been settled if you'd done what you promised. You said everything would be taken care of. Nothing was."

"It got you here," Kenric muttered.

"I would destroy any other man who lied to me so," Terran growled.

Kenric chuckled. "Then it's lucky we're family."

Terran glared at his cousin, then allowed himself a slight smile. *Family,* his mind repeated. *And friend.* Randolph had served him loyally for years. He would trust his cousin with his very life.

Terran sat back in the chair, rubbing his hands over his face. How had everything gotten so out of control? Was it already a month since he'd been overjoyed at the prospect of marrying Odella? Her dowry would have saved his lands and castle. But now . . . he shook his head, staring at the rushes on the floor. Must his entire life be a battle?

"I couldn't let you pass up the opportunity to save your castle and lands," Kenric said. "It was my duty to convince you to claim what is yours, by any means necessary."

"I don't want a wife," Terran said.

"Don't think of her as a wife, or even as a woman. Think of her as a key, a key to riches," Kenric coaxed. "She won't change your life. You can still have other women. You can still do as you please. You'd be marrying her for her lands and her dowry. She'd be your wife in name only."

Terran assented with a nod, even though he was lying now

to himself. He could do nothing but think of Bria as a woman. He would make her his wife in all ways, and he knew it. Just the thought of kissing her sent desire searing through his veins.

But she was the key, as Kenric had said. She would save his lands, his castle . . . and maybe even him. He sighed. "I suppose you're right," he agreed. He lifted his head to look at Kenric, only to see Bria standing slightly behind his friend. The sight of her clenched fists, her squared shoulders, her taut jaw, was enough to send any man running for cover. But what brought him to his feet was the sight of the glistening tears that lined her large eyes.

Kenric turned.

Bria's shining blue eyes never left Terran. "Don't worry about my getting in the way of your other women. You can rest assured I wouldn't marry you if there was a sword to my throat." With that, she whirled away and half stormed, half ran toward the double doors at the back of the room.

"You certainly have a way with women," Kenric mused.

Terran sighed heavily. "I'm afraid Lady Bria will never marry me willingly."

Kenric's black eyes glinted and a slow, sly smile spread over his lips. "Perhaps there is another way."

Bria sat on the hilltop, watching the knights practice their skills in the tilting field below. What difference should it matter how Terran treated her? He was the enemy, and he would never, ever be her husband. Then why had she felt so hurt and disappointed when she heard Terran and Kenric talking? Because they were speaking of her as if she were a possession.

She reached down to pluck a stalk of grass. Knowles was having a very strange effect on her. Ever since his kiss, she'd wanted to feel his touch again. She found herself dwelling on the way he made her feel for hours at a time. How could a man who had such a knee-shaking effect on her be so evil? How could a man who'd been so kind to a boy be so cruel?

A pair of boots came into her vision and she followed them up to see Kenric standing above her. Fear ignited inside her as quickly as dried rushes burst into flames at the touch of a lit torch. Bria pulled back slightly as Kenric loomed over her.

"It's good to see you again, Lady Bria." His smile only added to her terror. She remembered too vividly how he'd coldly struck down the herbalist. And Mary . . .

"What do you want?" she demanded with as much courage as she could muster.

A low chuckle issued from his throat. "So the little mouse has the roar of a tiger, eh?" He squatted down before her, his black, soulless eyes glaring into hers. "You weren't quite so brave when you came to Castle Knowles. Why did you come?"

Bria couldn't look away from his evil eyes. He'd kill her if he knew she'd seen him kill the herbalist. She knew that from looking into his eyes. Her eyes narrowed slightly in defiance. "I came to speak with Lord Knowles," she answered.

Was that a ripple of suspicion in his eyes?

I'm safe here, she told herself. *He's on my lands.* Bria raised her chin slightly.

Kenric's hand shot forward and seized the blade of grass from her. "When you are Knowles's wife, I'll deal with you as I see fit. I'll know what you know," he whispered.

He lifted his hand and Bria pulled away from him. Her head banged against the tree trunk.

Kenric's smile grew. He leaned closer to her, extending his hand to her face. He lightly ran the blade of grass over her cheek. "There will be no more secrets between us." With a lascivious grin, he stood and towered over her for a long moment. Then he threw the blade of grass down and turned his back on her to walk down the small hill.

Bria watched him go, her body trembling. She clenched her

fists to still their shaking, but it was a long time before she could get her fear under control.

The pond glimmered magically beneath the stars. Bria dismounted as she reached the clearing. She untied a bag from the horse's saddle and moved to a group of bushes near where she'd tethered her horse the night Mary was murdered. She paused for a moment, staring at the broken branch, its ragged edge a reminder of her efforts to get away from Kenric that night.

This place was full of memories. And promises. Coming here, she remembered her mission.

She unhooked her brown velvet dress and slid it from her shoulders, then carefully folded it and tucked it beneath a group of bushes nearby.

Bria stood naked beneath the moonlight. She knew she should be frightened. She knew she should be scared of discovery. But a strange calm soothed her, almost as if someone were watching over her.

Bria removed a cloth from the bag and began wrapping it tightly around her chest, circling her torso again and again so her breasts were pressed down tightly. When her breasts were flattened almost to the point of pain, she pulled the cloth tight, tucking the end beneath the fabric. She removed a black tunic from the bag and pulled it over her head, then retrieved black leggings from the bag and pulled them up her long legs. She bent to the bushes and pulled out a pair of black boots, which she slipped on. She removed the cloak from the bag and flung it around her shoulders, tying it in place. Bria had left the castle with her hair braided and coiled tightly to her head so it would be well hidden beneath the cloak and its hood. She bent and reached beneath the bush, feeling back and forth until she found the scabbard. She pulled it out and laid it on the ground at her feet.

Finally, she bent to the bag and retrieved the last item. The mask. She stared at it for a long moment. She would leave her identity as Bria behind when she donned this mask. She would become the hero of the people.

Bria picked up her sheathed sword. She had enough money from the two tax collectors she'd stopped to help three people. Deb had told her about three other people who'd been hurt by Terran's men. One poor woman had lost her husband when he'd tried to stop Kenric from beating her—and Kenric was still demanding taxes from her.

Bria ground her teeth. This couldn't be allowed to continue. If Terran didn't care, then she'd stop it. Mary would be proud of her. Mary would have wanted her to help her people.

Bria strapped the belt to her waist. The Midnight Shadow wouldn't let Mary's death be for nothing. She placed the mask around her eyes and tied it behind her head, then lifted the hood and settled it well over her face so her features were hidden in shadow. The transformation complete, she stood with her hands on her hips, gazing down into the tranquil pond.

The Midnight Shadow stared back.

Thump.

Max the baker opened his eyes. He sat up quickly, lighting the candle beside his bed. Was it a robber in his bakery, or had those tax collectors returned to eat all his bread? He grabbed a stick and descended the stairs.

His foot no sooner touched the floor of the first level than he saw the dark figure standing in the doorway. He raised his stick, but the figure did not move. If it was a robber, he would have run.

Max narrowed his eyes. "Who are you?" he asked, refusing to lower his stick. "What do you want?"

"The tax collectors stole bread from you?"

Max clutched the stick tighter. Was this a trick? "What concern is it to you?"

"I am justice," the shadow said. "I am the Midnight Shadow."

Max could only stare. Then something caught his eye. Flickering on the table in the middle of the room was a candle, and beneath the candle was a small pouch. Max cautiously moved over to the table, still clutching his stick. He reached out to the pouch and pulled the string. Something inside glittered, but he couldn't see because of the darkness.

Anxiously, he dumped the contents onto the table. Coins rolled out, hitting the candlestick and spinning before falling flat onto the table.

Max's eyes widened. It was enough for fifty loaves of bread! He lifted his eyes to the Midnight Shadow . . .

. . . but the doorway was empty.

Max raced to the door and looked out into the night. The shadows of the surrounding trees swayed in the breeze, but there was no sign of the Midnight Shadow.

Chapter Seventeen

The Midnight Shadow rode through the forest, urging her steed in and out of streams and paths with the ease of one who knows the land, returning to the pond whose waters twinkled beneath the stars of the clear midnight sky, glimmering like a magical lake.

She swung her leg over the horse and dismounted, tying her horse to the tree near the pond. She moved to stand at the edge of the pond, gazing into the water, studying herself for a long moment.

Then, with a sigh, the protector of the innocent reached up and removed her hood. She untied the mask and slid it from her face. The Midnight Shadow disappeared.

"I'm so sorry, Mary," Bria whispered. She lifted her gaze to the distant road where Kenric had killed Mary and the herbalist. Every night before donning the hood and cape, Bria silently remembered her friend, remembered why she'd chosen to become the Midnight Shadow. And every night when she removed the hood, she recalled her friend's bravery for facing Kenric.

She reached beneath the bush and pulled out her bag. She carefully folded her cape and put it on the ground. Then she unfastened her black scabbard and sword from her waist. She crawled between two bushes, their branches clawing at her tunic and hair. She reached beneath one of the bushes and shoved the sword and scabbard into a mound of fallen leaves. She strained beneath the bush to push the leaves over the top of the sword to hide it from all would-be discoverers.

Then Bria rose and carefully removed her black tunic and black leggings, folding them meticulously and lovingly. She set them on the ground on top of the cape. She pulled her gown from the bag and donned it, hooking it at the side.

The moon was far up in the sky when she finished dressing. Lastly, she knelt on the ground beside the Midnight Shadow's pile of clothing. She took the mask and placed it on top of the black clothing. She sat back on her heels. The mask stared up at her, a silent reminder of her obligation, her mission.

Bria gently lifted the pile of clothes and placed them into the bag. She pulled the cord tightly around the sack, closing it, sealing her secret from the rest of the world.

Then she mounted her horse and rode toward Castle Delaney. It had been a good night. She'd managed to leave a few coins for two farmers whose families were on the brink of starvation as well as Max the baker. All had been cruelly overtaxed by Knowles.

Knowles. Terran. Again the question surfaced: How could he be so evil when he had touched her with . . . with such tenderness? She could still recall the gentle touch of his lips. How could he treat his own people as if they were nothing but the means to more wealth, and yet allow Garret's squire to be his own squire? It just didn't make sense.

She crossed the drawbridge and entered the castle, riding to the stables. She saw to her horse, combing him down and

blanketing him for the night. She affectionately patted his neck
and slung the bag over her shoulder, heading for the keep.

The dark courtyard was still and silent, as if it, too, was
working with her to keep her secret.

Bria walked up the two steps to the keep and pushed one of
the double doors open to enter. She pushed it closed behind
her and moved down the still hallway. All the servants were
sleeping. The only sounds were the snapping, hissing flames
from the torches that lit the corridor and her own soft steps.
She moved up the spiral stairway and down the hallway to her
room.

When she entered and closed the door behind her, a sense
of relief filled her. She tossed the bag on the bed and lit a
candle.

"It's rather late to be out for a ride."

She whirled, her gaze searching her room. A shadow separated from the wall and moved into the circle of light cast by
the flickering candle. The light slowly washed over Lord Terran
Knowles, revealing his face as he moved toward her.

Bria's heart raced as panic filled her. She fought it down,
demanding, "What are you doing here?"

"I have a solution to our problem," he murmured, the timbre
of his voice moving through her body.

She stepped away from him, realizing her heart was racing not
with panic, but with something else. Unsure and frightened by
the strange sensations Terran aroused, she quickly moved out of
the light of the candle and into the darkness that helped conceal
her as the Midnight Shadow, the darkness she hoped would conceal her feelings as Bria. She skirted the edges of her room, but
Terran pursued her.

"What problem?" she managed to stammer.

"You're mine," he proclaimed.

The certainty in his voice sent waves of shivers through her
body. For just an instant, a wildly mad instant, she wondered
what it would be like to be possessed by Terran.

"You've been mine from before you were born," he said. "Your father knows it and you know it. You simply will not acknowledge it."

The backs of her knees hit the bed. She glanced over her shoulder. A ray of moonlight illuminated the deep red blanket and something black near the head of the bed. Suddenly, sheer, vibrant fear seized her as she remembered her bag lay hidden in the darkness near the headboard.

Her gaze snapped back to Terran. He was standing very close, so close she could see the smoky depths of his eyes. So close that she could feel his breath as it fanned her lips, the raw power radiating from the core of his being.

It wasn't fear that filled her as he lifted his arms to her shoulders. It wasn't dread. It wasn't loathing. It was breathless anticipation.

"I'm here to convince you."

Chapter Eighteen

Terran stared down into the largest blue eyes that he had
ever beheld, eyes that held a surprising strength shimmering
deep inside behind their beauty. He reached for her, and Bria
stood her ground. He admired her defiance and determination
not to be intimidated.

Or was it that she wanted him to kiss her? Because that's
what he was going to do. His fingers pressed into her soft
shoulders and drew her closer to him. Was that a gasp from
those parted lips as she came up against his chest?

Terran stared down into her eyes. Then his own gaze traveled
over her features inch by inch. Her lashes were long and dark,
closed partly over those liquid blue eyes. Her nose was pert
and delicate, her skin flawless and creamy. He feathered his
fingertips over her cheek. Her skin was warm and soft, everything he'd imagined.

Her lips captured his gaze. Full and ripe.

Terran lowered his head, moving his lips closer to hers. "It
will do no good for you to fight," he murmured. He'd come

here to compromise her and had expected some resistance. He hadn't expected her to be so . . . willing.

His lips touched hers softly, caressing them with featherlight strokes.

She wasn't fighting. She wasn't pushing him away. She was simply standing, unmoving, in his hold. She wanted him to kiss her. The thought sent waves of desire crashing over him.

He pressed his lips against hers, pulling her firmly to him. She was so soft against his hard body. He moved his hand down her shoulder to cup her full breast. She gasped slightly, arching against his hand. *God's blood!* he thought as desire flared through him. *She wants me to touch her!*

Where had she been? The thought came unbidden, and he reared back suddenly. A rendezvous. She'd been out with a lover. It was the only reason she would have been out so late at night, the only reason she'd let him touch her. Warmed by the caress of another man. Of course. It all made sense now.

Her partly closed eyes opened wider as the moment was lost. She jerked as if to flee his embrace, but Terran held her tightly.

Obviously her lover had left her unsatisfied. "It's too late for escape," Terran growled, fiercely angry. He stepped forward, using his body to push her back onto the bed. The impetus toppled him toward her, but he caught himself on his arms before landing hard on top of her and hurting her. "I will not have my wife running around at midnight like the village harlot."

She pushed against his chest. "I am not your wife," she ground out.

He'd fought for everything worthwhile in his life—his reputation, his skill as a warrior. He would fight for Bria. Even tainted, she was his. He seized her wrists in one hand and pinned them above her head. With his other hand, he reached around to undo the hooks that fastened her dress.

"Don't." She snarled and twisted, trying to break his hold. But his hold was tight and unrelenting. No wife of his would dare to cuckold him. When he couldn't unfasten the hooks, his rage and frustration mounted. He pulled fiercely at the fabric, and it ripped across her stomach.

"Stop it!" she screamed.

His lips curled as he gazed down at her torn dress; the shimmering skin bared to him aroused him more than he cared to admit. He lifted his face to hers and froze, letting the torn fabric slip from his fingers.

It wasn't her rage that halted his movements; it wasn't her defiance that cooled his anger. It was the tears that glistened in her large eyes.

"Stop it," she whispered through trembling lips.

What am I doing? Terran thought. When Kenric had suggested compromising her, he'd said Bria was just a woman and no woman could stand against Terran's charm. Terran's vanity had believed him. He thought she might fight at first, but he believed ultimately she'd enjoy his touch.

The desperate pleas from her lips were not those of a woman enjoying his touch.

The idea of forcing Bria to his will, of forcing any woman, was repulsive. What he'd been about to do to save his castle and his lands sickened him. He rolled off of her and shoved her away from him.

"I'm sorry, Lady Bria," he murmured. "Betrothed or not, I have no right to treat you like that."

He looked up at her, but she was hidden in the shadows. Moonlight streamed in through the window, bathing the bed and part of the floor in light.

Terran tried to see her face, but he couldn't. He saw the bottom of her brown velvet skirt near the floor, but that was all. He stood and moved to the foot of the bed.

He would leave come sunrise. He bowed slightly, planning to tell her so, but something caught his eye. A piece of black cloth was lying in the moonlight not far from the bed.

Had he ripped her dress that much? No, Terran remembered, she was wearing brown. It must have been from another dress.

Terran bent to retrieve the cloth. She stepped forward so quickly that he almost didn't reach it first. His hand closed over it and he straightened. When his eyes alighted on her, he noticed the strange coloring of her face. At first, he attributed it to the moonlight. But there was such utter dread and fear in her eyes that it caused him to glance down at the black cloth. Was this the source of her terror?

His finger was sticking through what could have been a tear in the black fabric. Fabric as dark as the night. The hair on the back of his neck stood on end. Something wasn't right. He lifted the piece of fabric and held it before him.

Two eyeholes stared back at him. It was a mask.

The same kind of mask his enemy the Midnight Shadow wore.

Chapter Nineteen

Her mask!

Bria couldn't move. Sheer terror engulfed her as Terran lifted the mask before him. Their struggles must have knocked the bag to the floor and the mask had somehow tumbled out.

He knew she was the Midnight Shadow. He'd throw her in the dungeon—or worse. Have her hanged. Or burned.

What was she to do? She had to come up with some reason the mask would be in her bag. She could feign innocence. *What is that doing in my bag?* It was ridiculous, but it was the only thing she could think of.

Terror closed her throat. She opened her mouth to offer an explanation, but nothing came out.

And then he turned black, condemning eyes to her. Bria recoiled as if he'd thrown a noose around her neck.

"What is this?" he demanded in a voice that brooked no argument.

Bria couldn't move. She could feel the imaginary noose tighten around her throat. None of her muscles responded to the silent command to run. He would kill her now unless she could think of some reason why she'd have the Midnight Shadow's mask in her bag. *Oh Lord,* she begged silently, *let something come to me.* But no flash of insight came to her, no way out.

"Answer me," he snarled.

Bria licked her lips to moisten them, but her mouth was dry. "I . . . I don't know what that is," she whispered.

"Liar," he snapped, closing his fist around the mask. He stepped closer to her and Bria retreated.

Suddenly the door flew open behind Terran. Her father and grandfather entered the dark room, two guards behind them. Bria raced around Terran, all but leaping over the bed to escape his wrath, and fell into the safety of her father's arms.

"What is going on here?" Lord Delaney demanded, his good arm tightening protectively around Bria's shoulders.

"I might ask the same of you," Terran retorted.

Her father's gaze shifted to Bria and lighted on her torn dress. His gaze snapped back to Knowles, and his jaw clenched furiously. His burning eyes pinned Knowles to the spot.

"You vile filth," Harry said through clenched teeth. He stepped forward as if he meant to beat Knowles, his hand clenched tightly in a fist.

Terran stepped closer. "Lady Bria will marry me."

"Enough of this," Lord Delaney declared.

"Yes, quite," Terran's eyes narrowed and he glared at Bria.

His anger sliced through her body like a sword. She wanted to cocoon herself in the safety of her father's arms, but they weren't enough to shield her from Terran's fury.

"Enough of *this.*" Terran lifted the mask before him, holding it out for all to see.

Bria turned her head from Terran's gaze to lock eyes with her grandfather. He alone knew she'd seen the fabric. He alone knew how dear she held the story of the Midnight Shadow.

But would he know now she'd chosen to take up her hero's cause?

Horror and anxiety glittered in Harry's eyes. His fingers clenched and unclenched.

"What is that?" her father demanded.

"If I'm not mistaken, it's the mask of a certain man who's been robbing my lands. He calls himself the Midnight Shadow," Terran explained.

"And what does that have to do with my daughter?"

"I found the mask here, in her room," Terran explained.

Bria shifted her gaze to Terran to find his eyes on her once again. She wanted to bury her face in the safety of her father's chest as she had when she was young, but this was something she had to face. Bria lifted her chin in the face of Terran's accusations.

"Tell your father, Bria," Terran said. "Tell your father of your rendezvous."

His voice was a mocking caress, teasing, coaxing, a trap waiting to be sprung. Bria closed her mouth defiantly. She met Terran's gaze evenly and could have sworn she saw hell's fire burning deep in his black eyes. But despite his heated glare, she would never tell her father she was the Midnight Shadow.

"Tell him your secret," Terran urged softly.

Bria straightened away from her father's embrace, bravely facing Terran's vindictive gaze, refusing to relinquish her secret.

"Tell us how you've been secretly meeting with the Midnight Shadow," Terran finished.

For a long moment, she couldn't move. She thought she'd misheard him.

But he continued in a dark, dangerous voice. "Tell your father how he tasted your charms before I was anywhere near you," Terran all but purred.

She wanted to laugh out loud as relief swept her body. He didn't know! He didn't know she was the Midnight Shadow!

She swung her relieved gaze to her father, but he wore no smile on his lips. Her eyes shifted to her grandfather. He wasn't smiling, either. Her happiness died within her.

"Have you been meeting this Midnight Shadow?" her father asked.

Bria's desperate gaze swung to her only ally. Harry stared at her, and she realized the seriousness of Terran's accusation. But how could she deny it? If she told the truth, she'd be locked up as a thief. If she didn't, she'd be labeled a harlot.

Terran crumpled the mask in his hand. "If Lady Bria does not marry me, she will spend the rest of her life in my dungeons for aiding a criminal."

Silence filled the room. Terran's threat hung in the air.

Bria opened her mouth to object, to deny his accusation, but she knew whatever she could say would only get her deeper into trouble. She closed her mouth and her gaze swiveled to her father. He wouldn't allow Terran to throw her in the dungeon. He'd protect her, as he always had.

But the silence stretched and her father's face remained as still as stone. He turned his gaze from Terran to Bria, and for just a moment Bria thought she saw disappointment shimmer in his eyes. Then he looked away from her, rubbing his left arm.

Complete and utter dread welled up from the very depths of Bria's soul.

Lord Delaney nodded. "We will work out the details."

Bria stepped toward her father, her hands stretched out beseechingly, her heart pounding in her chest. "Father, you can't!"

Terran seized her arm and glared into her eyes. "You will not share your virtue with any other man." He shoved the mask at her.

Bria began to shake her head and deny his accusations, but Terran turned from her and followed her father from her room, brushing past Harry.

Bria's desolate gaze fell to the black mask in her hand. "What have I done, Grandfather?" she whispered.

Harry placed a hand on her shoulder.

But Bria found no comfort in his touch. If she were living in Castle Knowles as Terran's wife, how could she continue to be the people's defender? How could she continue to sneak out in the middle of the night to defy her husband?

How could she marry her enemy?

The next morning, Terran sat in a chair at a table in the Great Hall, still simmering, still fiercely angry from the night before. Bria was sleeping with his enemy. His damned enemy! Where Garret was a rival, the Midnight Shadow was a criminal, stealing what little was left in his coffers. He'd kill the man with his own hands.

Kenric slid onto the bench beside him. "Congratulations on your betrothal," he said, motioning to a maid for an ale.

Terran grunted.

"So my plan worked," Kenric said gleefully. "Did you have to restrain her?"

Terran cast Kenric a hard glare. Kenric's insatiable desire to overpower the weak was repulsive, but it made him a good sheriff. People were afraid of him. They didn't defy him. There had been no refusals to give up their tithe. "It didn't go as planned," Terran said.

"You raped her?" Kenric asked joyfully.

Terran's open palm hit the table hard, causing a few heads to turn. "God's blood, man!" he thundered. "I do not rape women."

Kenric shrugged slightly as a serving girl eased hesitantly up to him, eyeing him with fear, and placed an ale in front of him. He took a long gulp of the ale as the girl raced away. "You might have to consummate your marriage," he finally said. "Rumor has it she wants nothing to do with you."

Terran snorted. "That is no rumor. Lady Bria has made it abundantly clear she doesn't want to be my wife." Terran's eyes turned watchfully to the double doors. "She has a lover."

"Lady Bria has a lover?" Kenric echoed.

"And he's not just any man," Terran said. "He's the Midnight Shadow."

Kenric almost spilled his ale, but quickly grabbed the mug with both hands.

"I want him caught," Terran demanded.

"You have a plan?"

Terran nodded. Unable to sleep, he had been thinking of one all night. "Spread the word two tax collectors will be riding in tonight with the southern part of the village's tithe. You'll be waiting for him."

Chapter Twenty

Bria clutched her bag tightly to her chest. She'd waited as long as she could to leave the castle. Deb had told her of two tax collectors returning from collecting the tithe on the southern edge of Terran's lands. It was too good an opportunity to pass up.

Bria sneaked through the dark, still courtyard to the stables. She sighed slightly as she pushed the door open. She had made it. No one had seen her. She entered and shut the door behind her. There was a thrill in sneaking out to become the Midnight Shadow, a danger that excited her. And every night upon her safe return, a victorious feeling soared through her, making her feel exuberant, as if she were floating on a cloud. Despite the fact she'd almost been discovered, she found herself again tempting fate.

A slight grin curled her lip as she moved through the stable. The Midnight Shadow would not be denied.

"Going to see him again, aren't you?"

Bria stifled the surprised cry that rose in her throat. She

quickly dropped the bag behind a bundle of hay, hiding it from view, before turning to confront her questioner.

Terran stood silhouetted against the window of the stables. He approached her. "Who is he?"

Bria stood her ground, trembling fiercely. She could not tell him. Ever. He was the cause of such hardship for his people. He'd never understand. Besides, she'd tried to tell him, tried to explain about Mary's death, but he would hear none of it. "I don't know who you mean," she replied sweetly.

He seized her shoulders, dragging her close to him. "You know," he hissed, so close she could almost feel the movement of his lips against hers. "Tell me," he commanded.

She lifted her chin slightly, but the movement only thrust her lips closer to his.

He looked at her mouth, and she suddenly felt a hot tingling in her lips. The next instant, he pulled her closer, pressing his lips to hers, kissing her with an angry insistence. Shock held her immobile. The vehemence in his kiss frightened her. Because beneath his anger, she sensed something else. A desperation. A need.

And her own body responded to that need, to the urgency building in her. She lifted her hand to touch his arm, and her fingers brushed the hard muscle hidden by his tunic.

Terran responded by pulling her tighter, closer against him. He plundered her mouth until all her resistance was gone. The swirling passion of her emotion caught her up in its whirlwind and buffeted her until she was dizzy.

He thrust his hand beneath her dress, his searing touch burning across her chest to her breast, enflaming it with heated strokes of his thumb, until her nipple was as hard as a pebble. She was breathless, panting against Terran's mouth, groaning with the awakened need that scorched through his body into hers.

She should stop him, but, God help her, she wanted him to

show her. She wanted Terran to teach her what was making her feel this way. She wanted him to . . .

He reached down and cupped her buttocks, pulling her against his hardness. She gasped as the core of her being brushed against him. Her emotions swept her up and up, until she was unable to remember who she was or what she was doing. His hand stroked her breast, teasing and caressing. His other hand moved lower and lower, closer to the spot where she needed him.

Terran pushed her back to the wall, shoving his leg between hers. Instinctively, her hips moved, rubbing over his leg. The mounting urgency, the growing need, filled her until it was all she knew, all she cared about.

Suddenly, he stepped back, releasing her.

She almost fell forward. She was breathing hard, panting for completion. She stepped toward him, but he grabbed her shoulders to hold her at arm's length. He studied her face.

Finally, Terran dropped his hands. "Go to your lover with my kiss on your lips and my touch on your skin and know that when we are wed, I will have you and you will belong to me. Completely." He turned away and headed toward the door.

Bria watched his straight back and almost cried out to him. She felt a longing and want whirling inside her the likes of which she had never known. For a moment, she thought of telling him she was the Midnight Shadow, just so he'd kiss her and touch her again.

But slowly, rationality returned. She wanted him to understand why she felt the need to continue her rides, but he would never listen to her. Betrothed or not, he was her enemy. There were people who needed her. His people.

She turned her back to him and moved to her steed.

Terran crossed the inner ward to the stairs of the keep with long strides.

Damn her! He was trembling with such desire that he felt powerless before her. He clenched his fists, fighting the feelings that threatened to overtake him. He wasn't used to battling an unseen foe. He couldn't fight these feelings with swords or lances.

He cursed silently. *She is just a woman. How do I battle this control she has over me?*

He turned back to stare at the stable. *Am I mad? I've left her to go to another man. I will not permit it!*

The stable door flew open and Bria emerged on her steed.

Instinctively, Terran stepped toward her.

But she raced past him toward the outer gatehouse.

I have to stop her, Terran thought. He took two steps toward the stables before realizing he'd never reach her in time.

By the time he got his horse out of the stables, she'd be gone into the Midnight Shadow's arms.

Frustration consumed him as he watched her ride out of the castle.

The Midnight Shadow hid in the foliage waiting for the two tax collectors. Suddenly, the sounds of horses' hooves came to her ears, the clip-clop against the dirt road as they walked. She stepped out into the road, still hidden by the shadows of the forest. The moon was but a sliver tonight, giving just enough light for her to see them in the open road, but not enough to expose her position. Slowly, she saw them coming down the road in the dim light. Only two men.

Something prickled the back of her neck. What kind of fools would be riding so slowly when their bags were heavy with coin? She wasn't the only thief to travel these roads this late. And where was their escort?

As they neared, she could make out the white horse one rode on. She waited until they were almost a horse's length away to rush forward and seize the bridles of their mounts. "Good evening, gentlemen," she greeted in her customary low whisper.

They glanced at each other. They didn't seem at all surprised to see her. Again that feeling clawed at the back of her neck. They hadn't even reached for their weapons. Her hand immediately dipped to the hilt of her sword. She drew her weapon.

Their gazes lifted to somewhere behind her.

A trap! The thought exploded through her mind.

Footsteps thudded on the road behind her. She jerked to turn, but a voice cut her off. "Don't move." The familiar voice left her cold with fear and foreboding. Kenric's voice.

Her limbs went stiff and her breathing shallowed.

"The Midnight Shadow," he scoffed. "Just a common thief. It'll be a great pleasure to see who you really are."

She whirled, bringing her sword up and smashing it against his. He growled and brought his weapon down, cutting into her left arm.

The Midnight Shadow bit back a cry of pain. She whirled between the horses, shouting loudly to spook them. They reared slightly, inhibiting Kenric for a moment.

Her left arm throbbed painfully, but she dashed behind the horses and swatted them so they jerked forward. She circled around one animal and found herself face to face with a guard. She met his lunge, knocking his blade cleanly aside, and parried with a cut to his stomach. He cried out and she sidestepped his fall, then turned toward the forest.

"Get him!" Kenric cried. "Fools! Don't let him escape!"

The pounding of a horse's gallop sounded behind her and she quickly entered the forest, moving abruptly to an area too thick for the horses to follow. Her left arm ached and she cradled it to her side as she ran through the branches.

Twigs exploded behind her and foliage crunched and crackled as her would-be captors gave chase.

Her mind slid back to another time when she was racing through the forest running from Kenric. She pushed the thought aside, gathering her cape beneath her arm so it wouldn't snag on the branches of the trees.

She had to think. Think of some way to escape.

She ducked behind a tree, quickly summing up her position. A fallen tree two paces to her left, a small clearing—large enough to fight in—to her right, and straight ahead more forest, more darkness in which to hide. She'd become very good at disappearing into and out of the darkness. Her cape was perfect for concealing her. She lurched forward, but froze as Kenric emerged, panting hard, from the copse of trees she'd just come through.

His dark gaze swept the area, but he didn't see her. "Spread out," he ordered as two more men emerged and finally a third. "If he escapes, it is your lives."

The Midnight Shadow eyed Kenric. Such pure evil. Hatred burned in her veins and righteousness roused her spirit. He was a head taller than she was, and stronger. She couldn't outfight this man. She had to use her brain.

Two of the men broke off from Kenric and headed toward the clearing. Kenric looked around and signaled the last man to head toward the forest—toward her. Kenric moved in the direction of the fallen tree.

The Midnight Shadow remained absolutely still, letting herself become one with the night, as one of the men passed within six feet of her. She held her breath until he moved out of sight, afraid he would hear the simple act of her taking air into her lungs. She had to wait until they'd passed and then double back for her horse.

There was no coin, no tithe. It had all been a ruse to ensnare her.

She'd been arrogant to think they wouldn't try to stop her. She was taking gold from Terran. He'd do everything in his power to catch her.

She watched Kenric's man disappear into the darkness and stepped out of her cover, moving back the way she'd come.

* * *

Bria rode for a long time that night, crossing and recrossing her path, making sure no one followed her. She pressed a torn piece of fabric to her wound, stanching the flow of blood. She was lucky. The blade had just grazed her; the cut wasn't deep.

Only a few hours before dawn, she rode back into Castle Delaney, stabled her horse, and headed toward the keep.

Someone called out her name and froze her in her tracks.

She hesitated for a long moment, fearing it was Terran. She knew she couldn't hide the pain shooting up her arm. But when she turned, she saw her grandfather. Relief filled her so completely she almost wept. Her steps quickened as she approached him.

"You shouldn't be out this late, Bria," he chastised. "If Knowles—"

He must have seen the pain in her eyes, for suddenly he grabbed her shoulders, demanding, "What's wrong?"

She winced as the agony shot through her arm to her shoulder. Harry's gaze quickly scanned her body, her shoulders, her waist, her arms for an injury. "You're hurt." He seized her hand, leading her into the keep and down the hall. "What happened?" he whispered urgently.

Bria shook her head, allowing him to lead her through the empty hallways. He brought her to his room and sat her on the bed, pausing to light a candle. "Where is it?"

"My left arm." Bria eased her arm out of her dress. Though her movements were slow, pain sliced through her shoulder. She hadn't hooked the side of her dress when she put on her regular clothes. The shooting agony had prevented her from reaching the hooks. She had wrapped it as best she could with a piece of her cape.

Harry unwrapped the material, inspecting the wound with a critical eye. He pressed the material to the wound. "Hold it here," he ordered. "I'll be back." He left the room.

Bria sat alone in the darkness. Her ally. Darkness had hidden her from Kenric. He'd be furious with her escape, would double his efforts to find her. There would be more traps. She'd barely made it out of this one, and with nothing to show but a sword wound in her arm. That would do nothing to help anyone.

The door opened, and Harry entered with a bowl of water and some clean rags. He sat down beside her, placing the bowl on the floor. "Would you like to explain what happened?"

Bria relinquished care of her wound to him, but wasn't sure she wanted to involve him in her scheme. "There was a fight," she lied. "I tried to break it up."

Harry lifted his eyes to hers, searching out the truth. She turned away from his stare, unable to look at him. "This is a sword wound," Harry informed her. "I'm not a fool, Bria, and I'm insulted you'd treat me like one."

"Oh, Grandfather," she whispered. But she couldn't tell him her secret, couldn't implicate him in her plan. She shook her head and her long locks fell over her shoulder. "I don't want to hurt you." She stared at her arm, refusing to meet his gaze. "I was coming home from the clearing and I saw two men fighting. I tried to stop it."

Harry's eyes saddened, and he looked down at her wound, cleaning and wrapping it in silence.

Bria wanted to tell him the truth. It was tearing her apart not to be able to confide in him, but what she was doing was far too dangerous.

Harry tied off the wrappings. "You'll be fine," he assured her. "Just stay away from sword fights."

Bria smiled and stood. Grateful, she placed a hand on his shoulder. "Thank you."

He grunted in disapproval, but kissed her hand. "Go and get some rest."

* * *

Terran sat in the Great Hall late into the night, awaiting word of the capture of the Midnight Shadow—his rival, his hated enemy. He held a mug of ale tightly as he stared into the crackling fire of the hearth. Around him on the floor, servants slept, content in the dreams of commoners. For Terran, there'd be no contented sleep until the Midnight Shadow was captured. His coffers suffered, but not half as much as his heart.

Footsteps echoed in the Great Hall, the sound bouncing off the heavy stone walls. Terran lifted his gaze to see Kenric approaching.

Terran rose and moved to greet him, calling, "Where is he? I want to interrogate him myself."

Kenric looked away from his cousin's piercing stare and his jaw clenched. "He escaped."

"What?" Terran roared.

"He's like a demon, my lord," Kenric defended himself. "He disappears and reappears—"

"Rubbish," Terran exploded. "He is a man. I want him caught."

"I wounded him. I know he bleeds. I'll try again tonight. This I promise." Kenric whirled toward the doors.

"No." Terran slapped his hand on Kenric's shoulder. "He'll be expecting something. Wait a while. Let him grow comfortable with his escapades." Terran's gaze drifted in the direction of Bria's room. "In the meantime, let's see if we can't secure the aid of my betrothed."

Terran stared at Bria's horse. The black steed eyed him as he moved about the stall, closely surveying the animal for any clue as to where she had gone to meet this . . . this man. But her horse's legs had been washed down and a blanket was thrown over his back to keep him warm.

Terran's jaw clenched. She'd taken care of her steed before returning to the keep. This was a smart woman he was marrying.

Fury and betrayal burned inside Terran. His fists clenched tightly.

Bria Delaney would know the full extent of his wrath. He would have answers.

Chapter Twenty-one

I will have answers, Terran thought again.

He hadn't been able to fall asleep with the little night that
remained after Kenric's return. He'd only managed to rest for
a few hours before rising. Now he found himself in the Great
Hall, waiting for his betrothed. And waiting.

His mood darkened as the sun lifted further and further in
the sky until it was directly overhead. He'd intended to question
her gently about her lover. But the more he waited, the angrier
he became. His plan to question her calmly was slowly changing
to one of getting what he wanted one way or another.

He rose and headed for the door, crashing through the rushes
that lined the floor. He hadn't missed her awakening. She was
still asleep in her bed. Well, no future wife of his would sleep
the day away.

Kenric entered the Great Hall, momentarily halting Terran's
stride. "M'lord," he greeted with a nod of his head.

"Have you seen my betrothed?" Terran almost spat the
words.

"No."

Terran stalked past him. Kenric had to walk quickly to keep up.

Terran rounded the corner, heading toward her room, and almost slammed into a group of serving women and ladies. He came up short and bowed slightly before them when his breath suddenly caught in his throat.

Bria stood before him at the front of the women. She met his stare evenly, those blue eyes luminous with a smile that slowly faded from her lips.

Terran realized he'd never seen her smile before. His anger vanished beneath the happiness he'd just seen touching her eyes, her lips, her cheeks. She was beautiful. Incredibly, amazingly beautiful.

"Lord Knowles," she greeted.

Some of the women curtsied, some hailed him with a barely audible acknowledgment. But Terran's gaze remained fixed on Bria. What had she done to make herself so vibrant?

She stepped around him.

For a moment, Terran watched her move past him, transfixed. Such confidence in her step, such beauty in her features, such—

"M'lord."

It was Kenric. Terran turned his head to his cousin, who was staring at him in confusion, as if something were wrong. It shook Terran out of his fog. He glanced back to Bria, calling, "My lady, I would have a word with you."

Bria halted and turned. Her eyes were so large and so startlingly blue. Her long, dark hair hung in ringlets over her shoulder to the middle of her back. The dark blue velvet gown she wore hugged her shapely figure. She nodded and her hair brushed her breast. She whispered something to one of the women and then stepped forward.

The group of women turned and continued into the Great Hall.

Terran watched Bria approach with uncharacteristically tentative steps. He shifted his gaze from the subtle sway of her gown to her eyes. She wasn't looking at him. She was staring at Kenric.

Terran glanced over his shoulder at Kenric to see a small smile of satisfaction on his lips. A frown carved its way into Terran's forehead. He didn't like the effect his cousin had on his future wife. He turned away from Kenric and took Bria's hand, tucking it into the crook of his arm, almost as if protecting her. He guided her down the hall into a more secluded area of the castle. Kenric trailed them like a shadow.

"You certainly rise late," Terran commented.

Bria glanced over her shoulder at Kenric. "Must we have an escort?"

"He's interested in what I'm going to ask you."

Bria stopped and faced him. "Whatever you have to ask, you may do so right here."

Terran studied her slightly upturned chin, the glint of defiance in her eyes. "Are you afraid?" he challenged.

"Yes," she admitted.

His admiration grew stronger with each passing moment. No man would dare to admit his fear, even though he felt it. For Bria to do so meant she had more honesty and confidence than any man he knew.

"I'm afraid to be alone with you," she clarified.

A grin quirked the side of his lip. After his behavior two nights ago, he thought that was a fair explanation.

"I have a right to be, after you murdered your last betrothed."

Her words caught him unaware. Murder Odella? Such fury as he had never known claimed his entire being. He grabbed her arm and squeezed it tightly. "You will not speak again of Odella. She was more of a lady than you will ever be."

Bria's face twisted in agony and she bent her body slightly, favoring the arm he was squeezing. Terran lessened his grip, but something beneath her velvet sleeve captured his attention. He ran his fingers up and down her arm until he found the top and bottom of the discrepancy beneath her clothing. He looked at the width his fingers spanned.

Bria pulled her arm away from his touch, holding it as if it were wounded.

Wounded! Terran's eyes snapped to lock with Bria's. That's what it felt like—wrappings from a wound. A sword wound, by the width of it.

He grabbed her forearm in a tight grip. "What is this?" he demanded.

Bria tried to pull her arm free. "I was hurt," she replied.

Kenric stepped up beside Terran. His small, ugly eyes glared at her.

Bria's gaze shifted between the two men. "I was wounded yesterday trying to break up a fight!" she said desperately.

Terran pulled her closer. "My enemy was wounded yesterday."

"Terran, you're hurting me," she whispered.

Terran immediately released her arm. "How is it you have the same wound as my enemy?" he demanded.

Bria rubbed her arm. She opened her mouth, searching for an answer, but nothing came forth. Finally, she closed her mouth.

"What's going on here?"

Terran whirled to find Bria's grandfather standing in the hallway. He was about ready to command the old man away, when he saw his left arm, which was wrapped in a cloth and cradled by a sling. Then a servant walked by, moving down the hallway. A fresh cloth covered the upper part of his left arm. Terran could have sworn he saw a mocking smile on the servant's lips. Another man walked by, his upper left arm wrapped, too. Terran's anger boiled and he snapped his gaze back to Bria. *Good lord! How many other men are wearing wrappings around their arms to cover for her lover?*

He glared at her with all the murderous intensity he felt simmering inside before whirling and stalking away from her.

She was the key to finding his enemy, but he couldn't speak with her when there was this much rage inside him. He couldn't face her and look into her eyes and hear her slanderous words about . . . Odella.

He paused at an open balcony to look out on the lands, but saw nothing of the world below. He ran a hand over his face. Bria thought he had murdered Odella. It pained him to the core of his being. No wonder she didn't trust him. No wonder she looked upon him with distaste. No wonder she never smiled at him.

Suddenly, a terrifying thought occurred to him. Would Bria do the same thing Odella had to avoid marrying him? Would Bria take her own life?

Chapter Twenty-two

Terran stalked away down the corridor, and Bria turned to find Kenric glaring at her. Her left arm throbbed with the memory of his attack. But he didn't frighten her any longer. She'd faced him in battle and had survived. It was the way he was looking at her—like all the fires in hell had gathered inside him and he was waiting for the right moment to unleash them on her.

Then Kenric cast a glance over his shoulder at Harry. When he looked back at her, there was a restrained look in his eyes, but a dark promise nonetheless. He moved off down the hall.

Bria turned toward her grandfather and slowly walked up to him, gazing at his arm. "That's a nasty cut."

"You don't know how nasty. Do you realize how much courage it takes to cut oneself with a dagger?"

A thousand sincere thank yous glimmered in her eyes. She knew now just how wrong she'd been in not telling him the truth. He was more than her grandfather. He was her confidant. "You knew."

"I may be old," he replied, "but I'm not a fool." He gently touched her cheek. "And I know my granddaughter. I had the others just put on bandages. They didn't cut themselves. I told them it was a joke I was playing on Knowles. They don't know what it means."

Bria threw herself into his arms.

"I was afraid for you, Bria," he whispered. "I knew Knowles would find out. But I can only protect you until that coward of a father of yours marries you off. Once you're gone, you're on your own."

"And it will be soon," she said, pressing her cheek to his chest.

"Aye," Harry replied, stroking her hair. "Within the next few days. Knowles is insisting you leave for his castle within the next week."

Bria's embrace tightened. She was scared. Everything she knew, everything she loved was here at Castle Delaney. She'd soon be leaving the safety of her home and venturing off into unknown lands . . . into her enemy's hands.

"Knowles will do everything in his power to find out who the Midnight Shadow is. Give it up, Bria, before it is too late."

"I can't," Bria whispered. She had to keep up the guise of the Midnight Shadow . . . for Mary, for Garret, for everyone she could help. "I won't."

Harry squeezed her tightly. "You must promise me something, then."

Bria pulled back. "Anything."

"You must promise me . . ." Harry studied her features.

Bria could have sworn that she saw tears in his eyes.

"You must promise me you will not die."

For the flash of a second, she considered lying to him, but he knew her far better than anyone else. He wasn't a fool. "The Midnight Shadow will never die," she answered, feeling tears rise in her eyes. "You taught me that, remember?"

Harry brushed a tear from her cheek before stepping away from her and turning to move off down the hallway.

Bria watched her grandfather, and a strange heaviness settled upon her chest. She'd be leaving him soon. But why? Why did she have to leave? Why wouldn't her father tell Knowles to go hang? Even if he thought the worst of her, she was still his daughter, his only heir. He could refuse this marriage.

Bria moved down the hall, then up another set of stairs to find her father. He was probably in the treasury studying the profits and figures from the tithes. Holding her skirt up slightly, she climbed the stairs. Her small, slippered feet made no sound as they moved across the steps. Finally, she reached the treasury. She tentatively opened the door, calling, "Father?"

"Come in, Bria," her father called from a small table. Stick tabulations lay spread out on the table, some banded together, some separate. A piece of parchment lay on the table with meticulous figures written on it. Her father paused, looking up from the sticks to gaze at her.

"Hello, Father," Bria called.

Her Father sat back in his chair. "I'm glad you came. I could use a rest from these figures," he said.

Bria nervously ran a finger through a gouge in the wooden table.

Her father reached out and clasped her hand.

Bria lifted her eyes to meet her father's. With his gentle gaze upon her, Bria couldn't speak the truth. She couldn't ask him why he wouldn't fight for her. She couldn't ask him why he wouldn't defend her. She knew why.

"I expected you to come to me much sooner than this, but you've always put the feelings of others before your own," he mused.

Bria glanced down at the gouge again, unable to meet her father's direct gaze. She couldn't hurt him. She adored him. He'd fought and been maimed in a horrible war. He was dealing with it the best way he knew how, the way that would keep him sane. She couldn't destroy him.

"You think me a coward for not protecting you from Knowles."

How could she think him a coward after what he had been through? She began to shake her head, to deny his words, but he continued.

"You do. As much as you want to deny it, you do." He ran his hand over his eyes, sighing. "I cannot fight him, Bria," her father admitted. "If I declare the betrothal invalid, he will challenge me in battle. It is his right."

Bria heard the anguish in his voice and dropped to her knees beside him. She reached out for his hand, but he moved his injured arm away from her touch with his good hand, absently rubbing his useless limb. Bria withdrew immediately, placing her hands in her lap.

"It would be pointless," he said softly. "I would be killed and then he would have the run of our lands anyway."

"But Grandfather—"

"Is old and would be killed, too. Knowles would have you in the end," her father explained. "He's a strong man, Bria. You will bear him strong sons and maybe you can raise them to be kind lords."

Bria sat back on her heels. "Then your mind is made up."

Her father's blue eyes rose to meet hers. "Your rendezvous with this Midnight Shadow doesn't help my situation any."

Bria began to shake her head.

"You brought this on as much as I," her father scolded.

Bria couldn't tell her father there were no rendezvous. He wouldn't understand why she risked her life. He wouldn't understand her reasons for trying to help the people under Terran's rule. He would forbid her from doing it.

"Tell me who he is," her father commanded.

Bria wouldn't look at him. She couldn't look at him. She

was disobeying a direct order of his. Women had been beaten for less, but she knew he'd never force her to tell him.

"Bria, I am your father. Tell me who he is!" His tone grew angry and stern.

She snapped her gaze to him. He'd never used that tone of voice with her before. Despite every fiber in her being urging her to confide in her father, Bria stood her ground. Revelation now would be the death of the Midnight Shadow. "I can't," she whispered. "I can't, Father. Please don't ask me again."

Her father sighed. "Why didn't you come to me with your love for this man, this Midnight Shadow, whoever he is? I could have betrothed you to him."

Bria wanted to laugh, but couldn't. This matter had gone far beyond the point of humor.

"Instead, you sneak off into the night to meet with a man I don't know. I should feel insulted. Betrayed."

"No," Bria objected. "Don't. I never meant to make you feel that."

"Maybe that's how you feel about me."

"No," Bria insisted.

"I'm sorry I'm such a disappointment to you," her father whispered.

"No," Bria repeated, running her hand over his cheek. "Father, you are not a disappointment. I don't blame this on you. I . . . I just don't know what the future holds."

Her father nodded. "That's how I felt when I took your mother as my wife."

Bria stared into her father's eyes. He'd loved her mother very much. She wanted her life to be like his. The love he had felt she wanted to feel. She threw her arms around him. "I'll do as you wish, Father."

"This is not as I wish. It is as it has to be."

* * *

Bria stood at the altar, staring up at the chaplain. Her palms were sweating, and she had to wipe them on her dress more than once. She half hoped one of the dozen witnesses would find a reason to object to the whole thing, and her eyes darted nervously around, looking for some kind of salvation: the chapel roof, the ornate glass windows, the elaborate statues that lined the church like guardians. Finally she looked at Terran. He was gazing at her with such calmness Bria was taken aback.

He reached out and placed his hand over hers. His gentleness startled her, but his touch soothed her. She turned her gaze back to the chaplain, her anxiety washed away by a simple touch from Terran.

The chaplain finished the uneventful ceremony and blessed the union.

She was the wife of Terran Knowles.

A simple ceremony had changed her life forever, a ceremony that she'd once imagined would be attended by all of her friends, by Mary, by Garret, by hundreds of guests, a ceremony that would be sealed by a kiss.

Instead, she didn't even have a special dress made for the occasion, but wore a simple dark green velvet dress she'd worn a dozen times before. And now the deed was done. The decree in the betrothal papers had been fulfilled. She didn't know what she was feeling, but it was certainly not the happiness of a new bride. A wife.

What a terrifying word.

In the next whirlwind moment, Terran ushered Bria out the doors of the keep. In the courtyard, a double line of mounted men awaited them, Kenric in the lead. Terran escorted Bria to a waiting horse and helped her mount, then mounted behind her without a word.

She couldn't help but notice the cart filled with bags of gold in the middle of the line. All these men, all these soldiers were here to guard her dowry.

Terran's arm swept around Bria, clasping her tight against

him as if she were his possession. Before she could register her annoyance, a tremor shot through her body at the touch of his strong arms.

The horse whinnied and reared slightly as Terran took the reins in his hands.

She'd barely lifted her hand in farewell to her father and grandfather, who stood in the doorway of the keep, dwarfed by the massive wooden double doors and looking as forlorn as Bria felt, before Terran kicked the horse forward.

Then she was moving through the inner gatehouse. The speed of the horses quickened as they rode toward the outer gatehouse. People stood at the sides of the castle watching, their expressions a mixture of pity and devastation.

Bria tried to glance back, but could see only Terran's shoulder. A strand of her long hair had come loose from her braid and Bria had to push it away from her eyes. As she turned back to the path of her future, she saw the last structure of her castle loom before them, the outer gatehouse. Panic flared through her, and she had a strong instinct to leap from the horse and run back to her home, the only life she'd known.

Instead, she lifted her head, letting the wind whip her hair behind her, and faced what the future had in store.

They burst forth from the castle, riding toward the village.

Who would have thought two weeks ago that she would be married to her enemy, sitting in his arms, approaching his lands?

My lands, she corrected herself. *My people.* A calmness washed over her. *My people. And I have a vow to keep to Mary. I will see to it that they are protected. One way or another.*

Chapter Twenty-three

As the entourage galloped through Knowles Village, there were very few cheers, and even fewer happy faces. Terran noticed more than one person shaking his head at the sight of Bria. Were they displeased with her? Not that it mattered.

The sun was beginning to set over the horizon as his castle appeared in the distance, marking an end to a very long day and several very long weeks. It seemed like another lifetime since he'd arrived at Castle Delaney to seek Bria's hand. Now that he'd secured it, he must instruct Kenric to get on with paying the king's tithe, paying his knights, and seeing that there was enough food to last the winter and . . .

. . . and these were things he didn't give a damn about. He'd sought Bria's hand for her dowry, and in the hope that the challenge of gaining her hand would rouse the spirit he had lost. But it hadn't been the challenge of winning Bria's hand. Bria herself had roused his spirit. At first her intellect had provoked him. Then it was her secrets.

Bria shifted in his arms, drawing his gaze to the top of her head. Little strands of rebellious curls had freed themselves from the tight braid. He hated that braid and wanted to see her hair freed from its constraints. She was at her most beautiful when her long tresses hung loose and free. Terran found himself leaning into those strands, inhaling deeply the fragrance of lavender. He rested his cheek against the top of her head.

Something else became very apparent. With each of the horse's steps, her bottom rubbed against his manhood like a lightning strike. He hardened instantly. Just the thought of her tiny buttocks pressing so intimately up against him sent desire spearing through him. He clenched his teeth, trying to get his passion under control, but it was next to impossible. He had to think of something else.

They rounded the hillside, continuing in an arc toward the castle. Castle Knowles rested near one of the highest mountains in the land. Surrounded by cliffs on all but one side, the fortress was virtually impenetrable. But Terran no longer admired its beauty or its strategic defenses as he once did. He'd lived here all his life and was unimpressed by its grandeur.

He needed something else to bring that spark of excitement back into his life. He'd thought he found it with Odella, but he'd been wrong. Fatally wrong.

His arms tightened instinctively around Bria.

They approached the castle head on. Terran glanced behind him at the long line of armored men. He had tripled the number of guards to his entourage, for the dowry was substantial—enough to pay his men and his taxes to the king.

And there was another reason. Terran knew the Midnight Shadow wouldn't let his lover go. He'd expected some sort of confrontation with his enemy, but their journey had been uneventful.

As the castle walls loomed higher in his vision, his tension eased. The Midnight Shadow wouldn't be bold enough to attack them in front of Castle Knowles.

Terran glanced down at his bride's head. He now knew his

attraction to her was much stronger than he could have imagined. They could have a good marriage. But could Bria ever let the Midnight Shadow go and let Terran be her husband?

It's irrelevant, he told himself. *She's mine.*

They rode through the outer ward and into the inner ward. Terran eased Bria to the ground and dismounted. He gave commands to Kenric to secure the gold in the treasury. Then he turned toward his castle. He had many things to see to, boring things. His steward, no doubt, had a list of things that needed his immediate attention.

As he turned, his gaze stopped upon the small woman standing where his war horse had been before the stable boy had led him away. Around her, his men were dispersing, but she stood motionless, her hands clasped before her, her large blue eyes trained uncertainly on him. Bria looked so lost that for a brief moment, Terran had the urge to sweep her into his arms and assure her everything would be all right.

He took a step toward her, but suddenly a voice called out, "M'lord!" Terran turned to find a blond woman standing on the stairs to the keep. Every detail about her was impeccable, from her horned headdress to her slippered feet. She was a marvelous woman to look at, and Terran used to love to do that. But now another woman needed his attention.

But the woman came toward him, holding out her slender hand. Terran brushed her knuckles with a kiss. "Lady Kathryn."

"Yes." Her haughty blue gaze swung to Bria.

"Lady Kathryn, meet my wife, Lady Bria." He turned his gaze to Bria and was crushed by her crestfallen expression. But she straightened her shoulders and marched up to them.

"A pleasure," Bria said, expressing anything but.

Terran stared in confusion at Bria. Her large eyes all but danced with fire as she gazed upon Kathryn. Kathryn's reaction was just as baffling. Her eyebrow rose in disdain. Then both women turned their gazes on him.

Terran smiled enigmatically, but he'd never felt so burdened and strained before. He felt expected to do something, but he didn't know what they wanted. "Kenric!" he called out.

His cousin strolled over to him.

Terran's eyes shifted from Bria to Kathryn and back again. "Show Lady Bria to her room." Something flashed in her blue eyes like the distant glint of lightning. Was that hurt or anger? She lowered her eyes before he could figure it out.

Terran's gaze shifted to Kathryn's, and he saw victory shining in her blue eyes. Strange, Terran thought. He'd never realized before how dull her eyes were. They were pale blue and hard, almost like stones set into her sockets.

Terran stepped past Bria and paused. "I will come to you tonight," he promised his new bride. Then he took Kathryn's arm and moved into the keep. Kathryn was aglow as they strolled through Castle Knowles's halls. She primped for the peasants who watched them, holding her chin high. Terran tried to restrain his impatience.

They turned down a dark hallway, their footsteps echoing. Kathryn was strangely quiet. She could talk for hours about herself, but now her mouth remained shut. Something was wrong.

"What brings you here, Kathryn?" he asked brusquely. Terran paused before the closed door of the room she always occupied when at Castle Knowles, although the last time had been over a year ago.

"My darling," she cooed, leaning back against the door. "Why are you so cruel to me?" She placed her hands on his chest.

Terran had once found her coy manner irresistible—before Odella. "I'm not cruel, Kathryn," he said softly. "I just know your games."

"Games?" She pouted with those once sensual lips. But now Terran could only see one pair of lips in his mind's eye.

"You wound me." She took his hand and placed it upon her breast. "Deeply." Her voice took on a husky tone.

Terran leaned forward. "Our relationship is finished. It ended long ago. You know that."

"Of course," she said, "when you were marrying Odella." She arched slightly so her breast filled his palm. "I couldn't come between you and my sister."

Terran's jaw clenched fiercely and he looked away from Kathryn.

"I came as soon as she died," she whispered.

"I see," Terran said.

"To comfort you," she said softly. Her lips were but inches from his now.

"So when your sister died, you came to Castle Knowles to . . . comfort me," Terran clarified.

She nodded.

"Only to find me married." He reached around her and opened the door.

Kathryn almost spilled into the room, but she quickly righted herself. She shrugged slightly. "A mere inconvenience."

Terran's eyes narrowed. Bria was his wife now, and the thought of her as a mere inconvenience boiled his blood. He entered the room and lighted a candle. "What do you want, Kathryn?"

Kathryn came up behind him to hug his broad shoulders. "I want things to be as they were before."

Terran grabbed her hands and removed them from his body. "Before what?"

Kathryn lifted her chin slightly and tried to look hurt. "I want you to love me."

"What we shared wasn't love, and you know it."

Kathryn didn't flinch. "You *did* love me . . . until you laid eyes on Odella."

"I never loved you, Kathryn—before or after Odella," Terran growled. "I always made that clear."

Kathryn crossed her arms and pouted.

"Why are you here?" Terran demanded.

"Truly, my lord, I came as a friend to comfort you. I know how much Odella meant to you."

Terran found this hard to believe. There wasn't an unselfish bone in Kathryn's body. She did things only when they benefited her. "Why didn't your father accompany you?"

Kathryn looked away from him, playing with a piece of fabric on the wooden table. "He wanted to, but he was busy."

Terran grunted. Something must have happened between Kathryn and her father. Last Terran had heard, Kathryn was bedding one of her father's friends.

"So who is this little mouse of a bride you've taken on?" Kathryn asked. "You obviously don't love her."

"Why do you say that?"

Kathryn lifted her smug eyes to meet his. "If you did, you wouldn't have left her alone on her arrival at your castle."

Terran stared at Kathryn, dismayed. He hadn't thought of that. Instead he'd wasted time seeking the reason for Kathryn's arrival at Castle Knowles. He hadn't considered his new bride's feelings. The memory of her standing so forlornly in the middle of his castle courtyard sent guilt rushing through him. "Damn," he murmured and started for the door.

He'd no sooner stepped into the hallway when Kenric came running toward him.

"She's gone!" Kenric exploded.

"What do you mean?" Terran demanded, anxiety prickling the back of his neck. Images of her in the Midnight Shadow's arms danced mockingly in his mind's eye.

"She ran away. I can't find her."

"Did she leave the castle?"

"By now she could have."

"Damn it, Randolph," Terran growled, "find her. She'll be heading back to Castle Delaney. Send men to search for her." He stormed off down the hall. "Find her!"

Chapter Twenty-four

Bria rode hard through the forest, tears burning her eyes. Terran had left her to be with his mistress on the very day he'd married her. She'd be damned if she'd wait patiently for him to come to her. She wanted nothing to do with Terran Knowles! She didn't want to live with him, she didn't want to share his bed, and she certainly didn't want to be his wife. She wiped aside the tears that ran over her cheeks. *Then why are you crying?* a mocking voice inside her asked.

The answer came to her abruptly. Because she'd begun to believe in his kindness. She saw him as something other than a tyrant.

But he'd given her to Kenric, the man who'd killed her friend. Bria had watched with disbelieving eyes as Terran disappeared inside the doors of Castle Knowles with Kathryn. But disbelief quickly left her, replaced by a cold assessment of her situation. Terran had apparently flaunted his lover before his first betrothed, Odella. Why not before her?

When Kenric reached for Bria, his hand wrapping around

her arm, Bria had turned confused eyes to him. The eyes that stared back at her were from hell itself. He smiled evilly at her, relishing the moment.

Bria lurched forward, catching him off guard. He'd lost his balance and fallen down a stair, losing his grip on her. Bria ran. She'd almost made it to the outer gate when she realized she needed a horse. She mounted one of the guard's horses that remained in the courtyard and raced for the castle gates. She rode as fast and as hard as she could, fearing that any moment they'd raise the drawbridge and lower the portcullis.

At first she had no idea where she was going. She rode past the eyes of curious peasants, past the inquisitive and even a bit amused gazes of the guards. It wasn't until she escaped the castle and reached the forest that she understood where she was heading. It wasn't home.

She was riding to the Midnight Shadow. Ever since Terran had found the mask, she'd left her Midnight Shadow costume hidden with her sword, and it was lucky she did. She needed it now. She needed to be brave, to stand up to those who were doing wrong. She didn't want to feel the stinging, burning agony swirling in her chest.

When the clearing came into view, anticipation sparked in her veins and a calmness settled her tumultuous spirit.

The Midnight Shadow was waiting for her.

Kenric searched the streets, the houses, but Bria was nowhere to be found. He grimaced. *That girl is going to pay for this,* he promised himself. *Ruining a good night of wenching and drinking.* He shook his head and reined in his horse, turning back to the castle. At least he'd collected some taxes and frightened some farmers. The night wasn't a total loss.

"Terrifying women is no way to get respect."

Kenric whirled.

A man clad all in black stepped from the darkness of the forest, a dark hood hiding his face.

"You," Kenric snarled.

"Only tyrants rule through fear," the Midnight Shadow whispered. He flung back his black cape and pulled his sword from its sheath. It hissed like the hot flame of justice.

Anxiety gripped Kenric. He looked around, but none of his men were anywhere to be seen. His horse danced nervously beneath him.

"Come, Kenric," the Midnight Shadow said. "Meet me in battle."

Kenric hesitated. Perhaps if he waited, his men would appear.

"Coward," the Midnight Shadow whispered into the darkness. The word carried to Kenric's ears on a light breeze. "By the time your men return, I'll be long gone. Face me now."

Kenric refused to dismount, holding tight to the horse's reins. It would be foolishness, he told himself, to fight in the dark. He looked around once more, hoping some of his men would appear, but the road remained empty. He turned back to the Midnight Shadow. "Your lover is now in our hands. Knowles married her to bait you."

"Here I am," the Midnight Shadow whispered. "Come and get me."

Kenric hesitated again, his horse circling. "We shall meet again," Kenric promised. "And the advantage shall be mine." He spurred his horse, moving down the path to flee into the night.

Terran stared out of his bedroom window at the late morning sun. Its bright rays bathed his face with warmth, but only coldness reached his soul.

"She knows who he is," Kenric said from behind Terran. "We should question her thoroughly."

Terran's mind refused to focus on Kenric's request. Bria was still out there somewhere. Had she reached Castle Delaney? Had brigands hurt her? Did she need him? Terran's jaw clenched.

"Terran," his cousin called, "he's robbing you, taking your coin, making a fool of you in front of your people. Why are you not more concerned with capturing him?"

Terran whirled quickly, fury binding his hands into fists. He approached Kenric, and Kenric retreated before Terran's anger. "I am no fool," Terran said. "But this Midnight Shadow is not important right now. The whereabouts of my wife is. And you failed to find her last night."

Kenric was silent a moment, unused to Terran's rage. Finally, he bowed slightly. "M'lord," he said, "I did not realize she meant that much to you."

Did not realize she meant that much to you. The words echoed inside him. *God's blood,* Terran thought. *She* does *mean that much to me! That's why I'm going mad with worry.*

"I will—"

A knock came at the door. Terran whirled, breathless in anticipation of any news. "Come," he commanded.

The captain of the guard, Sir William, entered. He looked at Kenric as if gaining approval, then glanced at Knowles. "We found her," he announced.

Terran took a step forward. "Where?"

"In the old garden, m'lord," he said.

Terran wasted no time in racing out the door toward the old garden. She hadn't left the castle! Or had she and then returned? What was she doing in the garden? Had she gone to that weed-infested patch to get away from him? Or was it as Kathryn had said, that he had hurt Bria's feelings? Guilt surged within him.

Terran cursed his rashness, but caring for someone so deeply was new to him.

Terran threw open the door to the old garden. It was smaller than the main garden and grossly neglected. Perhaps Bria felt she fit in here, Terran thought. He stepped through the door and looked quickly around, but there was no sign of her.

He moved down the stone walkway, continuing to scan the garden for her. Near the back wall something colorful caught his eye—a single rose, almost buried in the weeds. The rosebush had somehow managed to poke one of its branches out through the tangle of weeds, and one small bud was displayed proudly atop the stem, its petals yet unopened.

Terran stared at it for a long moment. Then something moved just to the right of the rose. The weeds had made a shelter, a cave of sorts. Vines grew down the wall and stretched over an old bench. In the sheltered, weedy cave, Terran could make out a head of dark hair. Bria's hair.

Was she hiding? Was she that fearful of him, of her new home?

Terran stepped closer, but she didn't move. "Bria," he called. She wasn't moving. Was she hurt?

Terran bent down before the strange shelter to look inside at his bride. She was nestled in the weeds, her knees pulled up gently, her hand up near her face, her head lying on a cushioned bed of moss. "Bria?" Terran crawled into the shelter. She shifted her head slightly, and Terran saw she was sleeping.

Terran stared at her, dumbfounded. Why would she choose to sleep here, alone and unprotected? Why wouldn't she come into the castle?

He ducked his head beneath the canopy of vines. He reached for her, but stopped suddenly as his eyes traveled to her face. Her long dark lashes rested against her ivory skin, her cheeks were tinted a luminescent pink, and her lips were full and red and parted.

He was transfixed by her beauty and could do nothing but gaze upon her perfection.

"M'lord?"

With a silent curse at Kenric for disturbing this moment, Terran leaned forward and gently brushed Bria's lips with his before he scooped her up into his arms, pulling her close against his chest.

She stirred and Terran whispered soothing words to her. Bria sighed and settled down once again, resting her cheek against his shoulder.

Terran moved through the garden toward the castle door, passing Kenric without uttering a word. He brought Bria to his room and settled her into his bed. She stretched a little, opening her eyes just enough to give him a teasing glimpse of their brilliance, then turned over and went back to sleep.

Terran settled a cover warmly over her body. Then he sat in a chair and stared at his wife. *Wife.* The word took on a powerful, potent meaning.

Somehow through her defiance and stubbornness, Bria had worked magic on him. She was his wife in more than just name, and all he wanted was to make her his wife in every way.

Chapter Twenty-five

Warmth splashed across Bria's eyes. Light burned into her lids even though they were closed. She turned away and stretched. The warmth of her bed was luxurious. She almost hated to open her eyes and greet the new morning. Reluctantly, she peeked out at the day.

The sight that greeted her caused her to sit up and clutch the blanket to her breast. Terran Knowles sat in a chair near the bed, his eyes trained on her.

"What are you doing here?" she demanded of Terran. "How did you get into my room?" But her voice died as she looked around. The window was in the wrong spot. The small table against the far wall that was littered with her collection of doves wasn't there. In one corner of the room hung a large tapestry she'd never seen before, depicting a richly colorful tournament, the jousting pole of one knight skewering the chest of his opponent.

She was not in her room. The last thing she remembered

was returning to the castle and ducking into the garden as she tried to avoid the guards.

"You are in *our* room," Terran softly corrected her.

Bria gripped the blanket tightly as the previous day's events came back to her. "I am your wife," she whispered.

"A disobedient wife," Terran growled.

Bria scowled. Yes, that was right. He'd gone with another woman on their wedding night. *Not that I wanted him to come to me,* she told herself, knowing it was a lie. *But I certainly didn't want him to be with another woman.* She bit her lip and looked away from him, trying to hide her disapproval.

"Why did you run away from Kenric?"

At Kenric's name, Bria's eyes snapped up to Terran's. "I didn't feel it was Kenric's place to escort me to my new home."

"So now you see fit to tell me how my castle should be run."

Bria's scowl deepened and she looked away again.

Suddenly, he was beside the bed, her chin in his palm. He lifted her chin until she was looking into his eyes. "I will not have lies between us," he said.

"Even if I would be punished for speaking the truth?" she asked.

He dropped his hand. Suspicion flared in his black eyes. "Is there something I would punish you for?"

The Midnight Shadow hung over them like a thick black cloud. She studied his face—his strong chin, his thinned and angry lips. But there was something gentle in his eyes. Most men would beat her for her disobedience, but Terran hadn't raised a finger against her. She had to grant him that much— that and so much more. He made her feel things she'd never experienced. She wanted to be with him. She wanted him to kiss and touch her. She wanted him to . . . fulfill her.

Bria shook her head, looking away sadly. It would never happen if she didn't reveal herself to Terran. "The Midnight Shadow is not my lover," she said.

Terran sat beside her. "All right," he said softly. His arm brushed hers, causing shivers to race up her skin to her shoulder. As if beckoned, she lifted her gaze to his.

He was staring at her, his dark eyes scrutinizing every aspect of her features. The sweep of his gaze was like a caress. Fire radiated from his eyes, warming her, reassuring her. And then he lowered his head to hers.

Bria closed her eyes, waiting for the kiss, anticipating the feel of his lips against hers. His hot breath fanned her lips. "Then tell me," he urged, "who is the Midnight Shadow?"

Her body tingled with the remembered caress of his kiss. She opened her mouth to tell him something, anything so he'd kiss her.

His lips touched hers, demanding, coaxing.

"Tell me," he whispered against her lips.

Bria wanted to tell him, but she'd tried before and he wouldn't listen to her. Would he now? Would he listen to how Kenric killed Mary? Would he listen to how he was mistreating his people? Would he change so she wouldn't have to become the Midnight Shadow? Tears rose in her eyes. She wanted to tell him. She wanted to give him everything he wanted.

His hot kisses moved over her chin, down her neck.

Her throat worked. "I can't."

He pulled back so fast that cold engulfed her and she trembled. "You side with him," Terran growled. "You side with your lover against me!"

Bria saw the fury in his eyes, the stark, vivid anger that seethed inside him. "No, Terran," she pleaded, tears blurring her vision. "He isn't your enemy. He takes the tax money and returns it to your people."

Terran ground his teeth. "How do you know this?"

"Someone has to help them, since you won't!"

"I asked how you know this," Terran repeated.

Bria swallowed hard, but closed her mouth, refusing to answer him. She couldn't tell him. And it was tearing her apart.

He grabbed her arm and agony flared up from her healing wound. "Tell me," he snarled.

"I can't," Bria replied. "I won't. What he's doing is good."

"He's stealing from me!"

"If you wouldn't overtax your people, he wouldn't have to!"

"I won't permit it!"

Bria stared into Terran's eyes just as determinedly as he gazed into her own. Stubborn resolve warred on both sides. Suddenly he moved, dragging her across the bed, through the soft velvet covers. She almost tumbled, but Terran yanked her to her feet. He flung the door open so hard it banged against the wall.

He pulled her out into the hallway, where he paused to look left and then right. Then he started down the hall with Bria in tow. Bria stumbled and almost fell as he pulled her behind him, but his grip on her arm kept her on her feet. He moved onto the spiral staircase, and Bria had to run to keep up, holding her long dress up so as not to trip over the stone steps. The wound in her arm flared again, but she bit back any protestations.

Terran did not pause at the bottom of the steps. He pulled her roughly down the hallway, stormed into the Great Hall, and paused in the doorway, scanning the room.

Bria had a quick moment to catch her breath, but it didn't last. Terran started toward the hearth where a group of men had gathered.

They turned as Terran approached.

Suddenly Terran shoved Bria to the ground. "If you will not tell me who my enemy is, I can only consider you my enemy as well."

"Terran," Bria cried, pushing herself up to a sitting position.

Terran's eyes shifted to someone standing over her. "Find out who he is," he ordered.

Bria looked up to see Kenric staring at her, a grin quirking his lips.

She scrambled to her feet. "No!" she shouted. "Please, Terran."

Terran turned his back on her, moving out of the Great Hall.

"No!" Bria shouted as Kenric grabbed her arm.

Chapter Twenty-six

As Bria moved down a long set of stairs, the sunlight faded and then vanished altogether. The only light came from the few torches on the wall. Behind her, the footsteps of two guards echoed softly.

Down they went into the darkness, until they reached what felt like the very bottom of the castle. The air was cool and damp. Bria scanned the small room, which was illuminated by a lone flickering candle on a table in the corner. The stone walls were moist and speckled with a mossy growth. Ahead of her stretched a dark corridor, from which emanated occasional moans.

"Well," a voice behind her said.

Bria turned to see Kenric emerging from the stairway. The flame flickered over the sharp ridges of his face as he approached. "Not exactly where you expect to find the lady of Castle Knowles."

Bria's skin crawled as he stepped near her. He studied her face, and she turned her gaze toward the darkness.

"You may leave us," Kenric commanded the guards.

Bria snapped her gaze back to Kenric. Shivers of apprehension raced along her spine.

The guards turned and moved toward the stairs. Bria had a sudden urge to call them back, to beg them to stay, but she closed her mouth quickly.

The guards quietly disappeared up the stairs, and she was alone with Kenric. Fearful images of her childhood rose to the forefront of her mind.

She blinked her eyes, trying to erase the visions. She succeeded in pushing the terrible images from her mind, but those black, black eyes of Kenric's still stared at her as if he read her thoughts. A smile curved his lips.

"Bria . . ."

Bria straightened slightly at the intended insult.

Kenric chuckled slightly. "Of course I meant 'my lady,' " he said mockingly.

Bria swallowed. There was no sword strapped to his waist, so he would not run her through. What could he do?

He moved slowly around her until he was behind her. "Do you remember the bramble patch?" he asked.

Bria stiffened as his breath fanned her neck. He was right behind her, standing near her, taunting her, making her afraid. He loved to have people fear him. She had seen it as Bria and as the Midnight Shadow. She lifted her chin, but refused to be baited by his taunts.

"That was quite some while ago," Kenric whispered. "Perhaps you've forgotten."

Bria still said nothing.

"Who is the Midnight Shadow?" Kenric suddenly demanded.

What could she tell him? She could no more tell Kenric than she could Terran.

Terran. He didn't care about her. He'd abandoned her to Kenric. A strange sadness came over her at his betrayal. She'd wanted to start the marriage out right, to try to make it work. But how could they make it work when he treated his people so horribly? When he left her standing alone on the stairs of the castle while he took his mistress inside the stone keep? When he let Kenric question her?

Suddenly Kenric's hands were loosening the hooks of her dress. Bria tore away from his touch, demanding, "What are you doing?"

Kenric's lips twisted in a grimace of dark amusement. "I'm questioning you." He took a step forward. "Who is the Midnight Shadow?"

Bria stepped quickly away until she came up against the cold, wet stone wall. She opened her mouth to reply, but promptly closed it. What could she tell him? "You'd never believe me," she said.

"Try me," he ordered.

At her hesitation, Kenric reached around behind her, almost in an embrace, touching her neck with his hand and her shoulder with his arm. Bria slunk back, trying to protect herself by leaning into the wall. She fought back a shiver as the cold wetness of the wall began to seep inside her.

"Go ahead and scream," Kenric whispered. "No one will hear you."

Bria swallowed the scream that rose in her throat. She would never allow him to know the terror she was feeling, the sheer unabashed fear that froze her limbs.

"Who is the Midnight Shadow?" Kenric demanded again. He pulled away from her, having undone all the hooks of her dress.

Bria wanted to dissolve into a fit of sobs and become the frightened child lurking just below her consciousness. But she was an adult now, and she fought back the urge.

Kenric reached up to her shoulder and eased her dress down over her arm. All the while, a smile etched his lips. He was enjoying her humiliation, her terror.

Finally, she lifted her chin and met his glare. "I remember the bramble patch," she retorted bravely. "And I am not that child any longer. You do not frighten me."

Uncertainty flashed in his dark eyes and Bria knew a moment of victory.

But then the cruel anger etched its way into his slanted eyebrows. "I should," he growled and pulled her dress roughly from her shoulders.

"Stop it!" Bria pushed at his hands, knocking them away. She grabbed at the dress, keeping it from falling any lower.

"Tell me who he is and I will stop," Kenric urged, a tight smile on his lips. "But it would be much more fun if you didn't."

Bria couldn't stop humiliation from painting her cheeks red. Fear ate away at her bravery. "Terran will never allow you to do this."

"On the contrary," Kenric said, wrenching the dress from her grip and sliding it down lower and lower. "He ordered it."

Bria grabbed the material before it slid completely from her body. "Liar! He didn't tell you to—to hurt me."

Kenric reached out to touch her fingers, sliding his flesh along the length of her knuckles to the tips of her fingers to pry them open. "All you need do to stop this is tell me who the Midnight Shadow is."

The dress dropped to the floor, pooling around her ankles. "You bastard," she hissed.

Her chemise was now the only barrier between his evil gaze and her flesh.

Kenric flashed her a grin, displaying sharp white teeth. His gaze assaulted the flesh beneath the sheer fabric.

"If you touch me, I'll tell Terran."

"My dear," he said silkily, "he already thinks you're a slut. Who will he believe?"

Slut. The word rocked Bria. Was that how Terran described her to his men?

Suddenly, Kenric stepped away from her into the darkness and Bria knew a moment of fierce relief. She reached down for her dress, but he suddenly caught her arm and pulled her forward, into the dark corridor.

"I'll let you think about it for a night," Kenric hissed. "I'll be back come morning to continue our discussion."

In the dull light from the distant candle, Bria saw Kenric open a cell door.

She tried to pull away from him, tried to free her wrist, but his grip was relentless.

"And keep in mind you wear only a chemise now," Kenric propelled her into the dark dungeon with a tug of his wrist. "It will be a short discussion."

Bria landed on the floor, her hand skidding in some grime. A bolt of pain seared through the wound in her shoulder.

"I want the name of the Midnight Shadow," he called, slamming the door shut behind her.

Bria rose and raced for the cell door. Through a small barred window, she could see the candlelight flickering on the table. Bria grabbed the bars and shook them frantically. He couldn't leave her in here! He couldn't leave her alone in the dungeon!

Then Kenric bent near the candle. The light disappeared with a quick puff of his foul breath. Blackness surrounded her. It was so complete and so thick she couldn't see her own hands on the bars before her face. Utter despair swept through her. How had this happened? How had it come to this point? Overcome by fear, she began to tremble.

Something shifted behind her. Bria turned slowly, eyeing the darkness.

She wasn't alone.

Chapter Twenty-seven

Bria stared at the darkness, listening intently. Had she heard rats?

Another shuffle. No, rats didn't shuffle.

"Is someone there?" she called, pressing her back to the door.

"Did he say the Midnight Shadow?" a hoarse voice called from the darkness.

Bria peered into the blackness, trying desperately to see the owner of the voice, to make out a shape. Was this one of Kenric's traps? "Who's there?" Bria demanded. The blackness was so thick she couldn't see anything.

Another shuffle, the sound now louder, nearer. Whoever was in the darkness moved closer to her.

"Are they looking for the Midnight Shadow?" The female voice, now a little stronger, sounded strangely familiar.

"Yes," Bria replied quietly, confused. Trepidation ran along her spine to her neck, sending tingles of apprehension along her shoulders.

There was a long moment of silence, a moment as quiet as the cell was dark. Bria thought she heard a moan from somewhere down the hall, but she couldn't be sure it wasn't from the person before her.

"Who are you?" the voice asked.

"My name is Bria."

"Bria?" the voice queried in disbelief. "Bria?"

Bria stared into the darkness. She knew that voice. But it couldn't be! She could barely form the name on her trembling lips. "Mary?"

Suddenly, something knocked into her, pressing against her. Arms wrapped around her shoulders. "Oh, Bria, Bria," the small form sobbed.

Bria lifted trembling hands to her friend's face, touched her hair. Mary was alive! She touched Mary's wet cheeks, her forehead, trying to convince herself this was real, that Mary was alive and this wasn't some wonderful dream. But as Bria stroked Mary's hair, feeling thick knots in the strands, she realized this might very well be a nightmare.

Bria held her close, putting her face against Mary's wet, tear-streaked cheek. "Oh, Mary!" Bria gasped. "Mary."

She was alive! And Bria had left her. She had abandoned Mary to Kenric as surely as Terran had abandoned her. "I'm so sorry," Bria sobbed over and over.

The two women collapsed onto the ground, crying and holding each other.

Terran shifted in his seat, staring at the fire. Its flickering tongues snapped like whips. With a sigh, he hung his head forward into his hands. How had everything gone so wrong? He should be enjoying his wife, kissing those delectable lips, spreading her thighs, teaching her how to make love slowly and thoroughly. Instead, he'd handed her over to Kenric to question. Terran knew his cousin had a penchant for cruelty.

He rose and took a step toward the dungeon. Then he came up short, his back straightening. Bria had brought this on herself. He'd been willing to make the marriage work, but she'd refused. With those wide eyes and full lips, she'd denied him. And if she wouldn't tell him the Midnight Shadow's identity, then Kenric was his only hope. After what had happened with Odella, Terran could never allow any man to come between him and his wife, especially a criminal who was stealing from him.

Terran groaned softly and threw himself back into his chair. Was this only about his pride? No. It was a matter of trust. How could she take the criminal's side against his? How could she think he'd treat his people cruelly and unjustly? He was certain they were fine. Kenric took care of that for him. It had freed up his time for tournaments and jousting, what he really loved, what he was really interested in—until now.

"Darling."

Terran stiffened at Kathryn's voice. He hadn't thought of her the entire day. His mind had been occupied by Bria.

"You look terrible," Kathryn said, resting her hand on his shoulder. "Why haven't you come to see me?"

"I have a wife," Terran replied gruffly.

Kathryn laughed huskily. "Most men do. That doesn't stop them."

Terran slowly turned to face her. "I am not most men."

Kathryn straightened. "You love her?" she asked in surprise.

"It doesn't matter if I love her or not," Terran replied. "She is my wife."

"But I can offer you so much more!"

Terran stared at Kathryn. Her eyes had once been the most brilliant blue he'd ever seen . . . until he'd seen Bria's. Kathryn's hair was lush and golden and combed to glittering perfection. But he preferred the way Bria's dark hair shone with streaks of red, as if her inner fire permeated her entire being. And that lock that curled down over her soft, smooth cheek in innocent beauty. And her boldness, her vibrancy, her passion for justice.

All the qualities a lord should despise in a wife. But Terran liked them. He liked Bria. Very much.

Mistaking his regard, Kathryn licked her lips and ran a hand down her side to her hip.

Terran rose to tower over her.

Kathryn accomplished a practiced swoon against him.

Terran's arms came up to capture her. He knew he was not mistaking the victory in Kathryn's half-closed eyes. But this time, the victory spoils were nothing he had any desire to claim. Terran set her aside and stepped past her.

"Where are you going?" Kathryn demanded.

"Where I should have gone from the beginning." He paused and turned to her. "Pack your things, Kathryn. I'm sending you back to your father." He whirled away quickly so as not to hear her pleadings.

Terran stalked down the steps to the dungeon. *I'm just going down to see how the questioning is proceeding,* he told himself. Kenric liked no one, including himself, to interrupt his interrogations. It was one of Kenric's favorite pastimes—that and counting gold in the treasure room.

Terran stepped into the first guard's room. The man on duty quickly straightened out of his chair at seeing him. "Lord Knowles," he said stiffly, trying to hide the dice he'd been rolling.

"Where is Sheriff Kenric?" Terran asked.

The guard's brows lowered over clear brown eyes. "He left hours ago, m'lord, and hasn't been back."

Terran frowned. "Did he take Lady Bria with him?"

"No, m'lord," the man answered. "She's in the first cell."

Outrage speared through Terran like a lance. Bria in a cell?

"Open it," he commanded. As the guard moved to obey, Terran realized he shouldn't be surprised. He had given Kenric free rein to question her. He supposed throwing her in the dungeon for a night wasn't going to hurt her any. Then why was he clenching his fists so tightly they hurt?

The guard grabbed a torch from the wall and led the way. Terran followed the man deeper into the dungeon. The creeping darkness was held at bay by the light of the torch. With each step, the stillness of the dungeon surrounded Terran in an eerie silence.

The guard led him down a flight of steps and past the second, deserted guard post. If they'd held an important person, someone who might inspire a rescue attempt, this post would be manned.

The guard moved to the first cell. He paused once to glance at Terran before sliding the bolt aside and swinging open the door. Terran stepped past him into the cell. He could see nothing until the guard shoved the torch forward and the light seeped into the dank, small room. The dirt floor was partly mud, damp from a continuous drip falling from the stone ceiling above. The cold stone walls were slick with mold and fungus.

Something erupted from the darkness, hitting Terran in the back, shoving him into the darkness. A wild demon attacked him, hitting his back with a rain of blows, screeching madly like some wild beast. Terran whirled on the witch, but received a blow to his face. He grabbed the thin arms that were striking at him, holding them back. The small hands were curved into claws. He tried to see into the wild thing's face, but the darkness was too thick. It took all his effort to hold her away from him.

Fear knotted Terran's stomach. Was this Bria? Had Kenric changed her so much in but a few hours? He'd seen it happen before.

But as the guard stepped forward to pull the woman from Terran, the light washed over her face. Through the thick, knotted hair, Terran saw she wasn't Bria. He shoved her away from him. His eyes quickly scanned the cell and came upon another woman. She was curled up in a far corner, long brown hair splayed out around her head, and had obviously just been awakened.

Terran recognized her immediately. Bria. His heart surged with concern as she began to lift herself up onto her elbows. Had the wild woman harmed her? Terran wondered frantically. Bria was in her chemise, the white garment now stained with mud and grime.

Terran lurched forward to kneel at her side. The light around him flickered, and the guard uttered a curse before a slap sounded.

"Bria?" he whispered. His knee sank into the mud as he scooped her up into his arms.

"No," she muttered tiredly as he headed with her for the door. "Mary. Mary!"

But Terran ignored her continued cries, contributing them to hallucinations. Who knew what that wild thing had done to her? He continued out into the darkness and moved up the spiral stairway until he came to the first guard's post. The light washed over the struggling Bria in his arms. She squirmed in his grasp, pushing away from his chest.

Terran set her feet on the ground. His eyes perused her face, her body, for any wounds. "Are you all right?" he demanded.

Bria stepped toward the darkness, calling, "Mary."

"Bria," Terran said, stepping into her path. He cupped her face in his hands. "Did Kenric hurt you? Are you all right?"

Bria seemed to focus on Terran's face for the first time. "Oh, Terran," she whispered and leaned heavily against him, exhaustion overwhelming her.

Instinctively, Terran's arms went around her, crushing her to him. Relief flooded through him. He brushed a kiss against the top of her head.

Bria looked up at him, her eyes clear despite her fatigue. "Terran, she's my friend. I can't leave her in there."

"Your friend?" Terran echoed.

"Please. You have to let her go."

Terran held her at arm's length, searching her face. "She attacked me. I can't let her go."

"She thought you were Kenric," Bria said defensively.

Why was she always taking someone else's side over his? Anger simmered his blood. "She's a criminal, or she wouldn't be in the dungeon. I will not let her go."

"What did she do?" Bria demanded.

"She murdered a woman," Terran replied tightly.

"What?" Bria asked in confusion.

"She murdered Widow Anderson, the village herbalist."

Chapter Twenty-eight

Bria's mouth dropped open at Terran's accusation. Mary hadn't killed that woman, Kenric had. But she'd tried to tell Terran that before and he hadn't listened. She shut her mouth and gritted her teeth.

"She's a danger to me and to my people. I couldn't let her roam the streets. She's lucky to be alive. Only at Kenric's insistence did I allow her to be locked up instead of beheaded."

Beheaded? The word sent chills through her body. And why would Kenric save Mary? Why not just kill her and be done with it?

The soft sound of footsteps reached her ears and Bria lifted her head to see the guard moving into the room from the dark hallway. She turned her gaze to Terran, her chin lifted slightly in defiance. "Now what? Do you plan to have me beheaded?"

"You mock me thus after I have saved you?" Terran growled.

"Saved me?" Bria retorted hotly. The fatigue she'd felt

burned away. She was very much awake now. "You sent me here!"

Terran opened his mouth as if to argue with her, but then shut it. The muscle of his jaw clenched. "For that I am sorry," he managed to grind out.

Surprise rocked Bria. Was that an apology from the tyrant? Had she heard him correctly? She stared hard at Terran, trying to see past his closed expression, but his eyes mirrored the flickering torchlight back at her.

Suddenly and unexpectedly, Bria felt a strange stirring in the pit of her stomach. Flustered, she glanced away and found herself looking at the guard. He was staring at her breasts. Bria glanced down, realizing she was still in her chemise. Mortified, she did her best to cover herself, crossing her arms over her chest and leaning toward Terran for cover.

Terran stepped in front of her, his eyes burning into the guard. The guard backed away from Terran, finally turning his back. Terran whirled to Bria, placing his hand on her lower back, and ushered her up the stairs.

They moved quickly through the hallways and Bria kept her head lowered to avoid the curious gazes of the peasants. Terran ushered her into the room she'd occupied before—their room. Just as she stepped over the threshold, someone called, "Lord Terran!"

Kenric approached them with quick steps. Bria straightened slightly, defiance and hatred sizzling through her.

Terran urged her into the room with a gentle shove and closed the door behind her.

Bria stood in the dark room alone. At first, she didn't know what to do. She had the strangest impulse to rush out of the room and into Terran's arms or to plant herself before him and protect him from Kenric. It didn't seem Terran truly knew just how evil Kenric was.

And then she heard the voices.

"Why have you removed her from the dungeon?" It was Kenric.

"She is lady of this castle now. A dungeon is not the place for her."

Again, surprise made Bria's heart jump.

"You told me to do what I must to find out who the Midnight Shadow is," Kenric defended himself.

"And did that include stripping her of her dress?" Even behind the wooden door, Bria could feel Terran's anger.

Bria reached out and ran her fingers over the wood of the door, wanting to touch Terran, to thank him for defending her.

There was a pause before Kenric replied, "I did what I thought I must."

"You've humiliated her for the last time, Randolph. I will not tolerate it again."

"Cousin, what's come over you? This Midnight Shadow is a threat to you and your lands! We must find out who he is, and she is the only one who can tell us."

"We'll find another way," Terran said.

"But I'm certain I can make her talk."

"I said we'll find another way!"

Bria whirled in joy and leaned her back against the door, smiling. Her heart bloomed with pride. Terran was defending her! She was so overcome with joy that she didn't hear the handle being turned until it was too late. She barely had a chance to step away from the door when it opened, smacking her in the shoulders and propelling her to the floor.

Terran stood over her, the torchlight from the hallway flickering behind him, casting his face in shadows. He reached out a hand to Bria.

After a brief moment of hesitation, Bria lifted her hand and placed it in his outstretched palm. His fingers closed over hers and he pulled her up, bringing her tight against his chest with a tug.

His eyes danced with curiosity. "Were you spying on me?"

Bria was too startled and embarrassed to offer any explanation.

"You were," Terran said.

A flash of white shone in the darkness and Bria realized it was the first true smile she'd seen on his face. She liked it. "No, I wasn't," she countered halfheartedly. She looked down at her hands splayed on his wide, broad chest. She could feel the muscles beneath his black tunic, the beat of his heart.

Bria lifted her gaze to his dark, midnight eyes. She could barely see his features in the dark room, but she could feel his breath on her lips as he drew her closer. He smelled faintly of sweet ale and leather. She half closed her eyes. She loved the scent of leather.

"Bria," he whispered, his lips nearly touching hers. "I know we could be happy together. Just tell me who the Midnight Shadow is."

"I cannot tell you that, but I promise you he is not my lover," she replied in a soft whisper, lifting her mouth to his.

Terran shoved her away from him. "You are as great a liar as Kathryn," he snarled, "and as great a whore. Wife or not, I cannot accept you as long as the Midnight Shadow stands between us." He whirled away from her and stalked to the door.

"Terran!" Bria called out desperately. "There has been no one," she pleaded. "What can I do to prove it to you?"

Terran turned to look over his shoulder at her. The light from the candles reflected in his black eyes. "There is one thing." He shut the door, sealing them in the dark room. "Show me your virgin's blood."

Chapter Twenty-nine

Terran watched Bria's mouth drop slightly. In a stray beam of moonlight from an open window, he saw the uncertainty in her bright blue eyes. Then resolution passed across her face as she pursed her lips, followed quickly by determination. She lifted her chin. "All right," she said.

Terran didn't move. Had he heard heard her correctly? Did she know what she was agreeing to?

She eased the chemise from her body, and the thin material pooled in a soft cloud around her ankles. She stood naked before him in the darkness.

Terran scowled. He'd been sure she would deny him. He'd been sure she'd make up another excuse. Was she challenging him? He never could resist a challenge. He stalked to her, grabbed her arm, and pulled her up to him. Most women would cower before him. Most women would beg for their very lives. But Bria looked him square in the eye as if she weren't afraid of him in the least.

Terran wanted to shake her. She should be afraid of him. He held her life in his hands.

Instead, she stared at him with those large sapphire eyes which held such clear simplicity and honesty that for a moment he doubted himself. Was he wrong about her? Was she a virgin unknown to men? Unknown to the Midnight Shadow?

No, he convinced himself. There was too much evidence against her. But why would she tempt fate and stand righteously in his arms?

Because she didn't believe he would make love to her.

How wrong she was.

He pulled her to him, kissing her with all the rage and confusion he felt. To his surprise and utter relief, she didn't stiffen or stand unaffected by his kiss. She returned it with a tentative stroke of her own lips, an encouraging caress, arousing in him a need greater than his mistrust.

Terran swept her up in his embrace, refusing to relinquish her lips, her kiss. He carried her to the bed and laid her upon the feather-filled mattress. Only then did he break the kiss. He was surprised at her slight objection. It seemed his wife liked the touch of men.

The thought angered him anew and he attacked her lips again wanting to punish her for her wantonness. He was her husband now. He was the only one who would be kissing her. He ran his hand along her side to her breast and cupped it.

A gasp escaped her lips. He fondled her breast, teasing the tip with circular motions of his thumb until it hardened and she became pliant beneath his expert touch. She groaned beneath his mouth, arching her back slightly so her entire breast fit into his palm.

Hot desire exploded through him. He realized with a sharp stab of shock that he wanted her as he'd never wanted anything in his life. He'd never felt this desire for Kathryn or even Odella. He bent his head to her breast, kissing it, teasing her gently with his teeth. The nipple hardened and he felt her gasps of joy beneath him.

She was no virgin.

He slid his hand down her slim body to the very tip of her womanly hair. She closed her thighs tightly against his exploration. He kissed her temple, her cheek, and whispered in her ear, "You are mine, Bria. No other man shall ever touch you." With that promise, he kissed her, plundering her sweet mouth. Her arms encircled his shoulders. Terran rained kisses down her neck to the valley between her breasts.

His hand slowly moved down toward the spot he knew she wanted him to touch, the spot he longed to caress. Carefully, ever so slowly, he urged her thighs open with gentle touches and hot, urgent sweeps of his fingers along the length of her thigh. Just as slowly, she opened to his exploration.

Terran could feel the heat mounting inside her, could feel her excitement, her pleasure. She arched her hips toward his touch, but he pulled away.

He separated himself from her, gazing down at her face. Her eyes glowed with passion and her cheeks were flushed, her brows drawn down in objection to his leaving her side. He quickly slid his leggings from his body and lifted his tunic above his head. Then he returned to her, pressing his body along the length of hers.

His desire pounded through him. He kissed her again, fully enjoying the sensation that rocked him. The tentative strokes of her tongue aroused him as no practiced strokes could. He could almost believe no man had ever touched her.

She ran her hands down the length of his back, sending waves of pleasure pounding through his body. *God's blood!* he thought. *A mere touch from her hands and I am almost brought to fulfillment?*

He moved his hand over her flat stomach and down between her legs. She objected with a cry and moved to close her legs, but Terran touched her softly, whispering quiet words to her.

He kissed her neck, her chin, her lips, until she gradually opened to him. As he soothed her with kisses, he stroked her most inner delicate folds with encouraging, gentle brushes of his fingers until she arched her breasts against his chest and groaned softly.

With each stroke, with each bold caress, she opened further to his exploration, allowing him full, luxurious reign over her delectable body. With each stroke of his fingers, he brought her closer to complete pleasure. He felt the explosion mounting within her.

Bria spread her arms wide and her fingers dug into the covers, pulling them taut. Terran watched her body arch against his touch. Her brows knit as though she were trying to control herself, but she was losing. And then suddenly she gasped and her body stiffened as pleasure danced across her face.

Terran gasped along with her. He'd never seen someone so beautiful, so utterly breathtaking. Her brown hair shimmered with the light from the moon, her cheeks glowed with exuberance, her lips were red from his kisses. She was stunning.

Terran could wait no longer. He lay atop her and guided his member to her moist folds. She opened her eyes to gaze questioningly at him, but he knew he would explode at any moment if he didn't have her.

He plunged into her . . .

. . . and knew in that instant that she had never had another man. The slight barrier gave way beneath his thrust.

Bria cried out and Terran froze. Then his expression and his heart softened. "I'm sorry," he told her. "The worst is over."

Bria nodded, but her body hadn't relaxed beneath his. He bent his head to claim her lips, kissing her softly at first. But as the truth of her virginity saturated his body and Terran realized she was his in every way, his kiss turned to one of possession.

She melted beneath his passionate caress and slowly Terran

filled her. His hips began to move, and she responded, tentatively joining the rhythm.

She is mine, Terran thought. *She always has been.*

With that thought, he exploded inside her. His body stiffened as waves of ecstasy cascaded through him. His world filled with a glow of love, healing his hurt heart. He felt whole again. He felt complete with Bria.

Terran opened his eyes to gaze down at Bria. She was watching him through concerned eyes. He bent to brush her lips with a kiss before rolling off of her. Then he swept Bria into his arms and pulled her against his chest.

"Do you believe me now?" she asked.

Terran nodded, but didn't speak. He didn't want the moment to end. He just wanted to hold her close. He liked feeling her body against his. He kissed the top of her head, held her tight against him, and slowly fell into a blissful sleep.

At least in this one regard she had told him the truth.

Bria turned over to gaze into Terran's peaceful face. She brushed a lock of dark hair from his cheek. Her body still quivered with explosive tingles from their lovemaking. "Are you sleeping?" she asked.

A smile curved his lips and his arm tightened about her shoulders.

Bria grinned up at him, tracing one of the planes of his stomach. "Is it always so . . . wonderful?"

"Not always," Terran replied.

Bria's hand stilled. "Was it for you?"

"Yes," he whispered. "Like no other time before."

Bria smiled and laid her head on his shoulder. She stroked his arm, marveling at her husband's strength.

"Tell me of your friend," Terran asked suddenly.

Shocked, Bria turned her head to gaze at him.

"Tell me what happened."

Hope surged in Bria's heart. "Mary and I were out in the woods near her home . . . on your lands . . . when we saw Kenric speaking with Widow Anderson, your herbalist. I saw Kenric kill her."

"Why would Kenric kill the herbalist?"

Bria shrugged her shoulders slightly. "He owed her payment for a potion she'd made for him, and he didn't want to pay." For a moment, looking past Terran into the darkness, she was silent, seeing the execution again. "Then he killed her. And Mary ran." Bria lifted her head to gaze into Terran's eyes. "I thought Kenric had killed her. I didn't know he locked her up."

"Why would Kenric killed the herbalist? And why lock Mary up for the crime?"

"Something's not right, Terran, but I know what I saw. I know what happened. Mary didn't kill Widow Anderson." Agony filled her at the thought of Mary locked in the damp, dark dungeon.

Terran gently kissed her lips. "I'll look into it tomorrow."

Bria slipped from the bed and quickly dressed. She hurried to the door, grabbing her velvet slippered shoes as she moved. There, she paused to glance over her shoulder at her sleeping husband. He was lying on his stomach, one arm dangling over the side of the bed. Bria gazed in adoration at his perfect body. His dark hair touched his shoulders in thick waves. His broad shoulders were strong and muscled, his sculptured back tapering into a thin waist. Bria grinned. He'd made her feel things she'd never dreamed of. He had made her feel loved, by him—by her husband.

Terran had a good heart. He would be a great lord, she was sure of it. He was going to do the right thing where Mary was concerned. And if she coaxed him, he'd investigate the overtaxing of the peasants, too. Everything was turning out wonderfully. She was so proud of him. So ... in love with him.

There was no longer any need for the Midnight Shadow. There was no tyrant to fight against, only Kenric, and Terran would deal with him.

This would be her last night as the Midnight Shadow. Then he would disappear forever.

Chapter Thirty

Dismounting in the clearing near the pond, Bria immediately spotted her hiding place. Her sword and disguise awaited her, hidden well beneath the bush. But first she approached the pond. She felt a jubilance she'd never felt. Tonight would be the Midnight Shadow's last ride. Terran would discover the truth about Kenric, and there would be no further need for the Midnight Shadow.

She gazed into the still pond. Terran would discover the truth. With conviction burning in her soul, she turned . . . and stopped cold.

Kenric was standing just across the clearing, watching her with his hands on his hips, two of his men on horses behind him.

He approached slowly.

"M'lady could not sleep?" he asked. "Or perhaps she is running away."

Bria scowled at his sarcasm. "Why did you follow me?"

"I was hoping you'd meet your lover here." Kenric scanned the clearing. "But I see that isn't the case."

Bria's eyes narrowed slightly. "What do you want?"

Kenric stopped just in front of her. "I want many things, m'lady."

Bria did not like his tone. She lifted her chin and moved to step around him, but he grabbed her arm, halting her.

"I'm not finished with you," he said softly.

Bria tried to pull her arm free, but he wouldn't release it. "Terran will have your head if you persist. I am lady of Castle Knowles."

"For now."

Dread slithered up her spine. Did he know she was the Midnight Shadow?

"You see, Lady Bria, it was I who suggested he marry you. It's true we needed your dowry. But I had another reason. A while back, the herbalist was killed not far from this very spot."

Bria swallowed hard.

His eyes narrowed slightly, his grip pressing ever tighter on her wrist. "Two women witnessed the murder. One I arrested and threw into the dungeon for the murder, but the other escaped. I chased her through the woods and onto Delaney lands. Who could have been out here in the middle of the night? I kept Mary alive to use as bait to catch the other woman. And now I have, haven't I?"

Bria raised her chin.

"My guard heard you talking with dear Mary. I know it was you, Bria, and this little trip of yours to the very same spot proves it. I can have no witnesses to the death of that old woman."

Bria turned wide eyes to him. What was he planning? He signaled the other guards with a wave of his hand. They began to move forward.

Fear flared through Bria like lightning. Why didn't Kenric

want anyone to know he'd killed the herbalist? "Why did you kill her?"

"She knew things," Kenric said. "I couldn't have her walking around telling everyone my secrets."

Secrets? Bria thought back to the night he had killed the woman. What was it the old woman had said? He owed her coin for the first potion. "What potion did she make for you? Whom did you poison?"

Panic flared in Kenric's black eyes, and Bria knew she'd hit the mark.

"You already know too much," Kenric retorted as anger replaced his panic.

The two guards drew nearer and Bria knew she had to escape. She brought her heel down hard on Kenric's foot. As he grimaced in pain and released his grip on her arm slightly, Bria shoved him away from her.

She turned and lifted her heavy skirt to dash away. She raced through the brush, managing to reach the dirt road nearby. But then something hit her from behind and she felt arms around her waist. She hit the ground hard, wiggling and twisting, trying desperately to free herself.

"Not this time," Kenric snarled from behind her, holding her tight. He flipped her over so she faced him, and he straddled her waist, holding her arms down.

Bria fought, expecting to feel a sharp pain in her side from a sword wound or the tip of a dagger run across her throat. But it never came. Instead, a sharp slap stung her cheek. Her head rocked to the side, and for a moment her world teetered.

Kenric tilted her head back and something bitter entered her mouth. She spit it out immediately. Kenric placed one hand over her mouth and his other beneath her jaw to hold her mouth shut. "Take it, bitch," he snarled.

Poison! She tried to open her mouth, but Kenric was stronger. She fought, hitting him and trying not to swallow. But the bitter taste slid down deeper and deeper into her throat until she could do nothing but swallow.

She opened her eyes in horror and saw his evil visage looming above her. His hands clenched tight around her face, and her head was locked in the crook of his arm. "You see, dear Bria, it wasn't all that bad. Had you not run from me the first time, I would have killed you then, and your horrendous marriage to Lord Knowles and subsequent rape by him could have been averted." He released her and sat up.

Bria pulled away from him, moving back on her bottom. "Terran didn't rape me." She spit as hard as she could. The bitter taste remained strong in her mouth. She turned and began to crawl away, but two legs blocked her. She followed the black leggings up to see one of the guards.

"You can't leave yet," Kenric said from behind her. "It takes a little time before the poison works."

"You won't get away with this," Bria proclaimed.

"I think I will. I have before." A smile split Kenric's lips.

Bria stared at him in shock. Before? Whom had he killed? Her eyes widened. Odella! Terran hadn't killed her, Kenric had poisoned her!

Bria stood. "You bastard," she hissed. She had to tell Terran! Her gaze swept the clearing. The two guards stood at the ready not feet from her. Kenric leaned against a tree. There was nowhere to run. "You killed Odella!"

"I told you you knew too much," Kenric replied.

"Why?" she demanded. "Why kill her?"

"It's of no concern to you," Kenric said. "You'll be dead soon."

"Then tell me," Bria insisted. "If I'm dead, I'm no threat to you."

"You were never a threat to me," Kenric retorted.

Suddenly, Bria's mouth began to water as nausea twisted her stomach into a wretched knot. Frantically, she looked around as the world spun dizzily about her. Then she turned her back to

Kenric and threw up. Spasms shook her body. She wiped the back of her mouth and realized through her agony that Kenric was talking.

"Good," he said. "That is the first sign. Soon, you'll feel drowsy and fall into unconsciousness. Then you'll die."

"No," she gasped. Bria had to warn Terran. She had to get to him. But suddenly her body felt heavy.

No, she thought. *I have to get to Terran.*

She fell forward to her knees. Kenric's boots appeared at her side, and she barely had the strength to lift her gaze to his.

"Don't fight it," he encouraged. "It will all be over within the day."

She grabbed his tunic in an effort to stand, but couldn't pull herself up. Somewhere, laughter drifted through her mind like a distant echo. She had to get to Terran.

Suddenly, she leaned forward and retched all over Kenric's boots before collapsing to the leafy ground.

She forced herself to lie absolutely still. She had to get rid of them. If she could get them to leave her, she could mount her horse and ride back to Castle Knowles. Ride? she thought groggily. She could hardly focus. She'd never be able to ride a horse.

She watched Kenric through her darkening vision. He and his men mounted their horses and in an instant were gone.

Bria tried to push herself to her feet. She had to reach her horse, which stood in the distance. But her body wouldn't move. Her hands lay still on the ground, her arms like heavy rocks. She couldn't lift them.

Tears entered her eyes. She was going to die here. She wasn't going to get the chance to warn Terran. *Oh, Terran,* she thought. *I have to tell you. I have to warn you about Kenric. He killed Odella. He's killing me!*

From far off, she heard a voice. Was Kenric still here? Hadn't she seen him leave? She struggled to turn her head toward the sound. A million black dots swam before her eyes. She could make out someone coming close. Or was he leaving? Was he running? She couldn't tell.

Then he was at her side, kneeling beside her. Brown eyes. Kenric had black eyes. Were these eyes brown? Yes. Yes! She recognized his warm eyes as a scowl of concern crossed his brow.

"George," she whispered. It was Mary's father.

He pushed his hands beneath her shoulders and legs and lifted her off the ground. She leaned heavily against him. "Don't worry, Bria," he said. "We'll get you back to the castle safely."

Bria closed her eyes.

"M'lord!"

Terran was out of bed immediately. He donned his leggings, noticing but not worrying that Bria was gone . . . until he threw open the door to his room and found her in Kenric's arms. A farmer stood just behind Kenric.

Dread welled up in Terran's chest. Had she been stabbed? There was no blood. What could it be?

But then he lurched into action, removing her from Kenric's arms. "What happened?" he demanded as he turned to lay her on the bed.

"This farmer found her in the road," Kenric said, motioning to the man behind him. "She'd taken poison. This pouch was beside her."

Agony pierced Terran's heart as he snatched the pouch. "Where the hell did she get this?"

Kenric shrugged. "Looks like she'd rather die than be your wife."

Terran turned burning eyes to Kenric. His jaw clenched so tightly that for a long moment he couldn't talk. "Go and find an herbalist."

"There isn't one in riding distance."

"Then fly," Terran snapped, "but find one."

Kenric bowed stiffly and turned, leaving the room, brushing past the farmer who waited by the door.

Terran returned his gaze to Bria. Her long brown hair was unbound and fanned out over the pillow. Her eyes were closed. Her face looked so peaceful that for a moment he imagined she was simply sleeping. Just sleeping—as he'd imagined Odella to be.

Ah, God, no! He collapsed to his knees beside the bed. *Why? Why is this happening again? Why? Why would she do this? Was I such an ogre to her?* He took her hand into his. It was so limp, so white. He pressed his forehead to her hand, kneeling in a position all too familiar to him.

"Terran."

He must have imagined the soft voice. It sounded so like Bria. Did he want to hear her voice so badly he was imagining it?

"Terran."

He lifted his head. Her eyes were open, staring at him with such agony and such pain that his heart broke. He held her hand to his chest, clutching it tightly. *What a fool I am!* his mind screamed.

"Herbalist . . . at Delaney," she whispered.

"At Delaney?" She must be hallucinating. He brushed a trembling kiss against her forehead. "No, darling. Kenric said there isn't one in riding distance."

"Terran." He looked into her eyes. "Go . . . to Delaney. Get . . . herbalist."

"An herbalist at Delaney?" Perhaps Kenric didn't know about him. Perhaps he was new. Whatever the case, he would retrieve him at once. He rose. "I'll send Randolph."

"No!" Her cry, so strong and so frantic, halted Terran immediately. "He . . ." Her voice faded as her energy waned.

Terran returned to her side, leaning close to her, brushing the strands of dark hair from her forehead. "I know," he

whispered. "Just rest. He brought you to me. You're all right."
He kissed her forehead.

"Kenric . . . killed Odella."

The words made no sense. First she'd thought *he* had killed
Odella. Now Kenric? "You're imagining this," he replied.
"You're speaking of things you know nothing about."

"Poisoned . . . me."

Disbelief overwhelmed him. He stared into her dull blue
eyes, seeing the desperation, the fear. "Poisoned you?"

"Forced poison . . . into my mouth."

The thought of Kenric forcing anything into Bria's lovely
mouth ignited a fierce anger in his veins, pulsing with the beat
of his heart. Would he really dare harm Bria?

"Please"—her small hand clutched his—"believe . . ."

Terran glanced down at her hand curled around his fingers.
It was so small in his larger hand. Suddenly, her fingers loosened
and began to fall from his hand. Desperately, Terran grabbed
her hand and gazed into her eyes. Her fading blue eyes. "Bria,
stay with me," he insisted, as his throat tightened.

"Don't know . . . if I can," she murmured.

Terran could feel the energy dwindling from her. "Bria,"
he called. Agony and pain twisted his heart, the very core of
his being. She had returned to warn him. "Bria," he pleaded.
"If I go for the herbalist, promise me, *promise me* you will
live."

A small smile curved her lips, but her eyelids fluttered closed.

"Bria," Terran begged. Anger, determination and a pain
he'd never felt warred inside him. He didn't want to leave her.
If what she said was true, if his cousin had poisoned her, he
couldn't leave her alone with Kenric. But how could he not?

He planted a firm kiss on her forehead and rose to move to
the door. His eyes came to rest on the farmer who still stood,
watching, his worried gaze locked on Bria. "Stay," Terran
ordered. He placed a hand over the peasant's. "Please, stay

and watch her. My servants will bring you anything you need. Whatever you want.''

The farmer looked into his eyes for a long moment, then finally nodded.

Terran raced from the room.

Chapter Thirty-one

Terran rode into Castle Delaney hard and reined in his horse in the courtyard. His face was flushed and sweaty, his lungs straining with the exertion of the fast ride. The sun was inching its way over the horizon. The castle was just waking up, and the courtyard was empty of people. Cursing, Terran spurred the horse on, searching for someone, anyone, to ask of the herbalist's whereabouts.

A young woman stepped out of the door to the keep, a basket of dirty laundry in her hands. Terran turned his horse toward her and kicked the animal to full speed. She took a few steps into the courtyard before he reached her and bent down to grab her arm.

She screamed and pulled back in fright, sending the basket of laundry tumbling to the ground.

Terran shook her. "Where is the herbalist, damn it?"

"The . . . the herbalist?" she stammered, trying to make sense of this wild man towering over her.

"The herbalist," Terran demanded. "Where is the herbalist?"

"In the garden," she replied, trying to pull her arm free of his hold.

Terran yanked the girl forward, grabbing her around the waist and hauling her onto the horse. "Where?" he ordered. "Show me where this garden is."

"Why do you want the herbalist? Who are you?" she asked.

Terran grit his teeth at having to explain to a peasant. "I am Lord Knowles. Lady Bria is in grave danger."

"It's that way." The girl directed him deeper into the castle. "He should be in there. He's in there early every morning tending to his plants."

He looked over to where she was pointing to see a small enclosure built of stone with walls about two feet high. He could see greenery beyond the low wall. He released the girl, lowering her back to the ground, then rode hard toward the small garden. The horse leaped the wall easily. Terran scanned the enclosure, looking for anyone who could help him. Anyone at all.

A man suddenly appeared from behind a row of blackberry bushes and came running at him, waving a fist. "What do you think you're doing? Get that animal out of here! You're trampling the—"

Terran urged the horse forward with a kick. He grabbed the man by his tunic front, shoving his face into his. He didn't have time for this. "Where is the herbalist?" he growled.

"I—I am the herbalist," the man replied quietly.

Anxiety tightened Terran's stomach as he loosened his hold on the man. "Lady Bria has been poisoned. You must come with me."

He heard gasps from behind him, but didn't turn.

"What kind of poison?" the herbalist asked.

Terran shook his head. "I don't know. We have to leave. Now!"

The man nodded. "I'll get my things."

Terran released him and the man raced toward a small thatched hut near the rear of the garden, leaving Terran alone for a long moment. He wanted to scream at the man, wanted to go in after him and pack his things, anything to make him hurry. Bria could be . . . He refused to finish the thought. He refused to think his wife, the woman he loved—yes, loved—was slipping away, and he couldn't be at her side.

Terran's hands gripped the reins so tightly his knuckles ached. How could this have happened? Why had she left him in the middle of the night? Where had she gone?

A sudden, vivid image of Kenric shoving poison through her lovely lips with his dirty fingers flashed through his mind. Terran's jaw clenched. Kenric had said there was no herbalist, and yet here he was at Castle Delaney at Bria's urging, getting an herbalist to save her life. Had Kenric not known about this herbalist? Why would he try to kill Bria? What would it serve him? Was Bria lying? *She didn't lie about being a virgin,* a small voice inside him reminded.

And what about Bria's declaration that Kenric killed Odella? Was it true? If Kenric had poisoned Bria, why not Odella, too? Rage simmered in Terran's veins. *All this time, I believed Odella's death was my fault. All this time.*

Terran cursed silently. *There's more to this. It doesn't make sense. Why would Kenric kill Odella in the first place? I'll discover the truth and see things righted.* He shook himself. Where was that cursed herbalist?

Finally, the man ran out of the house, holding a large sack in his hand. Terran grabbed his shirt front and hauled him up behind him. Then he spurred his horse hard toward Castle Knowles.

Terran held the herbalist's arm in a steely grip as he pulled him through the halls of Castle Knowles. He reached the door to his room and threw it open, then stopped cold at the sight that greeted him. Bria lay on the bed, unmoving, eerily still. But what made Terran's heart freeze was that Kenric stood at her bedside.

Where the hell was that wretched farmer? Had he abandoned Bria?

"She's still alive," a voice said.

Terran swiveled his gaze to see the farmer sitting in a chair not far from the bed.

Relief coursed through Terran. There was still time. The farmer had faithfully stayed to watch over Bria. *He protected her when I could not.*

"Where have you been?" Kenric asked.

The herbalist impatiently pushed past Terran and then Kenric to get to Bria. He quickly knelt at her side, checking the color of her lips, her skin.

"Who's that?" Kenric wondered, following the man's movements with his dark, suspicious eyes.

"The herbalist from Castle Delaney."

Kenric looked up and Terran could see the shock in his cousin's dark eyes. "I didn't know." But there was no remorse in his voice.

Terran's back stiffened. "You should have," he snapped. "Perhaps it would have saved Odella's life."

Kenric's jaw clenched, but he said nothing.

Terran stepped over to the bed, away from his cousin, and watched the herbalist administer to Bria. He felt useless standing there, but he couldn't leave her, as if his presence alone would give her the strength to live. Terran stared at her face, wondering if he'd ever see her smile again, wondering if he would hear her laughter. Her skin was so pale, her lips so red against the ghostly white of her skin. He wanted to turn away. He wanted to kill Randolph Kenric.

In that moment, Terran knew the truth, as if it had always been there and he'd known it deep down inside. He believed her. He believed everything she'd told him. With that revelation came an overwhelming sadness. What if he lost her?

"Will she be all right?" he found himself asking.

The herbalist straightened and a sigh escaped his lips. "I don't know. It appears to be some mandrake that she took, or something similar, but I can't be sure. I can't tell if she swallowed enough of the antidote, or if I've even given her the right one."

"When will we know?" Terran asked.

"If she lives through the day, she'll be all right."

Terran heard the door close softly behind them. Kenric. His jaw clenched tight.

Chapter Thirty-two

Terran rubbed his tired eyes, reaching for the ale a servant had brought for him earlier. His meal of mutton and bread sat untouched on the table near the mug. The room was dark, the shutters closed over the window. He had thought to keep the bright sunshine from disturbing Bria. Perhaps that was wrong. Should he open them? Maybe then she'd open her eyes.

Unable to decide, he returned the mug to the table, keeping his eyes to the floor. Every time he looked at Bria, his vision blurred and he had to look away. Somehow she'd worked her way through the wall he'd built around his heart, through it and over it like a vine of roses wrapping itself around a trellis.

If she lives through the day, she'll be all right. His hands trembled with fear as he gazed at them.

Terran shot out of his chair and paced the floor. If only he could do something to help her. But neither his sword nor his coin nor his power could help her. Bria had to fight this battle herself.

Terran raked a hand through his hair. *I can't lose her. Not now*. His heart ached, and he closed his eyes against the utter agony that was consuming him.

Terran dropped into the chair again. *I'm going to lose Bria.* The thought came unbidden, his fears finally taking shape in his mind. His throat squeezed tight, and his chest constricted painfully. He fell to his knees at her side, grasping her limp hand in his own. "Please, Bria," he whispered. "Don't leave me." He pressed his forehead to her knuckles. "Please."

Hours passed and night slunk over the land. Terran never left Bria's side, but his mind was reeling. It wasn't just coincidence that Odella and Bria had identical symptoms. Even if both had poisoned themselves, how likely was it they would have used the same poison? There was a traitor living in his midst.

Terran clenched his teeth, forcing his thoughts to the cause of her situation. *And what of Kenric?* he asked himself. He should be thrown in the dungeon or burned at the stake.

But it didn't make sense. Why in heaven's name would Randolph hurt Bria? It had been his idea for Terran to marry her. Why poison her? What would it gain him? No, he couldn't lock his cousin away—not until he found out why.

A groan.

Terran froze. Was he imagining it?

Her fingers in his hand jerked and moved slightly.

Terran's head came up to look into her face, but the room was so dark he couldn't see her. Holding her hand to his chest, he leaned close to her lips. "Bria?"

He waited with bated breath. But there was no response, no reaction to his voice. After a long moment of hopefulness, Terran bowed his head in disappointment.

The door behind him opened slowly and the light of a lone candle approached, engulfing him and Bria in its luminescence.

"Lord Knowles," a gentle voice from behind him called.

But Terran didn't move. He wouldn't release Bria's hand. He'd never relinquish her to the care of someone else, even the herbalist—especially the herbalist. The last time he'd abandoned his woman, she had died.

He felt the herbalist moving about beside him, checking Bria. Finally, the herbalist said, "Lord Knowles."

Dread filled Terran. He didn't want to hear the next words, for he was certain what they'd be. He didn't want to hear Bria was dead. He rose to his feet, towering over the small man. "Don't say it," he commanded.

"But, Lord Knowles!" the man objected.

Terran grabbed his tunic front and pulled him close until he could see the fear in the man's eyes in the candlelight. "I said I don't want to hear it."

Silently, the man nodded his head.

Terran released him and the herbalist quickly stepped away, moving toward the door. Terran watched him leave. He was afraid to look at Bria for fear her vibrant skin would be gray with death, afraid to touch her for fear her warm skin would be cold. He wanted desperately to escape this room of death, but he'd promised not to abandon Bria. He'd promised he wouldn't leave her.

Terran turned back to his wife, knowing the vision that greeted him would erase all the glorious memories he had of Bria and plunge his image of her into a deathlike slumber.

But she looked no different. Relief swept through him. She hadn't given up her battle yet. She hadn't succumbed.

Terran stood over Bria for a long moment, simply looking at her peaceful face. She was beautiful, even in this desperate battle for her life. Her glorious hair was spread out over the pillow like a blanket of silk. Her face was serene, showing none of the torment her body must be enduring.

He sat in the chair beside the bed, watching and waiting for any signs of what was to come.

What came was something he hadn't expected.

* * *

Bria's eyes fluttered and then opened. She felt tired, so tired, and groggy, as if she hadn't gotten enough sleep. She looked around her, disoriented for a moment. A candle, almost burned down to the base, flickered over the room, casting it in long eerie shadows. Her gaze continued to sweep the room, finally coming to settle on the one face that calmed her.

Terran was resting on the bed, turned toward her. His black hair spread out beneath his head, pillowing it upon the blanket. A smile touched her dry lips. She reached out a hand to his cheek, but before she could touch it, his eyes opened and he sat bolt upright, his hand moving to the hilt of his scabbard.

Bria stared at him, wide-eyed, breathless.

His eyes were wild for a moment, but then settled back into the calm darkness Bria knew well.

"Bria," he gasped, unmoving. He was frozen, his hand resting on the handle of his sword as if he were going to cut down some ghost in his memory.

Bria reached for him. "Yes," she said. "It's me."

"Bria!" His ragged exclamation was choked with emotion and worry. He clasped her in a warm, tight embrace, an embrace that bound her to him. She lifted her hands, encircling his back. Even though her arms felt heavy, she managed to hold him close.

"Oh, Bria," he whispered, pressing kisses against her hair. "I thought I'd lost you."

Bria sighed, relaxing in his hold. His strong arms engulfed her, pressing their bodies so tightly against each other that nothing could come between them. Terran cared for her. Relief filled every one of his kisses. Warmth flooded her.

Everything would be all right.

Terran pulled back and looked into her eyes. "How do you feel? Is there something I can get you?"

Bria smiled at him. "I feel like I slept for days." She sat up, looking around. "Is it morning?"

Terran glanced at the shutters, giving Bria a chance to study his rugged profile. He was a vision she didn't mind waking to—his strong Roman nose, his perfect, chiseled jaw, the soft strands of dark hair that curled around the tops of his strong shoulders. She reached up to touch his hair.

"It's dawn," Terran answered, returning his gaze to hers. He captured her outstretched hand in his, pressing a kiss to her knuckles. "You've been asleep for an entire day."

"A day!" Bria exclaimed. "No wonder I feel tired!" As she sat up, the room spun and she reached out for Terran. He steadied her with a firm hand on her shoulder.

"Shall I get the herbalist?"

"Herbalist?" Bria's mind reeled as a torrent of memories flooded back to her. Running from Kenric. A slap. Kenric forcing the poison into her mouth. She gasped, grabbing Terran's strong arm. "Terran, Kenric poisoned me."

Terran nodded. "Just rest right now."

"He had your herbalist make a poison and killed Odella. I saw him kill the old woman, your herbalist. That was when Mary was taken. I ran away. He tried to kill me because I saw him!"

"Shh," Terran soothed. "Don't worry. You have to rest."

"Terran, you have to believe me. He said Odella knew too much and that was why he poisoned her," Bria said.

A scowl crossed his brow. "Too much about what?"

Bria's troubled gaze met Terran's. She didn't know. She didn't have the answer to the puzzle. The more she thought about it, the more exhausted she became. "Please be careful, Terran," Bria finally said. "Kenric might try to kill you." She lay back on the bed, weak from fatigue.

Terran bent over her to lightly kiss her lips. "I will, my dearest," he promised. "You rest."

Bria's eyes closed and her worries faded away beneath a blanket of blissful sleep.

Terran entered the Great Hall to find Kenric lounging near the hearth, laughing with Sir William, Terran's captain of the guard. A dark scowl crossed Terran's features; his fists clenched tight at his sides. He moved toward his cousin.

Kenric turned to him, his smile fading. "M'lord, how is Lady Bria?"

Terran ignored him. "I would have a word with you, cousin."

Kenric nodded stiffly, if a bit apprehensively, and Sir William moved away.

"She said you poisoned her," Terran said through clenched teeth.

"What?" Kenric gasped. "Me? I would never . . . you can't believe that!"

"Did you poison her, Randolph?" Terran demanded.

"Why would I poison her? She is my lady!"

"Did you poison her?"

"No!" Kenric shouted, drawing stares from the others in the room. He lowered his voice. "Don't you see what she's doing? She is trying to turn us against each other."

"There's no reason for her to do that."

"No reason? The Midnight Shadow is her reason! They're working together against us. I'm trying to stop him, and all she does is defend him. She's trying to distract us. We must stay focused on getting rid of that thief."

Doubt settled in Terran's mind. The Midnight Shadow. He wasn't Bria's lover. What was he to her, then?

"Has she told you who he is?" Kenric persisted.

Terran looked away.

"How can you believe anything she says if she won't give you the name of your enemy?" Kenric asked.

Terran glanced at Kenric. His cousin was right. While the

Midnight Shadow still lived and breathed, he could never truly trust Bria. *She still keeps secrets. How can she expect me to believe her? Randolph wouldn't have poisoned her. She poses no threat to him.* But who had? And why?

Terran extended his hand. "Forgive me, cousin," he said.

Kenric nodded and clasped his hand. "Women are dangerous creatures, m'lord. Never to be trusted."

"Lord Knowles!"

Two men marched toward him—two familiar men. Terran faced them.

Lord Delaney glared at him. Harry Delaney stepped forward and announced, "We've come to take Bria home."

Chapter Thirty-three

A fierce protectiveness flared inside Terran. "She is my wife, sir," he replied stiffly.

"You tried to kill her!" Harry spat.

Terran's jaw clenched. They thought *he* had poisoned Bria!

"Father," Lord Delaney commanded in a stern voice, quieting the old man. He turned to Terran. "We see what a mistake this marriage has been. You don't want her any more than I want her to be your wife."

Terran fought back the urge to challenge Lord Delaney, to call him out for his slanderous words. "Regardless, the act is done," Terran replied.

Lord Delaney straightened slightly. "Be reasonable, Knowles."

"We will not tolerate your abuse of Bria," Harry said. "She means more to us than that. You can keep the wretched dowry if it means that much to you, but let Bria go."

Terran stared hard at Harry. He would never let Bria go! She was his wife, and she meant more to him than anything— more than the infernal dowry that would save his castle and lands. Why, he'd give it all back to keep her, every damned bit of it. Angry at the thought that the Delaneys put in his mind, he strode from the room, ignoring their calls.

"Do what you must," Harry cried, "but she is returning with us."

Terran tried to calm himself. They were just trying to protect her. But the very idea that he, her husband, her lord, would poison her was preposterous. He'd do everything in his power to keep her safe. To keep her from harm.

And how are you going to do that? an inner voice challenged. He'd have to watch her every moment of every day, watch what she ate, to whom she spoke, what she touched. Even then, he couldn't guarantee her safety.

The thought that he couldn't protect his own wife pierced his heart and his pride.

"M'lord!"

Terran turned at Kenric's voice.

"Shall I escort the Delaneys from our lands?"

For a long moment, Terran studied Kenric's face. His trusted cousin, the sheriff of his lands, and more importantly his friend. How could he be capable of harming Bria? Yet Bria insisted he'd poisoned her. He wasn't sure. Damn it, he just wasn't sure. Could he risk her life?

"No," Terran replied. "Not just yet."

Bria felt jubilant and more alive than she ever had. Terran had remained at her side for two entire days, only now allowing her to accompany him to the Great Hall to eat. His power and presence radiated over her like a shield, protecting her with its invisible force. She felt safe and happy. Terran was a good, decent man. He wasn't her enemy. He never had been.

She held his arm, her hand resting on his forearm, proudly accompanying him through the hallways.

The Great Hall was empty of servants and peasants. *How*

strange, she thought. She scanned the large room and saw all the tables and benches had been removed except for the head table. Near the head table stood a group of men, two of whom she recognized instantly. A huge grin lit up her face.

Bria broke free of Terran's arm and raced to embrace her father. Then she turned to hug her grandfather. She looked back at her husband. "Terran," she began, but stopped when she saw his expression.

His face was a mask of stone. He moved to stand beside Kenric. Dread and confusion filled her. She was standing but a few feet from her would-be murderer. Why wasn't Kenric locked up somewhere? Didn't Terran realize what a madman he was?

Bria stepped forward. "Terran," she whispered beseechingly, "what's going on?"

On Kenric's lips was a victorious smile.

Bria refused to acknowledge it, refused to let the shivers going up her spine alarm her. "Terran . . ."

"You may take her now," Terran said impassively.

Her father put his hand on her arm. She lifted a baffled gaze to him, then broke away, stepping toward Terran. "I don't understand," she said.

"There's nothing to understand," he said. "I don't want you any longer."

She recoiled as if struck in the chest by a war mallet. "What?" she gasped.

"Sheriff Kenric told me you rode out of the castle to rendezvous with your lover. You aren't fit to be my wife."

Bria's gaze shifted to Kenric. "But he tried to poison me!" she protested. "How can you believe him?"

"How can I believe you?!"

Tears filled Bria's eyes. "I wouldn't lie about this," she whispered. "You must believe me."

"How can I?" Terran asked firmly.

"Terran," Bria pleaded. "Please. How can you do this?"

"Then tell us who the Midnight Shadow is," Kenric said.

Bria's eyes didn't move from Terran. It was as if Kenric hadn't spoken. She saw the disdain in her husband's eyes, saw the clenching of his jaw. It wouldn't matter if she told him who the Midnight Shadow was. Terran would never love her.

And that realization shattered her. Bria felt her world crumbling around her. The incredible happiness she'd felt mere moments before disappeared without a trace.

Someone touched her arm. "It's all right, Bria," Harry whispered. "You can come home with us."

Bria swallowed hard and lifted her chin against Terran's coldness. "I am home," she proclaimed. "I am lady of Castle Knowles, and this is where I shall remain."

Fury flamed in Terran's eyes. "Didn't you hear what I said? You are not welcome here! I don't want you. I never have. You are to leave Castle Knowles at once." He turned his back on her and stormed from the hall.

Bria stood aghast, horrified and embarrassed, but mostly devastated. She felt as though he was ripping apart her heart.

"He'll try to kill you again, Bria," Harry whispered to her. "You'd best come home with us." He gently took her arm.

Bria savagely yanked her arm free of his hold. "Didn't you hear me? It wasn't Terran! It was Randolph Kenric! He tried to poison me!"

Harry and Lord Delaney's eyes turned to Kenric.

Kenric bridled. "She is mad," he said. "What reason would I have to kill her? I convinced Terran to marry her."

"You wanted me gone, out of the way. With my leaving Castle Knowles, you've accomplished that, haven't you?" She stood toe to toe with the man, glaring up at him with all the hatred and agony that swirled inside her. "This is your fault," she snarled, "and I won't let you get away with it." She swept up her blue satin skirt and raced for the door, running after Terran.

He will be long gone, she thought as she burst through the doorway. But to her surprise, he stood just down the corridor, speaking with a pair of guards. His earnest expression should have alerted her to the seriousness of his conversation, but Bria was too hurt to notice anything but the pain inside her.

She marched up to him. "I deserve answers," she said.

He turned to her, shock on his face. Then his eyes darkened. "You aren't going to make this easy, are you?"

"Easy?" she demanded, rage knotting her fists. "I'll make it as easy for you as you are for me."

He seized her arm in a tight hold and dragged her down the hallway, turning his head from this door to that. Finally, he settled on a room and opened the door. It was empty and dark. He propelled her inside with a none too gentle shove.

Bria almost fell to her knees, but caught her balance. He closed the door, sealing them in the darkness. There was complete and utter silence between them for a long moment. Bria could hear only her own heavy breathing.

"What answers would you like?" Terran demanded.

"Why? Why are you doing this?" Bria asked, trying desperately to keep her voice even.

"I told you. You are a failure as my wife."

"What have I done?" she implored, angry at herself for sounding so desperate.

"Your consorting with my enemy is intolerable," he retorted.

"I am not consorting!" Bria felt tears burning in her eyes.

"Then tell me where you go in the middle of the night. Tell me who you meet."

"I have never lied to you, Terran."

"Omission is just as much a lie," he snapped. "You plot against me with this criminal."

"No," she whispered, stepping toward his outline in the gloom. "I try to help you. Your people are living in fear—"

"So you've said."

"But you don't listen! How can you run a castle if your

people starve in the winter? Who will plow your fields then? Who will—''

"Enough!" The word resonated through the room. "Don't do this, Bria, please. Just leave."

"I don't want to leave you."

"The choice isn't yours to make," Terran answered.

The tears that burned her eyes ran over her cheeks. "Why save me to destroy me?"

"You aren't professing love, are you?"

"And if I am?"

He turned away before he answered. "I would pity you. Kathryn satisfies my physical needs. And my heart . . . belongs to Odella."

Bria's heart shattered into a thousand pieces. How could she have mistaken this cold, uncaring person for a man who loved her?

"Then why did you make love to me?" she cried.

There was silence before he finally said, "I thought to prove you were a whore. Imagine my surprise to find you a virgin."

Bria's entire body shook, trembling like a leaf being blown about in a violent wind, and she couldn't hold back a sob.

"Bria." The whispered tenderness in his voice confused her. "Why do you make me hurt you like this? Just go."

Bria didn't understand. She didn't *want* to understand the deceitful treachery behind Terran's actions. How could she have been so wrong about him?

She took a teetering step backward, her world blurring before her eyes, before whirling and running out of the room.

Chapter Thirty-four

Terran had never cared about the ledgers, but now he immersed himself in the harvest tallies. He frowned. The accursed tallies weren't making sense to him. He rubbed his eyes and looked at the entries again, but his thoughts weren't focused on the tally lines scribbled on the parchment before him. Where could he start?

How can I discover who poisoned Bria? His heart told him to start with Kenric. Bria wouldn't lie. But his mind argued there was no reason for Kenric to poison Bria or Odella.

No matter how hard he tried to focus his mind on something else, he couldn't get the image of Bria's tearful face from his mind. He'd wondered if perhaps she might be glad to be leaving him. But he'd been wrong. Very wrong. He knew that now.

Nonetheless, he did what had to be done. He had to get her out of the way in order to figure out what was going on. He couldn't risk her life. He couldn't risk someone's harming her again.

But now his mind was refusing to focus on the job at hand.

He shook his head firmly, gazing at the small lines and tallies on the page beside the names of the peasants and merchants and farmers who lived under his rule. They meant nothing to him, not compared to Bria.

Terran slammed the book closed and rose from the table, turning to head out the door. He hurried down the hall toward the main balcony. *I hope I'm not too late. I hope I can get there in time, just see her once more so I can concentrate on what I have to do.* With each step the urgency grew. He had to see her. He had to assure himself that she'd be all right. He was almost running as he reached the balcony, which over-looked the courtyard. He placed his palms on the edge of the railing, only to see the Delaney procession riding away in the distance.

He couldn't see Bria. With this thought came an anguish he'd never known. His wife was riding away from him, and he'd driven her away. His chest constricted painfully, and he bowed his head. She was gone.

It's the only way, he thought, struggling to convince himself he'd done the right thing. *The only way to keep her safe.* When it was all over, he would get her back. He'd make it right. He had to.

Thunder sounded in the distance, and he lifted his head to see dark black clouds churning in the sky just in front of the procession.

Soaked and numb, Bria sat before the hearth in her room. They'd reached Castle Delaney just as the downpour began and had been unable to avoid the torrential wall of rain. The flames snapped and danced, their movements reflected in her eyes, but she didn't see them.

She shivered in her wet clothing. Her maidservant Deb had suggested she change, but she'd refused. They were the last thing that held the memory of Terran's touch.

Someone hung a warm, dry blanket about her shoulders, but she didn't look up.

"Bria." Her father knelt before her.

Bria shifted her eyes to him, hoping to find comfort in his presence. But he wasn't Terran, and only Terran could stop the pain that burned in her chest. She turned her gaze back to the fire.

"We can petition the king for an annulment. We'll get the dowry back," he vowed. "That cur shall have none of your coin."

Bria almost laughed. As if she cared about the dowry.

Her father lifted a hand to stroke her wet hair. "Was it so horrible for you, darling?"

"Horrible?" she asked quietly. "No, Father." She blinked at the tears that entered her eyes. "Curse me for a fool," she said, and lifted a trembling hand to swipe at a lone tear that ran down her cheek. "I fell in love with him."

That night, Bria slept a barren sleep, her mind empty of dreams, her soul more dead than alive. By the time she woke the next day, it was late afternoon. She moved through the halls like a specter, pale, hauntingly slow. Peasants stopped to look at her and shake their heads when they thought she wasn't looking. She frowned. He had done this to her. Terran had made her an object of sympathy.

But she knew she was stronger than that. Then why didn't she have the strength of spirit to prove it? Why couldn't she be better than this phantom who walked the halls?

Without realizing where she was heading, Bria found herself sitting beneath the tree near the empty tilting yard. She pulled out stalks of grass one at a time, shredding each in her slender fingers, and then moving on to the next.

She didn't notice the passage of time, didn't notice the sun dipping lower and lower in the distance.

A sword dropped abruptly into her lap, as if falling from the heavens. She stared down at the leather handle for a long moment before lifting her gaze skyward to find her grandfather standing over her.

"The people need the Midnight Shadow," he said, "now more than ever."

Bria pushed the weapon from her lap. "I'm not worthy to be the Midnight Shadow."

"You've been wounded by your enemy and you just sit there, letting the wound kill you."

Bria shook her head. "It's not like that."

"Isn't it?" Harry knelt beside her.

"I don't have the spirit to be the Midnight Shadow."

"So he killed that, too, did he?" Harry shook his head. "And who will save those people? Do you think this is what Garret would have wanted? Or Mary?"

"Mary." Bria's head came up sharply at the thought of her friend. *How selfish I've been. While my friend rots away in Terran's dungeon, all I can think about is myself! I have to save Mary!* Bria quickly rose to her feet. "Grandfather, Mary is alive! I spoke with her. She's in the dungeon at Castle Knowles!"

Harry nodded grimly. "Then you have a lot to do, don't you?"

When Bria reached the clearing, the moon was high and bright in the night sky. She dismounted and moved to the pond, taking a moment to look down into the calm water. She was dismayed at her wretched expression, her swollen lids, her melancholy face. But there was a new resolve returning to her eyes.

Let everyone think I am wasting away from a loveless marriage. Let everyone think Terran treated me horribly. Let every-

one pity me, she thought. *I'll be safe from their suspicions. No one will expect me to be the Midnight Shadow.*

Bria looked around, watching the shadows, waiting, making sure Kenric hadn't set a trap. When she finally moved to retrieve her costume and sword, dark clouds had obscured the moon and the night cloaked her in nearly complete darkness. The blackness of the forest gave her courage; the stars twinkling above gave her hope. But mostly, the reborn determination within her gave her her spirit.

Bria took her sword, boots, and costume and mounted her horse, leaving the memories of her poisoning behind her. She had decided to move her hiding place to the bramble patch. There she once again became the Midnight Shadow.

Chapter Thirty-five

The Midnight Shadow hid in the trees near the dirt road that led to the gated entrance of Castle Knowles. She had debated swimming the brackish waters of the moat that surrounded the stone fortress, but quickly decided against it. She had no idea where the secret exits were built into the castle walls. She'd had no time to discover, or even ask about, their whereabouts in her few short days at the castle.

She thought of waiting until morning, waiting until the castle gates opened to let in the flood of daily business, but there would be no shadows for her to conceal herself in, and the thought of Mary's spending one more minute in that dark, horrible dungeon made her skin crawl and her heart ache.

Bria cursed. She'd brought along a plain brown hooded cloak to disguise herself as a monk, which she now wore. But when she arrived at Castle Knowles, she was dismayed to see the portcullis lowered.

There had to be another way in.

Her answer came rumbling down the dirt road on four wobbly

wheels, a merchant either returning very late or arriving very
early. He sat atop his wagon, driving his tired horses forward
with a feeble snap of their reins, pulling his covered cart behind
him.

The Midnight Shadow let the cart pass, then quickly moved
behind it to push the flaps of the covering aside and clamber
inside. The back of the wagon was filled with bags of spice
and other foodstuffs, fabric, piles of clothing, boxes of jewelry.
Two men snored softly at the front of the cart.

Just then, the wagon hit a hole in the road and the cart
bounced heavily, sending a box flying into the side of one of
the sleeping men. The Midnight Shadow caught her balance
and ducked down behind a pile of fabric, quickly pulling some
material over her head. She heard the man curse and rustle
about for a few moments before his snoring resumed. The air
quickly turned hot beneath her shield of cloth, but she dared
not move.

To enter the castle thus was impetuous and dangerous. But
it was the only way to free Mary.

The wagon continued on its way, the journey seeming to
take hours when only minutes had passed. The wooden wheels
clattered across more wood, and she realized they'd reached
the drawbridge. She heard voices, but couldn't make out the
words. The wagon stopped. She heard more voices, louder
now, the words still indiscernible. Footsteps sounded nearby.
Suddenly, the flaps whipped open and flickering torchlight rip-
pled across the fabric above her head.

One of the sleeping men grumbled, cursing the light in his
eyes. Then the flaps were shut, returning her to the safety of
darkness. A loud cranking sound signaled that the portcullis
was being raised. When the sound stopped, the wagon jerked
forward, moving them into the castle. Eventually, the wagon
slowed, then stopped. She started to rise, but quickly pulled
the material over her head as she heard one of the sleeping
men awake. The man stumbled through the wagon toward her,

stepping a mere inch from her booted toes as he made his way
outside.

The driver and the newly awakened man talked outside the
wagon, their voices fading into the distance as they headed
away. The other man still slept, snoring quite loudly. Quickly,
she slipped out of the wagon and moved to the dark shadows
of a nearby wall. She scanned her surroundings, seeing that
she was already in the inner courtyard near the keep.

The Midnight Shadow moved cautiously through the darkness. The moon was a sliver, its feeble light barely enough to
illuminate an entire castle, let alone a disguised woman sneaking through the blackness. She pulled the monk's hood up to
hide her mask and cape as she moved slowly through the inner
ward.

At the doors of the keep, she silently eased inside. As she
moved down the dark hallway, she pulled the cloak tight against
her body, holding her weapon against her so when she moved
it was lost in the folds of the cloak.

Most of the castle's occupants were asleep. She barely paused
to glance inside as she passed the Great Hall. It was littered
with sleeping bodies, most situated as close as possible to the
hearth for the warmth it offered. Bria continued on.

One other time she'd been up at this late hour at Castle
Knowles—her wedding night. She pushed the thought from
her mind. She had to concentrate on Mary, not on her husband.

She quickly found the stairway to the lower level and walked
cautiously down the stairs. She remembered the route to the
dungeons very well. She'd been brought this way when she
had been interrogated by Kenric. She forced the anger and
humiliation from her mind. She had to concentrate. She was
in her enemy's home. If she were to be caught . . .

She couldn't think of that. She descended into the darkness.
Torchlight wavered about her. She continued on until her feet
hit the dank mud of the dungeon level. Fear and excitement

mingled with the anticipation of seeing her friend again. She was so close to Mary, to finally freeing her.

Adrenaline pumped through her veins, heightening every one of her senses. She heard the moan of a prisoner in the distance as if he were right beside her. The first guard's post was empty, and she continued down the small, dark hallway to the second guard's post. She peered around the corner.

One guard sat at a small table. His back was to her, his head bent forward. For a moment, she thought he was sleeping. Then he straightened, spit something out, and bent his head again.

She thought of sneaking up on the guard, knocking him out with a quick strike to the back of his head with the hilt of her sword, but then realized that wasn't the way. Bria silently removed her brown monk's cloak and tossed it to the ground. She wanted Terran to know who had rescued Mary. She wanted him to know his enemy had infiltrated his castle. She eased her weapon from its sheath. Then she stepped forward, moving noisily out of the shadows.

The guard turned. When he saw her, his eyes widened and his hand immediately dropped to his sheath.

But the Midnight Shadow had the tip of her weapon against his throat before he could draw his sword. "Remove your hand from your weapon, sir," she ordered in her deep whisper.

The guard hesitantly removed his hand from the hilt of his sword, and the Midnight Shadow removed his weapon, tossing it to a far corner.

"Now open the cell Mary is in," the Midnight Shadow commanded in a whisper.

The guard nodded once, careful of the tip to his throat.

She took a step back and allowed him to rise and move down the dark corridor. He paused before Mary's door and then unlatched it, flinging it open. "Get her out," She commanded.

"The prisoner isn't in here," the guard told her.

"Explain," she insisted.

"Sheriff Kenric moved her," he said.

She was moved? Bria's heart pounded furiously in her chest. Anger and frustration speared through her. She had been so close! "Where?" she demanded.

"I don't know," he said softly.

The Midnight Shadow cursed silently and shoved the guard into the cell. She shut the door and latched it, sealing him in. She moved farther into the dark dungeon, ignoring the guard's shouts, and unlatched the other cells, freeing the prisoners. She'd need a diversion to get out of the castle in one piece. Hopefully the escaped prisoners would provide enough of a distraction to the castle guards. She bolted up the stairway, grabbing the monk's cloak on her way. As she moved, she shoved it into a bag at her side.

She'd been so close! She could have freed Mary. *Damn it, if I'd only gotten to her sooner.*

She looked up the stairway and froze. It was the way toward the solar, toward Terran's room. Would he be sleeping? Probably. Unwanted, the image of his powerful physique draped across the bed rose in her mind. She had to see him again. She wanted to look at him just once.

Before she had the conscious thought, she was moving up the stairs toward the solar, unable to resist the overwhelming urge.

She knew from experience that Bradley, Terran's squire, slept in the stables, keeping a close eye on Terran's treasured steed. Terran slept alone. Her foot landed on the second floor. The floor where Terran was.

Am I mad? she wondered. *What am I doing?*

To hesitate could cost her dearly. She would take only a quick peek in at him and then be gone.

The Midnight Shadow moved as silently as the night, pressing her back to the wall and merging with the shadows as she crept down the hallway until she stood before Terran's room. The wooden door stood as a barrier before her, a warning not to cross the threshold. She reached out to the handle, then let her hand drop to her side. This was madness. She had to get out of the castle.

She turned to leave when suddenly she heard the sound of approaching footsteps from down the hallway. Her gaze darted, but there was nowhere to run, nowhere to hide. She had no choice. She opened the door to Terran's room and stepped inside. She stood with her back pressed to the door, listening as the footsteps drew closer. Would whoever it was knock on Terran's door? She placed her hand on the hilt of her sword, preparing. She held her breath for a long moment . . .

. . . until the footsteps continued past the door, moving off down the hall.

She breathed a soft, relieved sigh and looked around the room. It was very dark, except for a stray beam of pale moonlight that shone in through the partially opened shutters and washed over the bed, illuminating a sleeping form.

The Midnight Shadow stepped away from the door, moving through the familiar room until she stood just before the bed. She watched the form breathe, the slow rise and fall of the blanket. She reached out a hand to touch Terran, to touch his shoulder, his cheek, his lips, but the shape suddenly moved, rolling over onto its back into the light. She gasped, snatching her hand back.

The face the beam of light illuminated wasn't Terran's. It was Kathryn who lay in his bed.

The Midnight Shadow stumbled to the door, betrayal piercing her heart like an arrow. Tears blinded her vision for a savage moment and she wiped at them with her gloved hands, smearing her mask away from her eyes. She took a quick moment to right it so she could see.

Then, she reached for the door and yanked it open, casting one last look back at Kathryn, cursing her husband. Seeing Kathryn in Terran's bed made his betrayal more real. She turned and almost ran into a wall of flesh, but pulled back suddenly.

Terran Knowles stood before her.

Chapter Thirty-six

The Midnight Shadow! In my castle!

"You!" Terran instinctively reached for his sword, but it wasn't there. He wasn't dressed for battle. He opened his mouth to shout for the guards, but the Midnight Shadow hit him in the chest, hard enough to choke his cry.

"You cur," the villain hissed. "How dare you betray your wife like this?"

Again Terran opened his mouth to call for guards.

But the Midnight Shadow drew his weapon and pressed the edge of the blade to Terran's throat, silencing him again. "I should run you through, vile betrayer."

Terran scowled. *Who is this dog to speak to me thus?*

The Midnight Shadow stepped closer to him, forcing Terran to take a step back. "Do you know how you've made her feel?"

The Midnight Shadow took another step closer, the tip pressing dangerously close to Terran's Adam's apple, forcing his chin high.

"She goes to bed crying every night. She thinks of you every cursed moment of every day. She can barely tolerate being away from you."

Terran's scowl and confusion deepened. How did this stranger, this mysterious man in black, know so much about his wife? She'd proven to him they weren't lovers.

"You've all but destroyed her," the masked man whispered grimly. "I should slit your throat for causing her so much pain." He pressed the tip of the blade closer to Terran's skin.

Terran's head was forced back as he lifted his chin, baring his throat to the Midnight Shadow. He awaited death. Expected it. But suddenly, the tip eased from his jugular. "But I won't kill you . . . if you tell me where Mary is."

Terran's gaze snapped up from the blade to lock with the Midnight Shadow's. Mary? Oh, yes. Wasn't she Bria's friend? The girl Kenric said had murdered the herbalist. "I don't know where the sheriff keeps my prisoners."

He saw fury flash in those blue eyes, the bluest eyes he had ever seen. "Who rules this castle, you or Kenric?" The whisper was full of disgust.

Suddenly, the sound of footsteps echoed down the hall. The Midnight Shadow's eyes shifted slightly in the direction of the sound.

Blue eyes. The bluest eyes he had ever seen. Why couldn't he escape that thought?

"You've much luck this day, Knowles," the Midnight Shadow said. "But we'll meet again. This I vow." With a flurry of his black cape, he lurched toward Terran with the tip of his blade. Terran stumbled back, away from the sharp blade. Was this madman going to kill him? He put up his arm to ward off the attack. But no pain pierced his arm, his shoulder, his torso. Terran lowered his arm and quickly scanned the hallway around him. The Midnight Shadow was gone.

Terran sprang into action, shouting for his guards. He had barely taken a step when his bedroom door swung open. Kathryn stepped into the hallway, clutching a blanket on her chest to cover her nakedness.

Terran halted immediately, his gaze sweeping Kathryn. *Betrayer.* Suddenly, his enemy's accusation made sense. What the hell was Kathryn doing in his room?

"What's happened?" Kathryn cried, clinging to his arm.

As Terran disengaged his arm from Kathryn's hold, two guards ran down the hall toward him. He had no time for her. His enemy was in the castle! He turned to the guards. "Search the castle. The Midnight Shadow was just here."

"The Midnight Shadow?" Kathryn gasped.

"Close the portcullis. Raise the drawbridge," Terran ordered. "We'll trap him."

The guards moved to carry out their lord's orders.

Terran took a step away from his room, down the hallway. He had to get to the gatehouse. Hadn't the guards seen anything?

"Wait!"

He stopped to look back at Kathryn. She let the blanket drop another inch.

"What about me?" she asked with a sultry, if practiced, pout. "I'm so frightened."

"I suggest you dress and return to your own room," Terran replied.

"But . . ."

Terran turned his back on her protests, moving off down the hall with long strides. How had it been so easy for his enemy to get into his home? Was he that clever? Was he that good? Was he really a he? He shrugged off that last question; he had no time to try to figure it out now. He could only concentrate on making sure the Midnight Shadow did not escape. He couldn't allow his enemy to return to his wife with the news of Kathryn in his bed. How could he explain that everything he'd said to her was a lie if the Midnight Shadow told her otherwise? How could he hope to fix things then?

* * *

Bria had donned the brown monk's cloak and was making her way toward the drawbridge and her escape when the cry went out. Bria froze, thinking she'd been discovered.

"Raise the drawbridge!"

The drawbridge.

She could still make it. It would take several minutes before the guards could turn the cranks and fully wind the drawbridge chains. She crept closer and breathed a silent sigh of relief as she reached the outer gate. The drawbridge was still down, her passage to freedom unhindered.

Bria chanced a glance back over her shoulder. No garrison of guards stormed toward her from the inner ward, no one cried out to stop her. Most of the guards would still be waking up, scrambling for their weapons in the darkness. A smile stretched across her lips. Success! She'd done it. Well, not exactly. Mary was still trapped inside somewhere.

She took a step forward to move quickly beneath the gatehouse toward the drawbridge. A sigh of relief welled up inside her. She'd been foolish to seek Terran out. It had been too great a risk, but she'd made it.

The sound of rushing metal reached her ears. The portcullis crashed down a mere few feet before her, its sharp metal teeth biting hard into the earth, slamming closed with a resounding boom, sealing her inside Castle Knowles.

Chapter Thirty-seven

"Get back from there!" a voice called from the battlements.

Startled, Bria obeyed the voice, trying not to give herself away, trying not to be scared, but already terrified.

If she was discovered as the Midnight Shadow, she'd be executed.

She took another step away from the portcullis, finally having to turn her back on the road to freedom. Fear knotted her stomach. What if she was caught?

She took a breath to calm herself. *Don't lose your wits,* she told herself firmly. *You'll think of some way out of this.* She moved back to the inner ward. *If I can get out of these Midnight Shadow clothes, I might have a chance to wait until they open the gates again.*

She continued to move along the wall of the castle in the shadows. She had to get her costume off. But where? She moved forward toward the keep. She was crossing the moonlit courtyard when the sound of running feet exploded from behind her.

"There he is!" someone cried. She froze in her tracks. Her

hand dropped to the hilt of the sword concealed in the long folds of her cloak. Dread pierced her heart as footsteps closed in around her. She slowly turned and chanced a glance up to see a group of soldiers rushing toward her . . .

. . . and then past her. She almost collapsed in relief as they hauled a man from behind a stack of large crates positioned near the front gate. He was skinny and dirty, his clothing in tatters. He screamed and struggled to be free. "No!" he hollered. "I won't go back to the dungeon!"

The dungeon. He was one of the freed prisoners.

A guard backhanded the man, silencing him. Bria winced, clenching her teeth. She wanted to help the poor man. He was vastly overpowered and outnumbered. After all, that was what the Midnight Shadow did—protected the weak. But to do so would be her undoing. She took a few steps back from the group of distracted soldiers.

She turned and entered the keep unnoticed. Bria moved down a long corridor, sticking to the walls and the shadows thrown by the torches. She walked slowly and cautiously to the Great Hall, pausing in the doorway. The room was strangely quiet except for the snapping flames in the hearth. She entered the room softly, trying to move as silently as possible. But the rushes snapped beneath her booted feet and a pair of dogs that had been napping amongst the peasants lifted their heads. One dog stood up, a peasant's arm rolling off the animal's back. The other stayed motionless, its eyes pinning her.

For a long moment, Bria couldn't move. She didn't know whether to go back through the large doors or continue on. She decided to head on. She moved through the Great Hall. With each footstep, she felt the dogs' watchful eyes on her back. She prayed they would go back to sleep, that they wouldn't start barking and wake the entire Great Hall.

They remained mercifully quiet. In the doorway to the kitchen, she paused and looked back. The dog that had been lying down had shifted its position, moving closer to one of the peasants. The other dog was sniffing around the rushes for some forgotten food.

Bria sighed to herself and moved into the kitchen. The room was empty and cold, the fire for the large ovens unlit. She scanned the kitchen and saw another doorway. She crossed the room and quickly stepped through the opening. More stairs. Blackness surrounded her as she descended.

At the bottom of the stairs, a flickering torch on the wall was dropping pieces of charred wood onto the floor. It illuminated the entrance into another dark room, where she found mountains of barrels and boxes. The moment she stepped into the room, the sweet smell of cinnamon surrounded her and her nose itched from the scent of pepper. The spice vaults! A perfect place to change out of her Midnight Shadow clothes. They wouldn't be looking for a woman dressed in a brown robe. She grinned. They wouldn't be looking for a woman at all.

She ducked behind three stacks of barrels and removed the cloak, then the hooded cape and mask. She shook her head, running her hands through her hair as the wild strands, free from their confines, cascaded down her back. She unbuckled her sheath and carefully, quietly, set it down so it leaned against one of the barrels. Then she eased her black tunic over her head, folded it, and laid it on a barrel beside her sword. She removed the tightly wrapped cloth that bound her breasts and rubbed the circulation back into them, then pulled off her boots and leggings. She folded the leggings, placing them on top of the tunic.

Suddenly she heard soft footsteps and turned, peeking out from between two barrels, her nakedness momentarily forgotten. She couldn't see anyone in the darkness, but she heard the rustle of clothing.

"What is it, Captain? You said it was urgent." Bria knew the voice instantly. There was only one voice that could be that cold, only one man who could speak plain words with such evil. Kenric.

"The men are getting restless. If they aren't paid soon, they might go to Knowles with your plan."

"Make sure they don't! They'll be paid tomorrow."

"How long before we act?"

"Soon. But make sure the men say nothing, do you hear? I've worked long and hard for this. Some overeager mercenary isn't going to destroy my plan."

Fear shot through Bria at his words. What was Kenric paying the mercenaries to do?

"How many men do we have?" Kenric asked.

"Enough to take the castle."

Horror flooded through Bria. Terran! her mind cried. She had to tell Terran!

"Some are still loyal to Knowles. I had to be very careful recruiting."

"Well done, Captain," Kenric said. "You'll be well rewarded."

Bria remained absolutely still. She didn't dare move for fear of discovery, but she had to find out as much as she could.

"And what of this Midnight Shadow?"

Kenric chuckled. "That useless Knowles has come up with a rather ingenious plan to capture him. When that happens, I'll give the signal to take the castle." Their footsteps faded as they moved out of the room.

Bria couldn't move. Kenric was planning to take Castle Knowles for himself! She had to warn Terran.

Despair seized hold of her. How could she think Terran would believe her? He hadn't believed her about Kenric poisoning her. Why would he believe her about something this important? Kenric was his cousin. She was nothing to him. Nothing. He had another woman warming his bed.

Pain sliced through her at the thought of Terran loving Kathryn. She should hate him. She should hate him for forcing her to marry him and then casting her aside like a worn cloak. She should hate him for showing her how to make love with such passion and such emotion that everything else paled in comparison. She should hate him for making her love him.

But she didn't. She couldn't. For not only had he taken her maidenhood, he had also taken her heart, and he hadn't given it back when he cast her from his home.

Bria shoved the Midnight Shadow costume into the large pouch she carried with her and then tied the string tight to close it. She tied the pouch around her waist, then slid her cloak into one of the wide sleeves of the robe. She quickly donned her boots and then stared down at her sword. She should just leave it, but she couldn't bear to part with it; it had been a gift from her grandfather. She picked up the weapon and put it under the robe, holding it to her side to prevent any obvious bulge in her clothing, then headed for the stairs.

Even if there was little hope he'd believe her, she had to warn Terran.

Terran cursed silently. The Midnight Shadow had escaped. Somehow. Some way. Every single one of the freed prisoners had been recaptured, but the Midnight Shadow had evaded him.

The castle was still being searched, but his hopes were dwindling with the rising sun. He stepped into his room and removed his tunic. He cursed again as he stood before the fire in the hearth, hands on his hips. Perhaps his enemy was still in the castle. But if so, where was he? The entire castle had been searched, but still the rogue evaded him.

Terran ground his teeth and shook his head slightly. Then he froze. There was movement behind him, a soft step, the rustle of clothing. Had the Midnight Shadow come to finish what he'd begun?

Terran whirled. A silhouette separated from the dark shadows near the bed. Terran saw the outline of wavy hair and relaxed slightly. A woman. He turned his back to her. "Kathryn," he said, "I told you to—"

"It's me, Terran."

Terran's heart leaped, but he was afraid it was all in his imagination. He'd heard that soft voice calling his name since the day he'd banned Bria from Castle Knowles.

"I've come to warn you," the voice went on. "Kenric is plotting against you, Terran. He's planning on taking over your castle."

How could this be his imagination? The things she was saying were nothing he could have imagined. Slowly, he turned to her, half expecting her to vanish. She didn't.

Bria stepped toward him, moving into the firelight to face him. The golden light of the fire kissed her skin, moving over it like an artist's brush. Her hair shimmered around her face and shoulders. An anguished longing encompassed him. She was real, very real, and he wanted her back. He desperately wanted to tell her so, but no words came to his lips. He could only stare in mute rapture at her beauty.

"He's overtaxing your people and keeping the coin to pay mercenaries."

Suddenly it all made sense, as if her words had cleared his mind from a thick fog, as if her soft voice had awakened him from a deep spell. There'd been discrepancies between the ledgers and the accounts of the few peasants he had spoken with. Now it made sense. Kenric's fanatical devotion to his work, his obsession with collecting taxes. The coin wasn't meant for Terran or the castle. It was all for Kenric, to be used in his own unscrupulous plans.

"I know it doesn't make sense, but I heard him. He's planning to do this when you capture the Midnight Shadow." Bria looked down at her clasped hands. "I know you don't want me here, but what I tell you is the truth! You must believe me." She nodded once as if convincing herself she'd done the right thing, then took a step toward the door.

He knew he should let her go. She'd be safer without him. Kenric wouldn't try to kill her if she were gone, and Terran couldn't bear the thought of her being in danger. He had to let her go. He had to.

Bria reached for the door handle.

The only problem was . . . he couldn't. "Stay," Terran said.

Chapter Thirty-eight

Stay. Bria halted at his soft word, more a request than a demand. It resonated through Bria's body. He'd asked her to stay. It was what she wanted, what she'd dreamed he would say.

"Bria," Terran said.

Was that longing in his voice, or had she imagined it? He was behind her, close behind her. Her hand tightened on the handle of her blade. She desperately wanted him to wrap his arms around her, but if he did, he'd feel the sword at her side. She couldn't explain away its presence easily.

"Do you really cry yourself to sleep?" he asked tenderly.

She swallowed, her throat tight. *Every night,* she admitted to herself, though she'd never admit to him how much she missed him, or how much he'd hurt her. She lifted her chin against the grief that pooled inside her. "I only came to warn you."

"I never meant to hurt you," he said, so quietly that for a long moment she thought she'd imagined the words.

"You have Kathryn now," she whispered.

Suddenly, his hands were on her shoulders, gently turning her to face him. Her folded costume shifted in its hiding place in her wide sleeve. She raised her arm slightly to prevent it from tumbling into the open.

"I never wanted Kathryn as much as I do you," he said.

A scowl of confusion crossed Bria's brow. "But she was in your room last night."

He looked at her seriously. "Not at my invitation. It's true she was my lover before Odella, but never since." He gently brushed a lock of hair from her cheek.

His touch sent ripples of pleasure through her body. She ached to rush into his arms, but held herself back. She must stay calm and keep her wits about her. She fought the swirling abyss that beckoned invitingly to her; she couldn't let him discover what was hidden on her person.

"I'm sorry I said those hurtful things. But I had to convince you to leave. To protect you." He kissed her forehead. "Oh, I have missed you! You've bewitched me, woman. You're all I think about. You're all I want." His hands moved up to cup her chin. "Bria," he whispered and slowly lowered his lips to hers.

She knew she should stop him. She knew she shouldn't let him say and do these things to her that made her feel so wonderful when she feared that he was lying to her. But his expert kiss sent wave after wave of desire pounding through her. She moved closer to him, wanting him with a fierce longing she'd never known. As his lips caressed hers, blazing a fiery path across her skin, desire fanned the flame of passion within her and she knew that she couldn't resist him; she knew that she didn't want to.

But she jerked away from him. Her weapon! She had to keep it hidden. She couldn't let him feel the metal or find her costume. He mustn't discover her secret.

Bria stepped around him to the bed. Hidden half in darkness, she slid the cloak from her shoulders, keeping the costume concealed within the sleeve. Revealing her nakedness, she carefully placed the brown cloak on a nearby chest, cautiously hiding the sword beneath it.

Terran stepped up behind her, startling her as he swept her against him in a tight embrace. "You come to warn me wearing nothing but a robe? I doubt your intentions are honorable," he teased. He pulled her against his hard chest. Bria wrapped her arms around him. Their kiss deepened and her consciousness seemed to ebb and then brighten more than ever, her senses alive with each of his strokes and caresses.

His hands moved gently down her back, pulling her closer to him, holding her as though he truly had missed her. Bria wanted to believe it. She'd missed him so!

His skin seemed to be on fire where it touched hers, and it ignited her own flesh. He pressed kisses along her neck and down her chest to her breasts. She gasped as he cupped one small globe and caressed it.

Lowering his head to the very tip, he pressed small, gentle kisses to her flesh. Her nipples firmed instantly beneath his lips. Waves of pleasure rolled over her, engulfing her in their rapture. Her knees weakened and she collapsed on the bed.

Terran lay down beside her, continuing his tantalizing exploration of her flesh.

Bria gasped as he opened his lips to take one nipple into his mouth. She arched her back, inviting him to delve further, but he pulled back to untie his leggings, and she helped slide them over his hips.

Terran pushed her back on the bed, holding her hands over her head, trapping her beneath him. Bria groaned softly, desperately.

Terran reclaimed her lips in a moment of unrestrained desire and love. He pressed kisses to her eyes, her cheeks, her neck. Then his hand moved over her taut stomach to her hip, caressing her skin in slow circles. His fingers burned into her skin, leaving a path of tingles in their wake. Passion pounded molten blood through her veins as his caresses moved slowly, teasingly, to the spot where she needed him to touch her. Bria groaned and tentatively thrust her hips.

But he continued to torment her with slow circles over her downy curls as he ravaged her with kisses.

Finally, he lowered his fingers to her womanly folds. He teased and stroked and touched her until her impatience grew to explosive heights. She arched and moaned until she thought she could stand no more.

He moved over her, the length of his body covering hers. She opened her legs to welcome him into her body. His manhood filled her completely, sliding deep inside her. He lay still for a moment, kissing her neck and lips. Then, he began to move, slowly at first, but then with a building crescendo. Bria's body responded immediately, and together they found a tempo that bound their bodies and minds as one.

Waves of ecstasy lifted her higher and higher with each thrust until she exploded in a fiery crest of sensations. She rode the wave into the sky, rising higher and higher until she touched the very heavens above. She returned to earth on a glistening wave of satisfaction and completion.

When she opened her eyes to look at Terran, his eyes were closed and his face was taut with a culmination of explosive joy and pleasure. She reached for him and pulled him close. His body trembled against hers.

For a long moment, Bria held him, enjoying the warmth of his arms and body engulfing her. She caressed his back, marveling at the sensations that pulsated through her body, the remnants of shared rapture.

With a sigh, Terran rolled off her and pulled her tight against him. Bria pressed her ear against the flat planes of his chest and listened to his heart beating. She could have sworn her heart beat with the same rhythm. She'd never known such happiness. Then—

"How did you come to be inside Castle Knowles?" Terran asked quietly. "And how did you know Kathryn was in my room last night?"

Bria froze, though her heart had started racing. "Are you going to send me away again?"

"Shh," Terran soothed, trying to draw her closer to him. But Bria resisted and Terran relaxed his hold. "Bria," he pleaded, "how can I trust you if you will not tell me the name of my enemy? I know he's near and you have spoken to him. Only he could have told you about Kathryn."

"The Midnight Shadow isn't your enemy. He is the protector of the innocent, the righter of injustice."

"Give me his name, Bria."

Bria sat up and looked at Terran. "Why won't you believe me?" She clenched her fists before her. "Why don't you listen to me? Why aren't you looking into my accusations against Kenric? *He* is your enemy, not the Midnight Shadow." She sighed and dropped her hands to her lap. She loved him so much. She wanted him to understand, to know what Kenric was doing and planning. She wanted to protect Terran and work with him. But he was refusing her. With a growl of frustration, she jumped out of bed and reached for her cloak. As she picked it up, her sword fell from its folds.

Terran watched with widening eyes as the weapon clattered against the stone floor. A scowl etched his brow. "What's this?"

The answer came to her lips in an instant, the culmination of her frustration and anger. "You did not think I would return to Castle Knowles, to Kenric, without a weapon, did you?"

He guffawed. "What good is a sword if you don't know how to use it? Wouldn't a dagger have been more fitting?"

Bria shrugged, but inside she seethed at his presumption, the presumption of all men who saw women as defenseless creatures, as stupid as they were weak. She answered with a similar presumption. "The bigger the weapon, the greater the defense."

Terran chuckled at such foolishness, not detecting her sarcasm.

Bria pulled on the brown robe, making sure to keep her back to him so the Midnight Shadow's cloak was well hidden in her sleeve. She tied the sack with her costume to her waist. When she looked at Terran, he'd pulled on his leggings and was slipping his tunic over his head. Their magical moment was gone. Long gone. "You're going to have me banned from the castle again, aren't you?"

"Listen to me," Terran begged, taking her hands in his. "I must make things right before I can ask you to join me. I cannot endanger your life."

"Let me help you. Let me be by your side."

"And have you poisoned again? Never." He lifted his fingertips to her cheek. "I will do right by my people. I will rid the land of the Midnight Shadow. Then you can return."

Just as joy had begun to brim in her heart, the bubble burst at his words. Rid the land of the Midnight Shadow? But that meant her. She wanted more than anything to stay with him, wanted to be his wife in every way. But now the Midnight Shadow stood between them. She threw her arms around him, holding him close. "I love you, Terran, with all my heart. I would do anything to make it right between us. And if you think knowing who the Midnight Shadow is will do that, then so be it. There will be no more secrets." She said it to herself as much as to him. With a deep breath, she pulled away and looked up into his eyes. "The Midnight Shadow is—"

Suddenly, the door flew open and Kenric rushed in, followed by four guards.

"M'lord," Kenric panted. "The entire castle has been searched. He . . ." Kenric's voice faded. "Lady Bria?"

"Search the castle again," Terran ordered. "I will not make

the mistake of opening the gates and have him slip through my fingers."

Kenric nodded. "As you wish, m'lord."

As the guards left the room, Terran called, "John!"

One of the men, the youngest by the looks of his boyish face, turned and came back. "Yes, m'lord?"

Terran held up a finger for him to wait. He turned to Bria. "You were saying?"

Bria swiveled her gaze to the guard and then to Terran. She wanted desperately to tell him, but she didn't know if the guard was one of Kenric's men and she hesitated, finally shaking her head.

Terran's lips thinned, and he addressed the guard. "I want you to escort Lady Bria back to her castle."

"No," Bria gasped.

"Take Pavia with you," he told the guard. "No harm is to befall her, do you understand me?"

"Yes, m'lord." John nodded.

"Terran, please don't do this," Bria begged. "You need my help."

Terran took her hands into his own. "John is one of my most trusted men. He'll see you safely to Castle Delaney."

"I don't want to leave you!" Bria objected.

"For just a little while longer. Do this one thing for me, Bria."

Bria started to shake her head, but Terran brought her knuckles to his lips.

"Please," he whispered.

Bria wanted to say no, to demand that she remain by his side. But he was looking at her with those large eyes, imploring her to do his bidding. Finally, she nodded and turned away to John.

She stepped out into the hallway to find Kenric standing there. "Do not worry, m'lady," he said mockingly. "We'll find the Midnight Shadow. He will not harm Lord Knowles."

Bria's eyes narrowed. ''The Midnight Shadow would never consider it.'' She quickly stepped past him. Satisfaction surged inside her. The ''man'' he was searching for was being escorted safely out of the castle.

By midday, Kenric and his men had searched the castle again. There was no sign of the Midnight Shadow.

''He's escaped,'' Kenric told Terran. ''We've searched the entire castle three times over.''

Terran thoughtfully chewed his venison. He sat in the Great Hall, eating his midday meal. A dog sniffed at the rushes near his feet, searching for a piece of dropped food. A servant stopped to refill his mug with ale. But not Kenric, the dogs, nor the servants occupied Terran's mind. Bria did.

''Damn that rogue,'' Kenric continued.

Bria had known Kathryn had been in his room.

''I just don't understand how he entered the castle undetected.''

Yes. And how had Bria gotten into the castle without anyone's knowing?

''Cousin, are you listening to me?'' Kenric asked.

And there was that sword. What in heaven's name was she doing with a sword? Even if Kenric tried to hurt her again, did she believe she could wield a sword like a man?

''He must have used some sort of disguise,'' Kenric went on, pacing back and forth before the table.

But something else was bothering Terran. It was the Midnight Shadow's eyes. So damned blue. The bluest eyes he'd ever seen, except for . . . he straightened slightly. Good Lord! Had he missed the signs?

''If we want to capture the Midnight Shadow,'' Kenric said, facing Terran once again, ''we'll have to put your plan into action.''

Terran lifted his gaze to Kenric, but he wasn't listening. It

uldn't be! Had he been blind to the truth when it stared him
the face? *It can't be!* his mind repeated. *She is a woman!*
e is my wife!

"My lord?"

Bria couldn't be the Midnight Shadow. God's blood! He had
know. He had to know that his wife was not the one stealing
om him. "Yes," Terran murmured. "Announce the execution
r tomorrow."

Chapter Thirty-nine

Bria arrived at Castle Delaney that evening. Her grandfather raced out of the keep to greet her in the inner courtyard, as did numerous servants and concerned peasants. Bria hugged her grandfather, but was surprised her father was nowhere to be seen.

"He is searching the countryside for you," Harry explained. "Are you all right?"

Bria nodded. "I couldn't find Mary, Grandfather. Kenric had moved her."

Harry stared at her in sympathy. "At least you tried."

"And I will try again and again until she is free."

Her father returned hours later and summoned her to his solar. When she was younger, a trip to his solar had spelled fierce discipline. She knew she was in trouble. And what father in his right mind wouldn't discipline his daughter when she'd been missing an entire night?

She entered her father's solar and closed the door behind her. A colorful tapestry depicting a coronation hung on one of the walls. To her right a warm fire flickered in the hearth, and a large bed stood near the far wall. Just before her, four chairs surrounded a wooden table engraved with knights and horses.

Bria stood at the door, wanting—nay, needing—to leave as soon as possible so she could plan her rescue of Mary.

"What do you have to say for yourself?"

"I didn't mean to stay out all night," she admitted, "but I couldn't get home."

"What do you mean?" her father demanded.

Bria looked down at her entwined hands. "I missed Terran, and I wanted so much to see him," she said quietly. At least that much was true.

"I told him," a voice said.

Bria whirled to find her grandfather standing just inside the door of the solar.

"Forgive me, child," he said. "But when you were missing this morning, I had no choice."

"I do not appreciate being lied to and deceived, Bria," her father said, drawing her gaze once again.

"It wasn't like that, Father," she pleaded. "I never meant to lie to you. But the less you knew, the better off you were. This was something I had to do."

"Something you had to do? Dressing up as a man and stealing the taxes? Don't you realize your life is in danger?"

"Every moment," she admitted. "But if I don't protect those people, who will? It is my duty as Terran's wife . . ."

"To behave like a criminal?"

". . . to take care of the people now."

"Your *duty* now is to do as your husband wishes. I'm sure he wouldn't want you stealing his coin."

"It's my coin as well," Bria argued.

"Tell her," Harry urged.

Her father's lips thinned, but he remained silent.

"She has a right to know," Harry said. "If you don't, I will."

"Knowles is going to execute Mary at dusk tomorrow," her father whispered.

"What?" Bria gasped.

"I heard it when I was looking for you."

"They're going to execute an innocent woman!"

"Talk to your husband," her father suggested.

Bria waved her hand. "He won't listen to me."

"You don't need to take up the sword. There are other ways."

"There is only one way!"

"Never mind that," Harry said. "It's a trap."

"I know," Bria said, turning to face him. "But I have to go."

"You will not go anywhere," her father ordered.

"Father, Mary will be killed if I don't go. I can't allow that. If I'd stayed with Mary in the beginning, maybe she wouldn't have been taken. But I left her. I ran away." Bria stood her ground. "I won't make that mistake again."

"No, you won't," her father said.

Bria didn't like the tone in his voice. She didn't like the intolerant look in his eyes. She scowled slightly. "Father, ever since you came back from the war—"

"You will not speak of it," he commanded, moving his injured hand behind his back with his good one.

"We must speak of it. You hide behind your wounded hand. Instead of conquering it, you let it rule your life. You should be proud of it. You received it fighting for something you believed in. I haven't seen you fight for something you believed in in a long time."

"Enough!" her father roared. "I've heard enough of your speeches and your schemes. You can do no more for Mary than I can. If Knowles chooses to kill her, you will not interfere.

He is your husband. You should obey him instead of fighting him and stealing from him.''

Bria glared at him for a long moment. Hurt and anger welled within her, but she refused to give in to it. ''I used to admire you. You used to be strong and brave, a man I wanted to be like. Now all I have for you is pity.'' With that, she whirled and stormed from the room.

Harry shifted his gaze to his son.

David Delaney turned away from his father's piercing gaze, holding his useless arm close to his body. Harry saw the agony on his son's face. ''She's right, you know,'' Harry said gently. ''You haven't been the same since the war.''

David turned his back on Harry and gazed into the dying fire.

''I think you're angry with her because you're envious. You'd do the same thing . . . if you could.''

''The devil, you say!'' Delaney spun and faced his father. ''I'd have stood against Knowles without lying about it.''

Harry stepped forward and placed a hand on his son's shoulder. ''You still can,'' he said.

Bria stared down at the tunic in her hand. Who would have thought all those years ago when she and Mary and Garret had played the Midnight Shadow together that she'd become him? That the Midnight Shadow would be real?

Who would have thought all those years ago that she would have fallen in love with the enemy? How could Terran execute Mary when he knew Mary was her friend? Bria clenched the fabric in her fist. *It will end now, one way or the other.*

Bria donned the black leggings and black tunic. A sense of destiny filled her, a sense of calm and direction. She bent to

the bed to pick up the cloaked hood and stared at it for a long
moment.

For Garrett. For Mary. For the people who had been wronged
and robbed and beaten by Kenric.

She would face Kenric and defeat him. She was no longer
afraid of him. But what of Terran? Could she confront him?
Could she beat him? Would she have to?

Bria finished dressing and raised the black hood over her
head to become the Midnight Shadow once more.

Chapter Forty

Terran stood silently in the Great Hall, staring into the flickering flames of the hearth, his arm resting on the stone mantel, a mug of ale dangling from his fingertips. But he didn't see the orange-red flames biting at the logs, nor did he see the brown bark turn to charcoal black as it burned, and he was completely oblivious to the gray and white smoke swirling up from the fire. All he could see in his mind's eye were two blue eyes. Two startlingly blue eyes that stared at him from behind a mask.

Kenric stood behind him, his words barely heard. "Oh, how she begged for mercy," he chuckled, "looking up at me with that piteous face. *My* mercy. As if I have any to give!" Kenric laughed aloud.

Terran ground his teeth. He'd known his cousin had a vicious streak, but to hear him talk about the girl like this made his stomach turn. She was just bait to catch much larger prey. *Innocent bait* . . . he pushed aside Bria's voice, defending her friend.

Not only would he capture the Midnight Shadow. His ploy would show who the traitors were. He wasn't sure which of his men sided with Kenric. He had to expose them all or he could never keep Bria safe.

"She was trembling so much she could barely—"

But how could he defeat him if he didn't know how many loyal men would fight Kenric's traitorous dogs? He clenched his teeth. "Is the trap all set for dusk?" he asked, cutting off his cousin.

Kenric nodded. "Aye," he replied. "I'll have men stationed around the walls and throughout the crowd. Double posts of guards near both gatehouses."

"Leave the gates open so it's easier for him to get in," Terran ordered.

"He'll get in, but he won't get out." Kenric smiled. "After tonight, the Midnight Shadow will no longer be a threat."

Kenric leaned against the wall of one of the battlements, his gaze trained on Terran. His cousin spoke earnestly with the farmer who'd found Bria after Kenric had poisoned her.

Sir William joined him. He glanced around, his eyes coming to rest on Terran in the courtyard below. "Everything is going as planned. The men are ready."

Kenric nodded his head, but remained quiet.

Below them, Terran nodded and clasped the farmer's arm before turning toward the keep.

Kenric shook his head. "He's never concerned himself with the peasants before." His eyes narrowed. "What's he up to?"

Terran stared down at the inner courtyard from his room in the keep. People packed the small square from stone wall to stone wall. He found himself transfixed by the play of events outside his window; he hadn't moved for hours, watching as

e usual traffic of carts and peasants and merchants gave way
 meandering knights and curious farmers. They formed a
assive sea of eager onlookers, all eyes locked on the execution
atform in the middle of the courtyard.

"It's time, Terran."

Kenric stood in the doorway. Terran nodded to his cousin,
it for a moment he couldn't move. The thought of what was
 come left him momentarily paralyzed. *Am I doing the right
ing?* he wondered. *Will this trap work? What if the Midnight
hadow gets killed? What if Bria . . .* He forced the questions
 stop lest they drive him mad.

Terran took a step toward the door. "Mary shall not be
armed," Terran ordered.

"Of course not," Kenric said. "The plan is to capture the
lidnight Shadow."

Together they proceeded downstairs to the open keep doors.
erran paused on the steps of the keep and looked out over
ie murmuring crowd. Two dozen guards had positioned them-
elves in two lines leading from the stairs to a viewing stand,
aaking a path for him. The viewing stand was a small, rectangu-
ir structure about three feet off the ground, providing an unob-
ructed view of the execution platform.

Terran walked past the guards, aware of the silence that
ollowed him like the wake of a boat. He could feel hundreds
f pairs of eyes on him, and he slanted a gaze at the crowd.
ome onlookers were clearly angry. Others looked afraid.

Frowning, he climbed onto the viewing stand and took his
lace at the front. Kenric took up a position behind him.

Suddenly, the people in the crowd shifted, craning their
ecks toward the commotion of shuffling peasants and shouts
f protests that began near the rear of the crowd.

Terran turned to see Mary being led toward the executioner's
latform. She was dressed in a drab brown tunic that reached
 just below her knees. Her hands were bound in front of her
ith thick rope. Her head hung to her chest, her shoulders

slumped. He felt sorry for the girl; he guessed how terrifie she must be, but comforted himself with the thought that sh was really in no danger.

The guards shoved her forward. The girl was so small th guards seemed like towering giants. She moved slowly throug the crowd, which moved ever closer to her, everyone clamorir for a look at the doomed girl. For a moment, it seemed the crow had actually swallowed her up. But she reappeared amidst th throng, moving ever closer to the executioner's platform.

The guards shoved people out of the way as they led Mar to the stairs of the platform. A few in the crowd surged forwar as if to help her, but the guards roughly pushed them back.

Sir William, the captain of the guard, stepped up the stair to join them on the viewing stand, his eyes scanning the crowd

"Any sign of him, Captain?" Terran asked.

Sir William shook his head.

Terran's gaze moved over the crowd. The sun had begun t dip over the horizon, and the anxiety bottled up inside hir drew his nerves taut.

Mary reached the stairs to the execution platform. A browr robed monk took her elbow and began to lead her gently u the wooden steps. She stumbled once as her legs gave wa beneath her, but the monk kept her on her feet with a firm gri on her elbow.

The guards stationed throughout the crowd drew closer t the executioner's platform, making a tight circle around it. A Terran's gaze moved back over the crowd, his eyes stoppe on Mary. She was staring at the large block of wood sittir ominously on the platform. A wicker basket was positione next to it, sitting beneath the indentation carved into the block The poor girl was visibly trembling.

The monk urged her on, and Mary finally reached the to of the platform.

The crowd became quiet, deathly quiet, as the executione mounted the rear stairs of the platform, his large boots thunde ıg on the wooden steps. At his side, he gripped a heavy axe ghtly in his beefy hand. He was dressed all in black, his head nd neck completely covered by a black hood save for two ırge eyeholes. He stepped onto the platform, shifting the axe ·om one hand to the other.

The monk guided Mary toward the block. Her eyes had gone lank, and Terran wondered if she had lost her reason. She eemed completely oblivious to her surroundings, her face as xpressionless as if she were asleep—or already dead. The ıonk guided her to her knees, and Terran's stomach tightened. 'his was going too far. Where was the Midnight Shadow? Was is trap going to work?

The monk stepped back as Mary placed her neck on the hopping block. Her hair dangled down into the wicker basket ·elow her head.

The executioner moved into position near Mary's head. He ·ripped the axe with both hands as he moved the head of the .eavy weapon into place at his feet.

Terran scanned the crowd, looking for a sign of his enemy, ·ut seeing nothing but morbidly curious faces awaiting an ınjust execution.

The executioner raised the axe over his head and glanced ·ver to the viewing platform, waiting for the final order to ·roceed.

He had to put a stop to this charade. Mary didn't deserve to lie. He opened his mouth to tell the executioner to lower his veapon.

Suddenly, there was another commotion, this time at the ·ottom of the stairs of the execution platform. Terran glanced ɔward the sudden flurry of movement and swore he saw a lash of black explode through the crowd.

The blur leaped onto the platform and hit the executioner, ·nocking the large man to the ground. The axe flew out of his .ands and landed with a loud thud in one of the platform's

wooden planks. Then, just as quickly, the shape was gone
Mary had disappeared into the crowd with it.

"The Midnight Shadow!" The shout erupted from some
where in the crowd.

The onlookers exploded in wild chaos, yelling and pushin
for a glimpse of the Midnight Shadow.

"Don't let him escape!" Kenric ordered, his gaze focuse
on the bottom of the stairway to the executioner's stand.

Another flash of black drew Terran's gaze as a cloaked figur
moved through the crowd. "There he is!" he shouted.

With a wave of his arm, Kenric signaled the guards forwarc

Quick as lightning, the Midnight Shadow engaged the firs
guard, slicing his sword down to block the guard's blow.

The crowd scattered away from the swinging weapons an
their deadly blades, clearing a small circle in which the combat
ants fought.

The Midnight Shadow parried and struck with the skill of
trained fighter. But as the second, third, and fourth guard
moved in, he was hard pressed to defend himself. Finally, on
of the guards grabbed his arm and another wrenched the swor
from his hand.

Terran's heart pounded in his chest. Was it her?

"Take off his mask!" Kenric shouted.

Terran stepped forward to the edge of the viewing stand
anxiously looking down into the courtyard.

The crowd shifted uneasily as people jostled for position t
see the unveiling. The entire courtyard again became unnerv
ingly, eerily quiet.

One of the guards reached forward and yanked the mask
from the Midnight Shadow's head.

Terran held his breath as the mask slid over the rebel's neck
chin, nose, and finally off his head to reveal . . .

. . . Harry Delaney.

Bria's grandfather!

"It can't be," Kenric hissed. "He never could have overpow-
red the tax collectors."

"He's not the Midnight Shadow!" a voice called. "I am!"

Terran swiveled his head to see . . . another Midnight Shadow
tanding at the outskirts of the crowd, sword at the ready.

Another Midnight Shadow!

Kenric fumed, "What's going on? Get him!"

But even as soldiers pushed their way through the crowd,
ne peasant and then another pointed toward the crenels. Terran
ooked up to see a third Midnight Shadow. This one grabbed
 nearby rope and swung down toward Harry, hitting two guards
vith his booted feet, knocking them down.

"Get them!" Kenric shouted. "Get them all!"

Terran's gaze shifted to the second Midnight Shadow, who
vas engaged in battle with two guards. He was skillful enough
o keep the two guards at bay, but there was something strange
bout the way he fought. His right arm wielded the sword
xpertly, but he never seemed to lift his left arm, either for
alance or for form. It hung at his side like a useless thing.
Iad he been wounded already, or . . .

Realization rocked Terran. He knew of only one man who
ad a crippled arm. And if Bria's grandfather was here, why
ot her father?

Terran's gaze swiveled to Harry and the other Midnight
hadow at his side. This third Midnight Shadow was quite
killed. His thrusts and parries were timed to perfection. Or
vere they *hers*?

Terran's jaw clenched as prickles raced across the back of
is neck. He had to know. He leaped from the viewer's platform,
it the ground and quickly moved forward, not taking his gaze
rom the Midnight Shadow beside Harry. A guard stumbled
ack from the fight and into Terran's path. Terran grabbed him
y his tunic and shoved him out of the way.

The Midnight Shadow deflected a blow and countered with

another, driving another guard back. Then he turned with his
sword raised and came face to face with Terran.

Terran wasn't surprised by what he saw. Crystal blue eyes
gazed at him through the two slits in the mask. The bluest eyes
he had ever seen. *God's blood! Why didn't I see it before?*

Bria. His heart ached to hold her and touch her. But as long
as she stayed hidden behind the mask of his enemy, he could
only stare.

Behind her, one of the guards lifted his weapon to strike her
down.

Chapter Forty-one

Terran lurched forward, lifting his blade to block the blow
and then knock the guard's sword aside, saving the Midnight
Shadow's life. Saving Bria's life.

He shoved the guard away in disgust, then looked back at
his black-cloaked enemy. His lover.

She said nothing as she slowly lowered her weapon.

He raised his sword and placed the tip to her neck. Which
one would she be when he unmasked her? Enemy or lover?

The fighting around them seemed to slow, the noise lowering
to a whisper, the figures fading into a hazy blur.

Bria lowered her weapon even further until the tip was almost
touching the ground. Terran's heart ached. He could see the
dazzling blue of her eyes shining at him from the dark holes
in her mask. He could see the sadness in them, the pain, the
anguish. But behind it all, her inner fire burned bright. If he
captured her, he would be sentencing her to death. The flame
would be extinguished forever—the only flame that could ever
warm his cold heart.

"Well done, cousin," Kenric said, approaching from th
viewer's platform. "Unmask him."

Terran kept the tip of his blade to her neck, transfixed b
her brilliant blue eyes. Despite the growing pain in his hear
he felt a sudden surge of anger racing through him as wel
anger at her betrayal. How could she stand against her husband

"I don't have to," he announced.

"What do you mean? Unmask him!" Kenric snapped.

Terran turned his full anger on Kenric. "You overstep your
self, cousin. I give the commands."

"Fool," Kenric gritted. He whirled away from Terran
throwing his arms high above his head. "Now!" he hollered
"Attack!"

The courtyard exploded with a cacophony of fighting a
Kenric's paid mercenaries moved in, clashing with Terran'
loyal men. The thunderous sound of dozens of blades colliding
of steel cracking against steel, clanged in the courtyard. Alle
giances quickly played themselves out as Kenric's men groupe
together, each ripping off his tunic to reveal a black snak
painted onto a chestplate or leather armor.

All of the snakes had eyes as cold and as black as Kenric's

Terran turned to his cousin. "You traitorous bastard." H
swung at Kenric, but his cousin ducked his blow and race
out of the circle of guards. Terran suddenly found himsel
surrounded by men bearing the snake symbol, men he didn'
recognize. *I've been living like a blind man in my own castle*

He turned to block a blow and found himself fighting sid
by side with Bria. He finished the guard with a quick strik
and felt pride swell in his chest as Bria dispatched anothe
opponent with great skill, defeating him with two solid blows

He opened his mouth to say something to her, but thre
mercenaries attacking one of his guards needed his immediat
attention.

Anger fueled Terran's rage, and he fought like a man pos
sessed. He quickly helped his man defeat the mercenaries, the

whirled to look for his cousin. Kenric had retreated to the viewer's platform and was watching the battle from afar. Of course. He was too much a coward to wage his own fight. Slowly his cousin smiled a chilling, triumphant smile.

Terran turned to survey the battle around him, needing to know the reason behind the smile. Kenric's men seemed to be swarming everywhere, outnumbering his loyal forces almost three to one.

Terran's gaze swept the peasants until he found George, Mary's father, at the front of the crowd. He nodded his head at him.

With a loud battle cry, the peasants rushed forward, brandishing pitchforks or pikes. They attacked the men with snakes on their tunics, clubbing them in the head, stabbing them in the side.

Terran turned back to Kenric. It was his turn to smile. He would not lose his castle to his cousin. His people would save the day.

The whizzing sound of a blade caused Terran to instinctively duck. A mercenary's sword sliced through the air above his head. Terran parried the blow and exchanged a second swing with the mercenary.

Suddenly, he found Harry standing at his side, intercepting the next swing. The old man turned to him and called out, "Go! They went into the keep."

They? Terran's mind screamed. He glanced at the viewer's platform and found it empty. *Damn it!* He quickly glanced around him to see his wife was gone. Bria was going after Kenric! But his men needed him here. They were greatly overpowered and outnumbered.

"Go!" Harry shouted at him. "We'll take care of these dogs!"

Suddenly, a squadron of soldiers entered through the open gates, bursting into the courtyard with swords in hand. It took a moment for Terran to realize that the crest they bore on their tunics was a flying falcon, the crest of the Delaneys. Lord Delaney had mustered up an army to help his daughter rescue Mary. And him.

Terran nodded to Harry and immediately charged toward the keep. But as he neared the keep steps, a familiar shape stepped out of the shadows thrown by the keep wall, cutting off his path of pursuit. Captain William stared challengingly at him, his sword in his hand. The eyes of the snake on his armor seemed to stare at him defiantly as well.

"Let me pass, William," Terran snarled. "You've done enough."

"But if I defeat you, Kenric might be lord yet. Then I'll have enough gold to call no one master but myself."

"You can try," Terran growled and swept in low, but William parried the blow, swinging his weapon around to the side to slice at Terran. Terran blocked the strike and answered with another swing.

Terran's mind kept returning to Bria chasing off alone after Kenric. He had to finish off William, or he would never get to her in time. He thrust, but pulled back as the captain aimed for his stomach with the tip of his sword.

Terran swung low, knocking William's weapon aside, and lunged in. The blow bounced harmlessly off William's chainmail, as if the snake itself were deflecting the strike. Anger filtered through Terran. He had to get to Bria! He had no time to waste with this buffoon, this traitor. "You're a fool to believe my cousin's word. Kenric has no allegiance to anyone but himself."

Terran feinted to the side, but then stepped back, launching an attack from the opposite direction. He caught William off guard and twisted his wrist in an attempt to disarm him. But William disengaged before his weapon went spinning. Terran grit his teeth and knocked his thrust aside. They crossed swords and the clang of the weapons reverberated through the air to mingle with the sound of other battles.

Terran swung to one side and then pulled back, thrusting. William didn't have time to recover and Terran's sword sliced deep into his stomach, driving through a gap in the captain's armor. William's sword clattered to the ground as he gazed at Terran in disbelief before crumpling to his knees.

Terran pulled his sword from Sir William's stomach and whirled without watching him fall. He raced into the keep after Bria.

Bria ran through the keep, chasing after Kenric. She wasn't going to let him get away. He had to pay for his crimes. He'd nearly succeeded in having Mary executed.

Kenric dashed into the Great Hall, and she sped after him. He was halfway through the empty hall when she reached the doorway. "You won't make it out of here alive," she called, making no attempt to disguise her voice.

Kenric halted and whirled.

She approached him purposefully. "Even if you do, where will you go? Word will spread of your betrayal, and you will not be trusted anywhere."

"Take off your mask," he commanded.

She shook her head. "Your reign of fear is over," she proclaimed. "You've given your last command." Bria halted an arm's reach away from him.

"I would have been lord here," he said, "if it weren't for you."

"No," Bria proclaimed. "Evil never triumphs. Terran would have defeated you with or without my help."

A crooked smile crossed his lips and he raised his weapon, attacking with a ferocity and strength that Bria was hard put to fend off. She had a moment's triumph as he grimaced under her defense. He hadn't known how good she was.

They crossed swords and Kenric grabbed her wrist.

"I know who you are," he chortled. "No one addresses Lord Knowles as Terran . . . except his wife."

Bria struggled to push off, but he held her firm.

"Remove your mask so when I put my sword through you, I can see your face."

"I'll remove my mask when you are banished from here and there is no more need for my services," Bria grit out.

Kenric shoved her back roughly and hooked his foot beneath her ankle. She stumbled back and fell to the floor hard. Kenric arced his sword down toward her head. Bria quickly rolled out of the way, but the tip of his blade sank into her cloak, trapping her.

Bria moved to raise her sword, but Kenric stepped on her wrist, pinning her hand to the ground.

Kenric loomed above her, a foot on either side of her body. He bent down to her, his booted foot digging into her wrist. Agony shot up her arm. "Let's see how much of a woman you really are." He ran a hand over her chest, grabbing at her breasts.

Bria backhanded him with her free arm.

His head rocked back from her blow, but when he recovered, anger burned in his black eyes. He grabbed her neck. "Bound your breasts to look more like a man. Ingenious." He squeezed tightly. "But you will die anyway."

Kenric's hand tightened around her throat and she struggled for a breath, gasping for any air she could get into her lungs. She refused to give in to him. The Midnight Shadow would not be defeated so easily. She brought her knees up behind him, pushing him forward. He tumbled over her head, releasing her. Bria tore her cloak tree from Kenric's blade and climbed to her feet, whirling on him.

He lurched forward, reaching for his blade. His hand closed around the hilt just as Bria put the tip of her sword to his neck.

Kenric straightened slowly.

Triumph crested in Bria as she pushed the tip of her blade

against Kenric's throat, forcing his chin higher. "You will never be lord here," the Midnight Shadow announced.

"Don't be so sure," Kenric said. "As soon as my men defeat the pathetic few knights who remain loyal to your husband, I will be lord of this castle."

"They may defeat Terran's brave men, but they will not defeat the army my father has brought with him today," Bria assured him.

Bria saw the uncertainty flash across Kenric's eyes. He didn't know whether to believe her or not, but his gaze still darted about as though he were an animal that knew it was trapped. An animal that suddenly became even more dangerous.

Suddenly, Terran skidded into the room. "Bria!"

Bria turned at the sound of his voice.

Without warning, Kenric lashed out, shoving her blade away from his neck and plowing a fist into her stomach. Bria doubled over, gasping for breath as pain exploded across her abdomen. Kenric locked one arm around her neck, holding her sword arm at bay.

Terran lurched forward, but came to an abrupt halt as Kenric tightened his grip on her throat. "Let her go," Terran commanded. "Your battle is with me."

"If only it were that easy," Kenric said.

"She means nothing to you!" Terran cried out.

"But she means the world to you—your one weakness. How ironic that your weakness is the enemy you sought so diligently to destroy." Kenric cackled darkly.

"You can have the damned castle, just let her go," Terran said.

"No!" Bria gasped, struggling. She still held her sword, but Kenric's hard grip kept it dangling uselessly at her side.

"How generous to offer it to me," Kenric sneered, "now that Delaney and his men have come."

"Terran," Bria began, but Kenric tightened his grip on her throat, cutting off her cry. He tried to pry her fingers free of her weapon, but Bria wouldn't release it. Kenric's chokehold intensified. Black dots swam before Bria's eyes. The next thing she knew, Kenric had her sword.

As her vision cleared, she heard Terran say stoically, "Bria was right. You were the one overtaxing my people, starving them, stealing their gold—and mine."

"Had you taken more interest in your people, it wouldn't have been so easy. But you were too interested in fighting in your beloved tournaments and impressing Odella."

"But why kill her? She was an innocent."

"She'd stumbled onto my plan. She'd gone over the ledgers and questioned the people, things you were too lazy to do. I couldn't let her warn you."

Terran's gaze locked with Bria's. Panic simmered just below the resolve in his eyes. For the first time, his eyes actually looked warmly brown, instead of black. Bria had to free herself and, in doing so, free Terran to right his wrongs.

"What do you want?" Terran demanded.

"Your life, cousin," Kenric said gleefully. "Only then can I claim this castle as mine."

"Release her."

"I think not. This is, after all, your hated enemy." A smile crossed his lips as he pushed the sword tighter against Bria's throat. He looked at Terran. "There is very soft skin beneath this hood, as I think you know. Let's find out how soft, shall we?"

"Noooo!" Terran yelled.

Bria lifted her elbow and rammed it into Kenric's stomach.

Kenric lost his grip on her neck and she leaped forward, out of the way of his swing. She scrambled on all fours toward the door, glancing back over her shoulder to see Kenric looming over her with his weapon raised to strike her down.

Bria closed her eyes tightly, willing her hands and knees to move faster, but knowing she couldn't outrun him. She waited for the stinging bite of his steel.

Instead, she heard the clang of metal against metal and

opened her eyes, looking back over her shoulder. Inches from her, two swords were crossed, one intent on killing her, one determined to save her life. Terran stood protectively above her, his eyes glaring into Kenric's.

His teeth clenched as he moved Kenric's sword with the sheer strength of his forearm, his muscles bunched beneath his tunic. Kenric planted his feet, trying to force the weapons down. But in the end, Terran was stronger. He flung Kenric's weapon up. Bria quickly rose and moved out of the way as Terran forced Kenric's blade away from her.

Kenric stumbled back, but righted himself in time to block Terran's swing. He stepped forward and shoved Terran back, pursuing with a flurry of hacking attacks.

Terran blocked his attack, each stroke of Kenric's expertly deflected.

Bria bent to retrieve Kenric's weapon, holding it tightly in her fist. She wanted to help, but she knew Terran had to defeat this foe by himself.

The two men crossed swords and Terran grabbed Kenric's arm. "You will die for your treachery," Terran promised.

Kenric tried to pull free, but Terran wouldn't let him go. Kenric lunged forward and bit Terran's fingers. Terran grimaced and released his grip on Kenric's wrist, pulling his fingers from Kenric's mouth.

Kenric immediately slashed at Terran, catching his tunic front.

Terran looked down at his tunic to see a clean cut right in the middle of his chest. When he lifted his eyes back to Kenric, they were narrowed and deadly. He moved forward, lunging after Kenric. When Kenric put up his sword to block one of Terran's swings, Terran caught Kenric's blade. With a flick of his wrist, he sent the sword flying through the air. As it clanged to the ground amidst the rushes, Terran stepped forward and put the tip of his sword to Kenric's neck. They stared at each other for a long moment, Terran's jaw tight with emotion.

Suddenly, Kenric dropped to his knees. "I yield," he whispered.

"This is not a tournament," Terran growled. "You have betrayed me. Die now, or die later."

"Please," Kenric whimpered. "Spare my life. Have mercy. I don't want to die."

Terran stared down at him, his lips twisting in contempt. Then he raised his gaze to Bria.

They locked eyes. Bria thought she saw the tension and the anger fade from Terran as they gazed at each other. His eyes softened.

"Then it shall be the dungeon," he sentenced.

Kenric didn't move. Reaching down, Terran pulled him to his feet and dragged him out of the Great Hall toward the dungeon. Bria followed.

They passed the first guard's post and then the second, both empty. She waited while Terran proceeded down the dark hallway and opened the door to the same cell that had imprisoned Mary. He shoved Kenric forward, then slammed the door shut behind his cousin, throwing the lock into place. He returned to the lighted section of the guard's post.

Behind them, Kenric pounded on the cell door, pleading for mercy.

"This place reeks of the doomed," Terran muttered. "Let's get out of here."

When they had ascended back into the Great Hall, Terran lifted his gaze to Bria. "Can you forgive me? I should have listened to you from the beginning."

A smile crossed Bria's lips. She raised her hands to slide the cloak from her hair and untie the mask. "Yes," she admitted as the mask slid from her face. "You should have. But you're a stubborn lout at times."

Terran nodded. "That I am. But I promise to change." He stepped closer to her. "If . . ."

"If?" She turned her head up to see the perfect smile that had eased across his lips.

"If the Midnight Shadow returns to whence she came."

"The Midnight Shadow will always be near. She is the defender of the people, Lord Knowles, the righter of wrongs, the guardian of the innocent. She is—"

"I don't care who she is, as long as she isn't my wife." He cupped her chin. "You'll have more important things to do—like bear me an army of knights."

Bria's eyebrows rose in disbelief. "An army, you say?"

"At least," he whispered against her lips before claiming them in a passionate kiss. When he pulled away, he looked deep into her eyes and said solemnly, "No one knows the identity of the Midnight Shadow. Let him return to legend."

Bria nodded her head.

Terran swept her into a tight embrace, kissing her with all the gratitude and love in his heart.

The Midnight Shadow's cape tumbled from Bria's shoulders to pool on the ground.

Epilogue

Five years later

". . . and he brandished his sword above his head, declaring,
'Tyranny will not be tolerated! All people will be treated fairly!'
With that, the Midnight Shadow whirled away on his horse
and disappeared over the horizon."

The small boy lifted his head to Harry. "The Midnight
Shadow beat the evil lord?" he asked, a strand of dark hair
falling into his bright blue eyes.

"He most certainly did." Harry squeezed the boy in a tight
hug, kissing the top of his head.

Bria exchanged a smile with Mary, who knelt on the floor
and picked up the boy's toys, placing them into a chest. It
seemed just yesterday her grandfather had first told her of the
wondrous deeds of the Midnight Shadow.

Strong arms wrapped around Bria from behind as a gentle
but possessive kiss pressed against her neck. She turned to see
Terran's strong profile.

"We really should set history straight on this 'evil lord,' " Terran murmured.

Bria chuckled as she turned to embrace her husband. "Surely m'lord does not take such tales seriously?" she teased.

Terran didn't smile. "Someday my son will discover the Midnight Shadow rode in his lands. I don't want him to think I was the evil lord."

"But you were. A tyrannical, unjust lord," Bria said with a wry smile.

Terran pulled her closer. "Neither tyrannical nor unjust. Just unaware. It took the threat of the Midnight Shadow for me to take an interest in my people and my lands." He pressed his lips against hers. "And thank the Lord she did."

Warmth spread over Bria as their kiss deepened. And she did, indeed, thank the Lord. He'd given her everything she ever wanted in life and more.

Behind her, she heard her son's happy voice. "Great Grand-father, tell me the story of the Midnight Shadow again."

"Of course," Harry answered. "He was known far and wide for battling against tyranny and for upholding fairness. He was called the Midnight Shadow . . ."

ear Reader:

A millennium has come and gone. And with its passing
merges a new legend. The Midnight Shadow.

I'm glad you've chosen to read *Midnight Shadow*. I hope
ou found the legend of the Midnight Shadow as captivating
s the stories of King Arthur and Robin Hood. I so enjoyed
hose tales that I decided to create my own legend, a hero (or
eroine in this case) who battles tyrants and fights for the
eople.

Please drop me a line and let me know what you thought of
he legend of the Midnight Shadow at PO Box 7241, Algonquin,
llinois 60102.

Or visit my Web site—*Lady Laurel's Castle*—at: http://
members.aol.com/laurelodon/ and warm yourself by the virtual
earth, or feel free to wander through my castle halls and read
he free previews, reviews, and reader comments from my other
ooks. Don't forget to join my guest list for a chance to win
ree autographed books, cover flats and more!

My readers are very dear to me and I truly hope you cher-
sh the legend of the Midnight Shadow. A hero for the new
millennium!

Laurel O'Donnell